CULT OF THE DEVOTED

ACADEMY OF THE APOCALYPSE: BOOK 2

K. A. RILEY

NOTE FROM THE AUTHOR

The Academy of the Apocalypse Series:

1. Emergents Academy
2. Cult of the Devoted (You are here!)
3. Army of the Unsettled (July 2021)

Dearest Reader:

The events of the *Academy of the Apocalypse* series take place immediately following the conclusion of the *Conspiracy Chronicles.*

Although the *Academy of the Apocalypse* draws upon characters and references some events in that nine-book series (made up of three interconnected trilogies), this is a stand-alone series and doesn't require intimate familiarity with what's come before.

But it couldn't hurt, right?

Either way, it's an honor to write for you, and I hope you enjoy meeting these characters and exploring this world!

KARiley

SUMMARY

Feeling an overpowering pull she can't explain or control, Branwynne slips out of the Emergents Academy in search of Matholook, the mysterious seventeen-year-old member of the Cult of the Devoted she first met five years ago.

Heading right into the enemy camp may not seem like the most sensible thing to do, but Branwynne has never been one to blindly follow the rules—or to shy away from danger. Especially when her instincts are screaming at her that Matholook may have answers to questions she's been searching for all her life.

With a bloody, three-way war for power looming on the horizon in a bleak and ravaged land, Branwynne has her loyalties tested as she closes in on the mystery of who and what she really is.

She's searching for connections and desperate for answers.

What she finds may not change her life or her mind.

But it could just change her *heart*.

DEDICATION

To those devoted—not to their own goals but to helping others to achieve their own.

EPIGRAPH

"A foolish consistency is the hobgoblin of little minds."

— Ralph Waldo Emerson, *Self-Reliance*

"Wrth gicio a brathu mae cariad yn magu."
[While kicking and biting, love develops.]

— Welsh saying

"When a couple of young people strongly devoted to each other commence to eat onions, it is safe to pronounce them engaged."

— James Montgomery Bailey

PROLOGUE

I'M SEVENTEEN YEARS OLD, and I live in a secret school on the top of a mountain in the Colorado Rockies.

That's probably the most normal thing about me.

I'm an Emergent.

(I'm sure that sounds brillie, but it's led to more trouble, bruises, and broken bones than I care to count. It's also contributed to me feeling disconnected from the world and with no idea what do about it.)

Being an Emergent isn't really all that special. I have slightly better than average senses and reflexes. I have a psychic connection with a white raven named Haida Gwaii through what's called a telempathic bond. And on exactly two occasions in the past—with help from Kress, my mentor—I've been able to walk through walls. (It hurts a lot, and I don't recommend it.)

Kress has got to be one of the most powerful and important Emergents in the world. My one-on-one Apprenticeship with her is just one part of my long list of classes that includes lessons in armed and unarmed combat, survival skills, strategy and tactics, game theory, and sniper training.

I grew up in London, England during the drone strikes that

turned my city to rubble. When I was twelve years old, Kress and her Conspiracy showed up at the Tower of London where I lived with my parents and recruited me. Five year later, I became part of the very first class of the Emergents Academy.

Now, in the western half of what Kress calls the Divided States of America, there's a war brewing between three major factions with each of them on separate sides and all of them gearing up to fight to the death over what's left of this bleak and defeated world.

The Emergents Academy will get drawn into the war percolating down below. It's not only inevitable. It's what we're here for.

According to Wisp—the Dean of the Emergents Academy—we're in school to develop our skills, take tests, endure competitive challenges, muscle through intense physical and emotional training, get yelled at, and occasionally get the snot beaten out of us by our teachers during our never-ending sparring sessions.

We've also been given one simple homework assignment. It's about as basic and straightforward as it gets. In fact, it's the cornerstone of the school's mission statement:

Save the world.

(There's no due date.)

Saving the world means facing death. But I don't care. I've tasted battle before, and I liked it. A *lot.*

Maybe too much.

Anyway, there's a new war coming, and one way or another, I'm going to help make sure we win it.

But all of that's a problem for tomorrow. In the morning, I'm supposed to have my first class of the day: Intelligence Ops with Kella, our resident expert sharpshooter. I'm supposed to be in bed right now resting up in the Dorms with the rest of my Cohort.

Instead, I'm hiking down the mountain in the middle of the

night, heading to the compound of the Cult of the Devoted, a potential deadly enemy and one of the three factions preparing for all-out war.

I met the Devoted five years ago. A few months ago, I met one of them again.

Matholook.

He freed a dozen kids, Emergents, like me. His own people had been holding onto them as potential weapons of war. Risking his own life, Matholook turned the twelve prisoners over to me and my friends for us to take back to the Academy where they could live and train without being experimented on, imprisoned, brainwashed, discarded, or killed.

In my life, I've felt fear, pain, and the thrill of combat. In the short time I spent with Matholook, for the first time, I also felt connected. Weirdly connected. More connected than I've ever felt before.

Now, hours before class and with absolutely no notice or permission, I'm sneaking out of the safest place in the world to go and find out why I'm so drawn to him.

PART 1

CULT OF THE DEVOTED

1

DESCENT

I've LEFT the Emergents Academy once before. And I got in a whole whack-ton of trouble.

I've been in combat out in the world. I've fought for my life. I've lived in the Academy for the last five years. And I've been in training for a few months now.

None of that prepared me for getting bawled out by my teachers for leaving like we did.

So why do it again? Easy. For the simplest reason of all: If I don't, I won't feel connected. And, in the end, isn't feeling connected—to something or someone—the only thing any of us really wants?

Sure, I've thought about ignoring the urge, pressing it down into a tight little knot and locking it away somewhere deep inside the core of my body. But it's bad enough being imprisoned by someone else. Imprisoning *myself* would be a whole new level of stupid.

So, I'm leaving.

This time out, I'm alone. I don't take the network of tunnels and the old gold and silver mines running like arteries through the mountains. War and Mayla have been working down there all hours of the night, and it'd be embarrassing to get caught so soon after sneaking out. Instead, I deactivate the single alarm on the flashing input panel just inside the main entrance hall of the Academy and slip right out the big front double doors.

With only thirty students and nine teachers in the huge school, every breath echoes, and every footstep sounds like the earthquaking boot-stomps of an advancing army.

But not *my* footsteps. Not *my* breath. Like a raven preparing to divebomb its prey, I don't make a sound.

Thanks to Kress, I'm learning how to access some of my white raven's stealthier abilities.

I'm even learning how to evade the motion and heat-detectors set up throughout the Academy. It's not easy. I have to concentrate to access my neuroendocrine and metabolic systems on their deepest, molecular level. I know the pulsing electric shock ripping through my temples and searing into the base of my skull won't last. But that knowledge doesn't make the pain any easier to bear.

(It hurts even more than walking through walls. I don't recommend it.)

Resetting the alarm behind me and re-activating the Veiled Refractor—the high-tech camouflage device that hides the Academy—I edge my way along the icy path with a towering wall of rock on one side of me and a deep, mist-filled abyss on the other.

The Academy has all kinds of defenses: It's on the top of a mountain. It's concealed. It's got a whole host of security systems. And there's a team of experienced, powerful Emergents running the school.

Right now, though, I'm more worried about navigating the long walkway leading away from the front door. The dizzying, meandering path is about a foot wide, jagged and uneven, barely visible, and coated in sheets of lumpy ice. It curves and drops to a steep, downhill slant for a few hundred yards with the end of the trail invisible in the darkness of the whipping wind somewhere up ahead.

All of my enhanced abilities and coordination won't stop me from dying in a puddle of my own goopy organ-soup if I lose my footing and slip off this thing.

Inching along, I try to keep my mind on my destination and on not dying ten feet from the school's front door. It'd be just my luck to have all these grand plans for answers and adventure only to go arse over elbow on the ice and end up somewhere down on the distant rocks as a slushy buffet for coyotes, turkey vultures, banana slugs, and other assorted scavengers a thousand feet below.

Focus, Branwynne. You've been through too much to die like some clumsy plonker.

I'm headed down to New Harleck, I remind myself. But long before I get there, I need to go through a ghost town first. The path from the Academy to what's left of the roads, paths, and hunting trails leading down the mountain goes through the Valta.

Kress explained the history of the tiny town to me a long time ago. "First, it was nothing," she said. "Then, it was a pass-through point for Puebloans and the nomadic Utes. Then, it was a mining town. Then, a haven for outlaws and gamblers. Then, a tourist attraction and a hub for skiers, climbers, kayakers, and all kinds of outdoor thrill-seekers. Then, it was a quaint town full of life and happy families. After that, it was a target, a prison, and a recruiting center. Then it was a cemetery. And now, after all these years, it's nothing again."

The one thing she doesn't mention much...for her and her friends, it was home.

I breathe a sigh of relief when the long, treacherous path between the Academy and the Valta finally widens and levels out. I breathe another sigh of relief when I'm able to pluck my way along a field of fist-sized rocks, slide down a dry river basin, and worm through a deep cluster of slanted, interlocking bristlecone pine trees and thick banks of crispy, tangled vegetation.

But I *lose* my breath when I clamber over the warped and rusted metal guardrail and step into the town.

The red crescent moon overhead is casting a crimson haze over the patches of snow. The glow lights up the overgrown knots of surviving thorny vines that have clawed and scraped their way across what's left of the Valta's yards, parking lots, laneways, and buckled roads.

It's my second time passing through here. But it's the first time I've had a chance on my own to see what remains of the place where Kress and her friends grew up. I've seen the town dozens of times from the roof of the Academy where I have my one-on-one Apprenticeship lessons with her.

One time, about two years ago, I even got to take a break from caring for the ravens and stood with Kress and her Conspiracy as they gazed down and reminisced, pointing and calling out locations from their old lives.

"That's where we tried to dig a second well," Rain said, her legs dangling over the edge of the rooftop wall.

"Tried and failed," Brohn laughed, his blue eyes dancing under the blazing afternoon sun. He directed everyone's attention to a spot near a dried riverbed out past the town. "That's where we had Final Feast. And where Kress and I first met."

Terk snapped his head toward Brohn. "What do you mean? We've all been together since we were little kids."

Brohn flicked his thumb back and forth between himself and Kress while slipping his arm around her waist. "True. But that was the first time I realized *we* might become *us*."

Kress leaned her head on Brohn's shoulder and gave me a little wink to let me know I was included in the moment.

I always thought Render is what finally made Kress feel connected. Could I have been wrong? Could it have been Brohn?

She and Brohn were quiet for a minute before Kella cleared her throat and ran her fingers through her short blond hair. She redirected the others to a clearing at the far end of town near the unpaved road leading down the mountain.

"Over there is where we first boarded the truck on Recruitment Day to get shipped off to the Processor and trained to fight the Eastern Order." She swallowed hard right before she added, "Cardyn was with us then. And Karmine. And Manthy."

"We were eight very innocent, very ignorant kids back then," Brohn sighed after a moment of heavy silence.

"We're not innocent anymore," Rain said. "Or ignorant. Or kids."

"So how come I feel so much the same?" Terk asked.

Kress and her Conspiracy lowered their heads, and I couldn't tell if the tears on their faces were from all of them laughing or from all of them crying. Maybe a bit of both.

From up there, the town always looked dead but peaceful, and I imagined the Valta as an old woman who'd lived a long life, now buried and lying in her coffin, her arms folded across her chest while her loved ones watched over her from high above.

Walking through the Valta tonight is a different story. Despite the graveyard stillness, there's nothing peaceful about any of it.

The town's remains are ghostly and mummified. The steel posts that once held street signs are melted down into pathetic, misshapen slags. Other than charred stumps, nothing is left of the trees that must have once risen high up over the town's narrow roads.

The larger main road cutting through the Valta feels like an open wound. Piles of rubble and collapsed structures of wood and steel squat down on either side with smaller, barely visible laneways branching off in one direction or the other. Shops and stores stood here once. But now, there's nothing left but their rubble-filled footprints.

Clusters of dried, splintered bones lie in and around what's left of the entranceway to the high pile of debris that was once Shoshone High School, where Kress and her friends lived and struggled to survive for so long.

Passing the school, I continue to walk through the tiny town. I should run. There's no reason for me to linger. I have a mission. But I feel like flying through with blinders on would be disrespectful somehow.

The entire town was built on an angle, and from here, it feels like what's left of it could just give up at any second, lose its grip, and go cascading down the mountain, taking me along with it.

Figures. Feels like my entire life's been an avalanche waiting to happen.

I've seen blasted out buildings before. And I've seen animals picking at the bones, flesh, and tendons of the casualties of war. This is different. In a lot of ways, it's worse. Maybe it's because I grew up in such a huge city. Despite the carnage, the drone strikes, and the deadly battles for survival, there was always the hope that some part of London somewhere remained intact.

Here, in the Valta, I can stand on the big hill at the top and look down the main road and see the entire town. There's no question. No guessing. No wondering. There's nothing here. No hidden pockets of resistance. No protected neighborhoods where survivors could have gathered and regrouped. There's no safe zone, no underground tube stations, no bomb shelters or radiation-proof bunkers, no intact structures, no tucked-away places to hide, and definitely no hope.

I may not have lived here, but Kress did. So did her friends. And they saw lots of people die in drone strikes or get taken away for Recruitment. I don't know if it's my imagination, what I've overheard, my memories of the stories Kress has told me over the years, or if it's some new Emergent ability I'm growing into. (Ravens are known to have excellent memories.) But I swear I can *see* the kids of the Valta. I can *hear* their voices.

And their terrified screams.

The sights and sounds come at me in flashes, like in a dream where you remember every single detail until the second you wake up and let them go.

The sensation actually staggers me for a second. Looking out over the remains of the town, I sway and feel dangerously close to throwing up.

Get a grip, Branwynne. There are enough real enemies in the world without adding ghosts to the list.

I spend the next hour just walking around. I feel like I owe it to the town, somehow. There's not a lot left, so I mostly just wander between piles of rubble, down laneways, and around the mountain of jagged, snow and ash-covered debris where Kress and her Conspiracy—before they *were* a Conspiracy—lived, feared, and, ultimately, survived.

Part of me wants to sprint back to the Academy. Part of me wants to stop and explore some more—maybe rifle through the basements of old shops and imagine what it was like to live here during the worst days of the Atomic Wars. The rest of me can't get through the town fast enough.

The main road leading out of the Valta and down the mountain is nearly impassable, even on foot. Smothering under the weight of countless fallen trees, the patchy path disappears and reappears until its existence loses all meaning, and I'm just walking downhill through the woods.

I'm still not used to the temperature fluctuations around

here. In London, it was hot almost all the time. Here, I can get frostbite two minutes outside of the Academy and then get a sunburn a few hours later as I make my way down the mountain.

The rest of my winding trip down toward New Harleck is slow going...until I'm able to get myself focused and centered.

Haida Gwaii is still in her roost back at the Academy. Mentally channeling her over this distance is hard but not impossible. Since I'm spending a good chunk of my time watching where I'm going so I don't slip and crack my head open, I have to really concentrate to reach her. By giving up a part of my own consciousness, I'm able to make room for some of her keener instincts and abilities. Even though she's asleep, her kinship and comfort with the natural world seep into my brain and body.

After a few minutes, being able to channel her abilities makes navigating the uneven, unpredictable terrain fairly easy. I'm pleasantly surprised when something new clicks on in my mind. It's a pull—a new sensation of being led and comforted at the same time by some outside, invisible force—and I realize I'm sensing thermals and magnetic waves in the air.

With a little more focus, I'm able to solidify the feeling and visualize the waves. And then, I'm not only able to follow them... I can *ride* them.

And whoosh—just like that...I'm able to surf my way down the mountain, and it's got to be the next best feeling to flying.

I wish I could feel like this all the time.

Liberated now, I skim over the rough terrain and move easily down some of the steepest, most perilous parts of the countless ridges and cliffs. I glide under cracked-in-half trees and over stretches of jagged-topped rocks. With my hands dragging lightly on the ground behind me for guidance and support, I slide down long trenches gouged into the side of the mountain.

And then I run, gliding over the rough surfaces with reckless abandon, laughing at how much stronger I am than gravity.

You're doing it Branwynne. You're becoming more by needing less.

I'm out in nature, away from the death and destruction of a homicidal and suicidal world, free from the confines of school, lessons, and homework. I'm in harmony, happy, and skimming along like a bird in flight.

Everything's going easy-peasy...until I slam face-first into a real-life giant.

2

GIANT

THE WOODS HAVE JUST STARTED to thin out and I'm right in the middle of speeding up when I slam into what I think must be a very large tree or else the side of a parked dump truck. Instead, it turns out to be the biggest person I've ever seen in my life.

And that's saying something.

Technically, in the dark and in the instant of stunned surprise, I don't even see him right away. It takes a full second for the stars to fade and for the world to stop spinning. And then I need another second to scrape enough air together to get some oxygen back into my very empty lungs.

The guy towering over me is more massive than Terk and War combined. Bare-chested and wearing what has got to be the world's largest custom-made pair of blue jeans—probably patched together from a repurposed café awning by the looks of them—he's got to be ten feet tall if he's a bloody inch. He's twice as bulky-round as War and even more thick-muscled and broad-shouldered than Terk, and he's exponentially bigger than both. He's got a shock of dark, silky hair hanging halfway down his face with the rest pulled back into a ponytail. He brushes the stray hair away from his eyes with a hand the size of a manhole cover and with fingers as thick around as my forearm.

In his free hand, he's carrying an axe, but it's bigger than any tool even the most strapping lumberjack has ever dreamed about carrying. The thing looks like someone hammered a helicopter blade through a tree trunk.

After a rapid-fire set of painful blinks, I recognize the giant from our brief meeting five years ago. How could I not? Even back then, at twelve years old, he was as big as some of the few intact bronze and marble statues I used to see still standing amid the flattened ruins of London.

Back in my home city, there was nothing left of the statues of Nelson Mandela, Winston Churchill, or Mahatma Gandhi except for their pedestals with their lower legs and feet still attached.

The Meeting Place statue at St. Pancras Station of a man in a suit snogging a woman in a skirt was scarred with blast marks and had fallen over on its side, giving it the appearance of two people frozen solid in the middle of a stiff, fully-clothed shag.

The Statue of Achilles at the easternmost edge of Hyde Park, though, had always been a favorite of mine and was one of the only statues left standing. Achilles' sword was broken in half, his shield arm was lying in rubble fifty feet away, and he was leaning on a forty-five-degree angle, but at least he was still imposing and mostly intact.

This giant is like that: ghastly and battered but still heroically huge, a monument to the aftermath of combat and war.

I can't remember the giant's name at first, but then it comes back to me:

Bendegatefran.

It's a name from the same myth that gave me mine.

I remember him being a kind of quiet and serious member of the Cult of the Devoted. I don't remember much about him, only that it hurt my neck to look up at him. Like trying to take in the entirety of a redwood, I had to scan him one piece at a time.

I'm fuzzy-headed and still on my backside as he stares down at me through dark, puzzled eyes. He raises his giant axe, not in a threatening way but more like in greeting. Like he's a gentleman tipping his hat to a girl he accidentally bumped into on the street.

It's practically charming.

Until he swings the damn thing at me.

I'm almost too stunned—or is it *scared?*—to react.

My training, instincts, and agility kick in just as the wedge-shaped blade is about to connect with the side of my neck.

Already on the ground, I pitch to one side and barrel-roll to the bottom part of a nearby broken tree with its long, gangly roots exposed like they're skeletal arms trying to claw their way out of the ground.

I slide under a bunch of the knotty arms just as the giant's axe comes crashing down, right next to my head.

The dried wood of the dead tree roots explodes into the night air in a hail of splinters and dust, and the giant grunts his disgust at missing his target.

In the near-dark, I slip around to the far side of the tree, hoping it'll give me a second to gather myself, get my bearings, assess my surroundings and my enemy, and maybe—just maybe—give me a chance to stay alive for the next minute or two.

No such luck. With a primitive, throaty howl, the giant swings the axe again. This time, he hacks what's left of my protective shield of a tree into nothing more than a three-foot high stump. The rest of the tall tree's twisted trunk cracks and crashes to the side, shaking the ground and kicking up a cloud of dead leaves and a million petrified twigs and sediment from the forest floor.

The dark air around me turns even darker as it goes smoky and dense with dust and debris.

Fighting blind. Exactly what I need.

And I don't mean that sarcastically. I've been in training to see the world beyond the limited scope of my binocular vision. I even defeated Granden—the Academy's vice-principal and a seasoned veteran of the Atomic Wars—in one-on-one combat...*while I was completely blindfolded.* Of course, it was part of a competitive training exercise, so maybe he wasn't giving it his all.

And he wasn't a ten-foot-tall storybook giant with an axe the size of the Washington Monument.

But I'll take my chances.

Like Kress taught me, I focus and let my consciousness find Haida's. Synched-up, I gasp at the deluge of new thoughts, instincts, and abilities flooding into my mind and body.

Whipping out my Serpent Blades—my twin, S-shaped, retractable knives—I slip down a shallow, frost-covered embankment and clamber around to the side, outflanking the giant. I send one of my weapons spiraling through the darkness. It zings just past his face, and he bellows out a startled bark before lumbering around to try to find me.

That was a decoy, you stonking oaf.

He brings his axe down hard in the exact place I was just kneeling.

With a combined hiss and a crack, the steel wedge buries itself into the firm, frosty ground.

He misses me by a mile.

Coughing on the sawdust and the puffs of snow and soil he keeps kicking up with his blade and with his shuffling, cinderblock-sized boots, he pries his axe loose and swings again.

Another miss.

Dancing around behind him and without making a sound, I

catch my spinning Serpent Blade with one hand as it returns to me through the darkness, and I vault myself up onto a sloping mini-cliff of pointy-headed rocks.

Leaping through the air, I land on the flailing giant's back. I can barely get my arm around his barrel of a neck, but I manage to plant my Serpent Blade close enough to his throat for him to gasp and thrash in terror.

Startled, he drops his axe, and I swear the thing slams to the ground with the force of a skyscraper crumbling under a full-on assault by a team of Demolition Drones.

I hiss into his ear, "We can stop here and now, or you can die...here and now."

It's not a bluff.

Bendegatefran is a resident of New Harleck, the exact place I'm going and a friend of Matholook, the exact boy I'm secretly hoping to see.

I don't want to kill the giant. But I'd rather not be killed *by* him, either.

Let's just hope he makes the right choice.

Bendegatefran stops staggering, nods, and grumbles something so low I can't make out the actual words. But I get the gist. He drops his hands to his side, and his shoulders slump down in sad, resigned defeat.

Looks like he made the right choice.

I remove my Serpent Blade from where I've got it pressed to his throat and slide down his back like he's an amusement park ride.

When my boots hit the ground, I half-land on a square-headed rock protruding from an embankment, turn my ankle, and fall flat on my backside.

So much for enhanced coordination.

And now I'm exposed as the giant, moving faster than I

would have thought possible for someone so big, reaches down and scoops up his axe.

Great. I've got to go through all this again?

But the giant doesn't assume an attack posture.

Instead, he rests the mammoth axe on his shoulder with one hand while he extends the other in an offer to help me up. I can't imagine accepting his gesture. My own hand, and probably the rest of me, could easily disappear in his.

Instead, I squint up at him through the darkness. "I remember you," I tell the giant.

A small animal could burrow in the deep wrinkle of confusion between his eyes. His voice is thick and dark as the belly of a blue whale. "Remember me? From where? Who are you?"

A voice from behind him says, "You can drop the axe, Bendegatefran. That's Branwynne."

And then Matholook steps out from behind the giant to offer me a hand up.

Trying not to seem too pleased or too shocked (and I'm both), I accept his offer.

He helps me to my feet and reaches toward my face in the process. I cock my fist and am about to offer him a double-decker knuckle sandwich when he shows me the thorny twig he just pulled from my hair.

He gives me an apologetic grin and tosses the twig into the woods as I holster my two Serpent Blades and tie my hair back into a ponytail with the leather band I keep around my wrist.

"You must've really taken it to him," Matholook chuckles. "Enough for him to respect you, anyway. Bendegatefran doesn't surrender to just anyone."

"I can imagine."

"She's really fast," the giant bellows. "*Deadly* fast." In the dark, his teeth glow white like a clutch of ostrich eggs. I give him a little salute for the compliment before turning back to Matholook.

"I came down hoping to find you," I tell him as I catch my breath and brush crumbling bits of wood and dirt from the seat of my pants.

Matholook's gemstone-green eyes sparkle in the dark as he laughs.

"What's so funny about that?" I scowl.

"What's so funny about it is that I came up here hoping *I'd* find *you*."

3

BODYGUARDS

"F<small>IND</small> *ME*? F<small>IND ME FOR WHAT</small>?" I ask.

"We need help."

I look from him to Bendegatefran, who nods his boulder-sized head. With an easy flick, he slides the handle of his mammoth axe into a steel loop on his thick leather belt.

(I'm impressed. I doubt I could move that axe with *two* hands.)

"Help? I ask Matholook. "Help with what?"

"We, um...we lost someone."

The giant clears his throat to correct him. "We may have lost a *lot* of people."

Matholook says, "You're right" before turning back to me. "We may have lost a lot of people. There was a raid. We had to get out of there fast, so we don't know how bad it was in the end. There was a person we took with us, a person we were assigned to protect. And, well, we failed."

"As much as I enjoy a good riddle..."

Matholook offers what turns out to be an oddly unhappy chortle. "I'm sorry. I didn't mean that to sound so mysterious. You see, we were attacked."

I flick my eyes toward Bendegatefran. "You and him?"

"Not us. Our town."

"New Harleck?"

"Yes."

I slap my fist into my open palm. "It was Epic, wasn't it? I should've known. I should've warned you a few months ago when I had the chance. He's got these big barmy plans. He thinks he can bring everyone together by ending all the little wars with one big one—"

I'm about to go on. I haven't had a lot of opportunities to rant about Epic and his theory about saving the world by basically harnessing the Emergent techno-evolutionary gene (which may not even exist) and burning everything and everyone else to the ground, but Matholook holds up a hand to cut me off.

"No. It wasn't Epic. It was the Unsettled."

A lump as big as a baseball forms in my throat, and I have to squint and swallow twice to force it back down. "The Unsettled."

"I know you know them. I know you've fought them before."

"Twice," I remind him, holding up two fingers to emphasize the point.

"Right. Well, they took someone. They raided our compound and took someone, and we need her back."

"Her?"

"A girl. The Unsettled knew what they were doing. They knew exactly who and what they were after."

"It was yesterday," Bendegatefran explains. "We were sent away with the girl. To protect her. We were supposed to be her bodyguards."

I don't know if it's from invisible nighttime clouds passing over the glowing red moon or some trick of the silvery, pink-hued light streaking its way through the thin canopy of spindly branches overhead, but Matholook's emerald-green eyes lose their luster and morph into a steely charcoal gray. His voice trembles when he admits, "We failed."

"Failed?"

Shaking his head, his eyes glossy with tears, Matholook invites me to follow him and Bendegatefran to their campsite.

"It's just down that way," he says, pointing vaguely into the dark distance. "We'll tell you all about what happened. But not here. Not like this. It's too dark out here. Too cold. Too exposed."

I don't know either of these boys well, but I know Matholook well enough to know he's not afraid of the dark or of the cold. There's more going on here than he's letting on.

"I don't know if that's such a good idea," I tell him.

"It's not my place to force, convince, or persuade you," he grins. "All I can do is ask."

"And if I say, 'No'?"

"Then we'll go our way, and you can go yours." While I'm pausing to ponder this, Matholook adds, "Of course, going your own way is a lot more fun when someone else is going along with you."

"If this is a trick or some kind of trap..."

"You'll kill us and be back in your Academy in time for breakfast."

"I *am* a pretty ferocious warrior," I say with a laugh.

"Great. Then let's get moving. There's a girl out there who needs our help, and we need yours."

I guess I didn't come this far down the mountain just to turn my nose up at a possible adventure.

"Okay. I'm in. Lead the way."

Matholook claps his hands, and Bendegatefran offers up a wrinkle-cheeked smile.

Rain, one of my teachers at the Academy, once told us, "Be worried when what you do makes your enemy happy."

It seemed like pretty reasonable and straightforward advice

at the time. But what if you're not sure if the two boys standing in front of you are even enemies?

Having decided to offer my help, I join Matholook and his giant friend on a downhill trek through the woods to what I hope is really their campsite and not a trap that ends with my head on one part of the mountain and my body on another.

4

CAMPFIRE

AFTER ONLY A FEW HUNDRED YARDS, Matholook pushes aside a curtain of hanging creeper vines and leads us into a clearing where a small fire is crackling inside a circle of round stones near the opening to a deep, wide-mouthed cave.

Off to the side, a jeep with an open top and thick, studded wheels lurks in the darkness.

"We're camping here for now," Matholook explains with a sweep of his hand from the campfire to the cave.

"You got here in that?" I ask, staring at the ominous, shadowy jeep.

"There's a road back there," Matholook informs me, pointing past the jeep toward a dense section of woods. "It took some doing, but we got this far."

"And then the trail just ended," Bendegatefran groans. "So here we are."

"The girl you're looking for...," I ask. "She was here with you?"

"No," Bendegatefran tells me through a mournful break in his deep voice. "We got ambushed before we got here. The

Unsettled took the girl from us and were gone before we knew
what happened."

"We tried following them," Matholook says, his own voice
heavy and apologetic. "But it was useless. They did something
that disabled our jeep from half a mile away. By the time we got
it running again, they were long gone. The Unsettled know the
terrain too well. We knew we'd never find them. We couldn't go
back to New Harleck empty handed. And I knew about you and
your Academy…"

I point over to the jeep. "And you thought you'd mosey on up
in that thing and ask for help tracking down some girl you lost
in a raid?"

"Um…actually, yeah."

"What a load of bollocks," I say with an undisguised sneer.
"You were about to go on a recon mission to try to find the
Academy so you and your Devoted buddies back in New
Harleck could destroy it."

I almost laugh at how offended Matholook and Bendegatefran suddenly seem. Matholook's eyes flash fury, and Bendegatefran, his mouth open wide enough to match the entrance to the
cave behind him, plants his massive hand over his heart like he's
a prissy little granny about to faint over hearing someone
cursing at tea-time.

"I promise—" Matholook begins, but I cut him off.

"Okay. Let's say you made it to the top of the mountain,
which I doubt you'd be able to do in that jeep. As you noticed,
there's no real roads leading up there anymore. The Academy's
hidden. What was your plan?"

Matholook blushes candy apple red. "I guess we hadn't
really thought that far ahead. I just figured…"

"He figured," Bendegatefran rumbles, "that something…
some *connection* would magically lead him to you." If a voice

could do an eye-roll, his would be doing cartwheels right about now.

The two boys each sit down on one of the five petrified logs lying on their sides in a pentagon around the fire. Bendegatefran has to spread his legs wide, his long arms poised in the air behind him, as he lowers himself to his log a foot at a time like a giraffe easing down to drink at a watering hole.

I'm still standing when Matholook waves his hand at the unoccupied log across from him and insists I join them.

Wary and with one eye on Bendegatefran, who I worry might accidentally stretch his arms out or lean too far over and crush me, I ease down onto the log, tug my red leather jacket around me, and ask what the frack is *really* going on here. "And exactly who the hell is this missing girl you're looking for?" I add, for good measure.

His shoulders back and sounding vaguely offended, Matholook tells me, "I *was* being serious. I really was hoping to find you."

My heart leaps a little when he says that. If I came down looking for him and if he came up looking for me, maybe this feeling I have—this urgent, unexplainable drive pulling at me—isn't just in my imagination after all.

"I was hoping to find you...for *her*," he adds.

"For her?"

"The girl. Gwernna. She needs help." Matholook tilts his head upward in the vague direction of the top of the mountain. "I figured since you had your Academy up there, maybe you could..."

Great. So I risk getting expelled from the Academy to trek down here looking for him, and I find him, only to be told that he wasn't even really *looking for me. And, if he was, it was only as a bloodhound and potential rescuer of another girl.*

Frack that.

"I don't know what you want from me."

Matholook gives me a half-shrug. Like I'm supposed to know what he's on about.

Staring into the fire, Bendegatefran wraps his python-long arms around his knees and tilts his head toward the woods. "I should have been back there fighting off the Unsettled. I'm part of the Vindicators. We're the warriors. The protectors. Fighting off the Unsettled was supposed to be my job."

Matholook reaches over and curls his fingers around Bendegatefran's forearm. ("Curls" might not be the right word. It would take six or seven of Matholook's fingers—lined up end to end—to encircle the giant's forearm.)

"They sent you because I'm just a Caretaker," Matholook assures him. "I couldn't protect her by myself."

Bendegatefran drops his heavy head and drags a sleeve across his eyes. "I couldn't protect her, either."

"And you're sure it was the Unsettled?" I ask Matholook. "I thought they were mostly staying out in the desert."

"They were. For a while. But they've been getting more and more desperate."

"Desperate?" Desperate for what? Food? Weapons? Supplies?"

"No. They're self-sustaining. It's why they're always on the move."

"They *used* to be purely nomadic," Bendegatefran explains, his eyes still watery and red-rimmed. "Just circling through the desert in that big, city-sized caravan of theirs."

"Not anymore," Matholook sighs. He reaches down and fiddles with a petrified twig at his feet before snapping it in half and sending the pieces pinwheeling out into the brush and trees surrounding the clearing. "They went out of their way to come after us. This was a deliberate incursion."

"We know Epic's been trying to negotiate with them," Bendegatefran adds. "Sending out envoys and such. Probably trying to form an alliance to take us down and get us out of his way once and for all."

"I don't think you can negotiate with the Unsettled," I laugh.

"It's true," Matholook concedes. "We have a whole Guild called the Negotiators. They haven't had any luck. But apparently Epic thinks *he* can communicate with the Unsettled. It's all part of some grand unification plan."

"I know all about it," I mumble.

"Oh, right." Matholook passes a glance over to Bendegrate-fran. "Branwynne was the one I told you about. The one who got away from Epic."

"This is the girl?" Bendegatefran asks with a low-pitched laugh. "This is the one who beat you up and took off with our Emergents?"

Matholook holds up his hand, his fingers spread wide. "It was her and *five* others," he reminds the giant with a pout. "And I'm not exactly on a Vindicator's level when it comes to combat."

I make eye contact with Matholook across the fire before flicking my eyes as quickly and subtly as I can back over to Bendegatefran.

From the corner of my eye, I see Matholook give me the tiniest shake of his head.

So...the giant doesn't know about Matholook deliberately releasing the twelve Emergents from their captivity and into the care of me and my Asylum a few months ago. (Or the crack to the jaw I gave Matholook to make it look like he'd been forced into letting them go.)

I guess it makes sense. If the Devoted knew he'd betrayed them like that, I doubt he'd be sitting here across from me, alive and well with his head and limbs still attached to his body.

From what Kress has told me, the Devoted are known for

their hospitality toward strangers but also for their ruthlessness toward any of their own who betray the Cult.

I decide not to fink on him. But I *do* mentally file away his lie in case I need it later. I hope I won't need it, of course, but when you're hanging around and getting chummy with a potential enemy, it never hurts to have a little extra leverage.

As I stare into the flickering, dancing campfire flames, Matholook and Bendegatefran take turns telling me about the recent attack by the Unsettled.

"You've really fought them before?" Bendegatefran asks.

"Yes. Five years ago. And again when we came down to find out who broke into the Academy and stole Haida Gwaii."

"Haida—?"

"That's Branwynne's white raven," Matholook reminds him.

"She's back at the Academy," I explain.

"I remember now." The giant swings over to squint down at me. "Then you know how the Unsettled fight."

I nod, and Bendegatefran says, "They're insane. They're animals." He grimaces and sweeps some of the stray hair away from his sweaty forehead. "Worse. They're cannibals."

Matholook seems sad as he nods his reluctant agreement. "They came in just before dark. Not even twelve hours ago. Not all of them, of course. Just a small platoon. But enough to do damage. They disabled our perimeter alarms. Attacked our security detail. Then went through New Harleck, building by building. We fought back, but they had the advantage of surprise, numbers, and total savagery. They charged right into the compound. No grand speeches. Just ruthless violence. They overpowered us. We don't even know how many got killed or injured."

Bendegatefran nods and cracks his doorknob-sized knuckles. He doesn't try to hide the tears pooling up in the corners of his eyes.

"Justin and Treva...they made us take Gwernna," Matholook tells me. "They made us promise to keep her safe. No matter what. We got her out just in time." He sucks in a deep breath like he's about to dive into the deep end of a pool. "She's an Emergent."

"I don't get it," I say, planting my gaze as firmly as possible onto Matholook's hypnotic green eyes. "There's other Emergents out there. Why her? Why would the Unsettled kill so many of you and risk all-out war just to capture one girl?"

"She's not just 'one girl.' And to be completely honest, she's not really even an Emergent. She's a Hypnagogic."

I repeat the word out loud. I know about Hypnagogics, a rarer and more unstable version of Emergents. I even helped to fight against a Hypnagogic named Noxia back in Buckingham Palace when she was working with the Royal Fort Knights. Depending on who I ask, we may even have a few Hypnagogics in our ranks at the Academy. Our teachers don't talk about it, and they definitely don't answer questions. But I've overheard bits and pieces from Kress and her Conspiracy about Lucid and Reverie, the quiet, magical twins from the Battery of Quail Cohort. And about Sara, the perpetually negative and nasty girl from my own Cohort. At one time or another, I've overheard all their names mentioned in connection with the mysterious sect of Hypnagogics.

Bendegatefran twitches and picks at the chalky, petrified squares of bark on the log he's sitting on. "The Unsettled...they don't speak right."

"Two of them did," Matholook corrects him. "Those boys."

"Right. The boys."

"The boys?" I ask.

"Not much older than us, really. When they were in our town, one of them kept screaming about Gwernna. They marched right down our main road, shouting for us to turn her over to them."

"Justin and Treva managed to get enough of the Devoted together to fight them off."

"They're crazy," Matholook says. "But not organized and definitely not prepared for the defense our people were able to mount."

He flicks his thumb back and forth between himself and Bendegatefran. "While everyone was fighting, Treva pulled me and Bendegatefran aside. They dragged us into one of the supply sheds. She said we had to get Gwernna out of there. She told us that the lives of everyone we know depended on her survival. She's all that mattered."

"And you're sure she's all the Unsettled were after?"

Bendegatefran growls into the campfire flame. "We *know* it."

"I still don't get it. What's so special about this girl?"

As if they're communicating telepathically, Matholook and Bendegatrefan exchange a curious look over the campfire.

"The Unsettled have this idea that she can bring people back from the dead," Matholook says at last.

My mind flashes to Manthy. I didn't know her that well, but I definitely heard the stories about her somehow coming back to life after getting killed by Krug in Kress's final battle against him and his Patriot Army.

But that couldn't have anything to do with this, right?

"Come on." I half chuckle. "Even the Unsettled aren't *that* crazy." When the boys don't answer right away, I remember Manthy and drop my smile.

I don't tell them about her miraculously coming back to life after dying in the final fight between Krug and Kress's Conspiracy in Washington, D.C. I wasn't there for Manthy's resurrection, but I heard the stories, and I personally saw her disappear with Cardyn into the *Lyfelyte* five years ago on the rooftop of the Academy.

"The Unsettled think this girl can bring people back from the dead?" I ask through a half-laugh and a skeptical squint. "Why would they think that?"

With his head tilted down, Matholook glances up at me at me, sighs, and pokes at the fire with another dried stick. "Because she kind of can."

5

HEALING

"Okay, maybe she can't *really* bring the dead back to life," Matholook confesses. "On the other hand, maybe she really can. I've heard different versions of the story. Justin and Treva have been working with her for a couple of years now."

"Bollocks," I interrupt. "You mean they've been *experimenting* on her, right?"

What is it about Typics that makes them swear they're splashing out for you when they're really just being self-serving arsemongers?

Matholook holds up both hands and shakes his head hard. "Not experimenting on her. I swear. More like experimenting *with* her. She's never suffered."

"Sure. Other than being a test subject. Forget being a princess. Being a guinea pig...*that's* every girl's dream, right?"

I really want to be mad right now. I want to smack Matholook and his giant buddy around and scream at them that being an Emergent doesn't come with an open invite for any random plonker to experiment on us. But Matholook sounds so sincere about his claims and just as offended about my reaction, so I hold my tongue.

For now.

Taking turns and sounding excited and a little proud, the two boys go on to tell me about Gwernna's ability to heal small animals that were infected with radiation poisoning.

"First it was just little things," Matholook says. "A bug or a scorpion. One of our younger members—a boy named Kelvin—had a praying mantis that lived on the ledge outside his window. I was there when Kelvin came running out crying one morning when he found the mantis dead on the windowsill. A bunch of us went back to his room. Gwernna was sitting cross-legged on the floor. The mantis was alive and well in her cupped hands."

Matholook forms a small bowl with his two hands and locks his pleading eyes onto my very skeptical ones.

I'm not anywhere close to convinced, and I do my best not to scoff. "So maybe Kelvin was wrong," I suggest. "Or crazy. Or pissing around. Or telling porkies. Maybe he was sick of having a bug as his best friend and was looking for attention."

"Um...what are 'porkies'?"

"Pork pies. Lies."

"You think he was lying?"

"He wouldn't be the first."

"I don't think so."

"He's weirdly moral," Bendegatefran insists.

"Okay, then. Maybe it was just a big, dumb coincidence."

"Of course," Matholook says, pointing a finger at me and nodding his agreement. "A coincidence. That's what I said. That's what a lot of us said. But things got weirder. After that, it was dead marmots or woodrats the Gatherers brought back from the mountains or from their trips into the desert. Other times, someone would come back dehydrated or sick with heatstroke or injured from a fall. A few times, injured Scouts got carried back after drone attacks. Gwernna did something to all of them."

"Something *real*," Bendegatefran assures me, his voice a bass rumble so deep and low I'm barely able to hear it, even though I can feel its waves vibrating in my stomach.

"It got to be too much to be a coincidence," Matholook promises.

Standing and edging past Bendegatefran's monumentally peaked legs, he walks around the fire to kneel down in front of me. He reaches out and curls the fingers of one hand around the side of my neck. He rests his other palm on my upper chest just above my left collar bone. It's an intimate, familiar gesture, and I'm about to smack him, but his touch is gentle, and his voice is apologetic when he explains what the girl did.

"She would touch people here...and here."

"And what? They would be magically healed?" This time, I *do* lean away. Matholook drops his hands and locks his green eyes onto mine before walking back to his own log and sitting back down.

"No. Not healed. Not right away. In fact, we thought maybe she was making things worse."

"But then the Cysters...," Bendegatefran begins.

"Right. The Cysters."

"The women survivors of the Plague?" I ask.

"You know them?"

"No. Not really. But I've heard of them. Some of my friends at the Academy know about them."

"Have you ever met one?"

"A Cyster? No. Why?"

Matholook and Bendegatefran exchange a look I can't read. "The Cyst Plague is a nasty business," Bendegatefran rumbles.

I tell him I know. "I saw it in London."

"Then you know what it does to a person."

With my mind full of memories of so many of London's adults lurching around, covered in blisters, angry red rashes, and raised ridges on their bodies from the long, multi-legged parasites burrowing into the decomposing muscles under their skin, I nod and tell him I do. "I *definitely* do."

"A Clique of Cysters—that's what they call themselves—they found their way to New Harleck about two years ago. That was the first time we saw Gwernna do her trick on a person outside of the Devoted."

"Trick?"

"When she touched them, like I showed you, they got better."

"Kind of," Bendegatefran clarifies.

"Right. Kind of."

"You mean she healed them?" I ask.

"Yes. And no. Their symptoms went away."

"Far away," Bendegatefran says with a hippo-wide smile.

"What's that mean?"

Matholook clears his throat. "The Cysters—there were three of them—they got healthy. *Really* healthy. Their eyes got bright. Teeth, hair...even their fingernails seemed cleaner. And their skin looked...polished. They'd been lost and wandering through the desert for at least a week before they found us. Apparently, two of their Clique died along the way. A team of our Scouts went out to confirm their story. They found what was left of the two bodies. Before Gwernna tended to them, the three who made it to New Harleck were a hot mess. Afterwards, after she did her thing with them, there wasn't a blemish in sight."

"Sculpted. Smooth," Bendegatefran clarifies, dragging the backs of his fingers down his long, burly forearms. "Glossy. Like perfect marble statues."

Marble statues? The last person I saw who looked like that...was... Epic. And he kidnapped me and Haida, and there's no telling what he would have done with us if my Asylum hadn't come to our rescue. Another coincidence? Real-life giants, magic healers, marble people... What the frack have you gotten yourself into, Branwynne?

"She could bring people back," Matholook explains. "Not all the time, but often enough to make her skills too valuable to leave to chance."

"So she became an experiment in a Petri dish."

"Worse. She became a weapon."

"A weapon? Just because she could *maybe* heal people? Doesn't that make her more of...I don't know...a doctor or something?"

"Sure. In the best of times. When all that's wrong in the world is a little illness here and there. But when it's the worst of times, when the world's at war...an army that can't die..."

"Can't lose," I finish.

Matholook gives me a knowing nod. "So she was...*is* valuable."

"Valuable?"

"To us, yes. But also to the Unsettled. And to Epic. Our leaders met with him a few times. He said he wanted to help her, that he was the only one who could bring out the full extent of her abilities and possibly save her life."

"Save her life? I don't get it. Wasn't she the one saving everyone else?"

"Sure. She could heal people. With some limits and conditions. We figured that out soon enough. But it turns out it wasn't that simple. There was a cost."

"There were some...side effects for the people she healed," Bendegatefran explains, his eyes planted to a spot on the ground between his boots.

"Other than the marble skin?"

"There were some weird personality changes," Matholook says. "Obsessive behaviors. Compulsions. Oh, and whatever person or animal she brought back lost its voice."

"Really?" I swing around to face Bendegatefran who nods his confirmation without looking up.

It's a lot to absorb, and it takes me a full minute of staring into the fire before I can even *begin* to process it all. Finally, I point out that losing your voice is a small price to pay. "Especially if it means having an immortal army at your command."

Matholook gazes at me for a second over the flicker and snap of the campfire flames. "Even if it weren't a small price, people like Epic and the Unsettled are willing to pay a lot more than that. They're willing to go to war and pay with their own lives if it means having hers."

"So where is this girl...what's her name again?"

"Gwernna."

"Right. Gwernna. If you were supposed to be protecting her, what the frack happened?"

"Don't underestimate the Unsettled," Matholook warns. "They may not be as big as Bendegatefran here or as tech savvy as Epic or as techno-genetically enhanced as you and your fellow Emergents way up there in the mountains. But they have ways of getting what they want."

"They got the drop on you?"

"That's an understatement, but yeah."

"I don't get what you want from me. I don't know where they took her any more than you do. I'm not a tracker. I can't find her."

Matholook points to a spot above my head. "I know. It wasn't just you I was looking for up here. I was kind of hoping maybe *she* could help."

I whip around to see what he's pointing at.

Ruffling her hackles and breaking into a cocky strut along one of the crooked branches of the tree behind me—her white feathers standing out against the dark night around us—is Haida Gwaii, the white raven I've known and been connected with for as long as I can remember.

6

VISION

"Haida!"

The white raven opens and closes her talons on her perch and gargles out one of her signature *gurgle-clacks*.

The guttural call rings through the calm, dark night.

Whipping around, Bendegatefran leaps up and spins around to face the white raven. Pointing like he's seen a ghost, he cries out in a slow, deep stammer, "That's a raven! And...and he's...he's an *albino*!"

"Haida's a girl," I correct him. "And yes—she's a raven. But she's not an actual albino."

Bendegatefran points a quivering finger at Haida. "But he... it...I mean, *she's* white."

"The condition is called *leucistic*," I tell him, holding back a laugh at the thought of someone the size of a double-decker bus being afraid of something the size of a loaf of bread. "It's a genetic abnormality related to another condition called vitiligo. It causes patchy pigmentation patterns. In Haida's case, it makes her nearly all white. Albinism is a lack of melanin and carotenoids. That's a type of pigment that comes from certain foods in her diet. Haida doesn't have the pink eyes of most albino animals."

Haida flutters down to land on my forearm while the two boys stare at me as if I'm a multi-headed pod-creature that just crash-landed in a spaceship and threatened to attack them with an alien rectal probe.

"What?" I ask them. They don't answer. "You want to know how I know this stuff, right?"

Both boys nod their heads.

"It's because of the Auditor," I sigh.

"The Auditor?" Matholook asks.

"She's a cyber-intelligence with access to all kinds of point-less information. And she's not shy about sharing it. She's integrated with Terk's Modified systems. He's one of my teachers back at the Academy. She's part of his digs-tech network, so she kind of goes along with him for the ride."

"Terk. I remember him! The big guy, right?" Matholook runs his hand over his own left arm, hip, and ribcage. "He has a bunch of synth-steel and cyber parts."

"That's him."

"You and this bird...," Bendegatefran begins but then seems to lose his train of thought.

"They might be able to help us track down Gwernna," Math-olook gushes. "Like I told you."

"You said she's done it before."

"A few months back. Branwynne and Haida Gwaii helped us get away from the Unsettled and back to New Harleck."

Bendegatefran clamps his hands to the sides of his hulking head. "I don't know. This seems pretty strange. And risky. There's no precedent."

"Precedent is kind of our bible," Matholook explains. "In the Cult of the Devoted, we rarely do what hasn't already been done. On the other hand," he adds, pivoting back toward Bendegatefran who is ringing his hands hard enough to make me think they might burst into flames, "what choice do we have? We can either trust her and her raven or else we can go back to the compound empty handed."

"Or we can follow a girl and a bird, try to rescue Gwernna, fail, and get killed and eaten by the Unsettled."

"That's the spirit!" Matholook says with a sarcastic fist pump in the air.

"I'm just being cautious," Bendegatefran pouts.

"Caution is reserved for people who still have something to lose," Matholook advises. "If we fail...if we don't bring Gwernna back with us, the Unsettled will raid New Harleck again. Only this time, it won't be to look for Gwernna. It'll be to use her to help them wipe out everyone in our Cult. We won't have a chance if we can die and they can't. And when they're finished with us, they'll be on their way to fight Epic in Sanctum." Matholook swivels away from Bendegatefran and lets his eyes settle on mine. "And then, they'll head up the mountain, find your Academy, and..."

He doesn't need to finish, and I tell him so. If what they say about this girl is true—if she can somehow miraculously bring the dead to life—the army with her in their ranks would be able to fight forever and without fear. They'd be completely unbeatable. She could wind up being more powerful than any Emergent, even Kress. *If* what these boys are telling me is true.

"I'll see what she has to say."

I let my mind drift away from itself, and my consciousness melts into Haida's.

Where'd you come from?

~ Home.

You hate flying at night.

~ It's almost morning.

Get back to the Academy.

~ *Not without you.*

Matholook needs help. There's a girl...

~ *I know.*

You know?

~ *She's in a caravan.*

A caravan?

~ *A small team. They're on their way to reunite with the Army of the Unsettled. They're on the move. Not far from here.*

How do you know?

~ *I can see.*

How?

~ *There's more to vision than meets the eye.*

I don't understand.

~ *Here. I'll show you.*

Some kind of furious, flashing mental pitchfork stabs a few million pinpricks of pain into my brain.

I gasp and am just able to latch onto the tiniest bit of breath. In the blank, arctic white of my mind's eye, a flood of images takes shape...

I'm soaring over a wide expanse of desert. The sand is red and pushed up into long, low dunes by the hot gales gusting over the land.

There are trees. Not many. But a few dozen scraggly survivors lean into the whipping wind. Their thin, knotted arms reach out into the distance, stretching toward some better place that may or may not exist. Parts of the landscape are dotted with spiky scrub brush.

An old highway winds through it. Bubbled and black from the heat, it rolls over hills and cuts through outcroppings of layered rock. Lining the road's sloping shoulders, the useless remains of a fleet of old military vehicles—picked clean of anything even remotely salvageable—lie half-buried on their sides.

A brown cloud of powdery dust churns in the distance. As it rolls toward me, it splits in the middle, sending huge curls of smoke and sand to either side.

From in between the big, looping plumes, a fleet of small, motorized vehicles emerges.

Skid Steers. Six of them. I've seen these things before. They're the scouting vehicles of the Unsettled. And there are six dirt bikes. Three of them are belching smoke. The other three have the shimmering distortion of a mag-field around them.

Like a lot of what I've seen—here and in London—the technology has become a chaotic hodgepodge of sophisticated and antiquated.

As the vehicles grind along, the six two-person Skid Steers and the six dirt bikes form a protective ring around a single, quaking and dirt-covered RV. The camper is big and armored. It's got long sheets of steel plating over its windows and thicker, darker shielding covering its wheels. Gun turrets are welded onto its top and onto one of its sides.

From this distance, even plugged into Haida, I shouldn't be able to make out this much detail. But it's beaming at me with crystal clarity, and I realize it's not nighttime anymore.

The moon is high but washed-out. It's daytime. Morning. The sun is crawling its way over the distant horizon.

I think maybe it's a vision of the past, but Haida corrects me.

~ You know this as "what will be."

Wait. What I'm seeing isn't happening right now?

~ It's happening soon.

How can I be seeing the future from the present?

~ What's the difference?

I SNAP BACK into focus-mode where I catch Matholook staring at me. "Can I just tell you how creepy that is?"

"What's creepy?" I ask with a huff.

"Your eyes. They go from nearly all black to nearly all white."

"Epic calls them Galaxy Eyes."

"I can see why."

"I think the color of my eyes will be a lot less interesting to you than what they saw."

"Which is...?"

"Your friend. Gwernna. The girl you were supposed to be protecting..."

The boys both lean forward nearly far enough to fall over. "What about her?"

"I think I know where she is."

"What? Really?"

"Well, not exactly." I look up and out over the tree line to where the dark night sky is dissolving into a faint sheen of pinkish mist.

"It's almost morning," I say out loud. And then I swing around to face Matholook and Bendegatefran. "I may not know where she is. But I think I do know where she's *about* to be."

7

MISSION

Bendegatefran's mouth hangs open. I can tell he wants to ply me with a million questions. But we don't have time, and Math-olook cuts him off, anyway.

"Branwynne's an Emergent," he reminds his giant friend. "They have magical powers."

"Hardly," I scoff. "I'm not some frog-boiling, warty witch."

Matholook leans in, his green eyes reflecting the snapping, dancing sparks from the fire. "Really? Then what would *you* call what you are?"

"I call it being just one of the infinite versions of 'normal.'"

Matholook gives me a raised eyebrow of amused skepticism. "That sounds nice in theory. But out here in the real world, being an Emergent makes you a million miles away from 'normal.'"

"Fine," I sigh, taking a deep breath before leaping into the explanation I've been taught. "We're the convergence of an evolutionary leap possibly having to do with the thirty-ninth or fortieth parallel of the Earth with a little help from a confedera-tion of evil techno-geneticists determined to harvest us for our abilities and sell us off to the highest bidder." I'm laughing to myself as the boys give me matching, silent, puzzled stares. So I add, "We're *not* superpowered. Some of us can barely do anything. Others can't control what they can do. That's why we're in school."

After another round of uncomfortable stares, Matholook speaks for both boys.

"Well, whatever you can do—and however you can do it—we'd be happy and grateful if you could lead us to Gwernna."

He sounds so sincere when he says this. Sincere and charmingly overprotective. But I have to remind myself: These boys aren't trying to save her for her sake. They're trying to save her for their own. I'll help them find her, but there's no way I'll sit by and let them re-imprison, analyze, and weaponize her.

"I can't swear I'm comfortable with this whole rat-arsed scenario of yours. But okay, I'm in."

Matholook slaps his palms to his knees, jumps up, and heads over to the jeep. "If you're right about seeing what hasn't happened yet, then we need to get moving if we're going to catch up to the future."

"Right now?" Bendegatefran asks as I stand up and go over to join Matholook.

"Do you have somewhere better to be?" I call back to him. "Maybe you're secretly the Greek god Atlas and have to get back to holding up the sky? Or you're a Cyclops about to get tricked by Odysseus? Or killed by David and his little sling?"

Bendegatefran groans himself up to his full, tree-sized height. He snatches up his axe and a large canvas duffel bag sitting just inside of the cave before stomping out the campfire with his canoe-sized boot. "You know, there's also Paul Bunyan and John Henry. Not all giants are evil."

In the dark shadows cast by the fading campfire, I can't tell if the side-mouthed smirk the giant gives me is one of amusement, pride, or irritation.

Before I can figure it out one way or the other, he strides toward me.

"You better be right about this, Emergent," he grumbles as he lumbers past.

"Hey," I call out to his barn-sized back. "This Gwernna girl really means that much to you?"

"More than you do. If you betray us...If you try to attack us..."

"You'll never see it coming," I sneer.

Bendegatefran stops dead in his tracks, but I don't bother to wait for his reaction. Instead, I skip ahead and hop into the jeep's passenger seat as Matholook presses the pad of his thumb to the ignition port, and the vehicle hums to life.

Bendegatefran slings his duffel bag into the jeep's shallow trunk and folds himself sideways into the backseat. I notice he hangs onto his axe.

With Haida flying ahead toward the rising sun, we drive downhill, bouncing over some brutally rough terrain. I've got to brace my hands against the jeep's front control panel to stop myself from hurtling through the windshield. My arms are tight from the strain, but I hang on until we push through a final wall of thinning trees and drive out into an open plain of empty desert.

I've come this way before. A couple of times actually. Once, when I first arrived out west with Kress and her Conspiracy five years ago. And then again, a few months ago, when Matholook risked his life to turn over his Cult's twelve captive Emergents to me and my Asylum.

But right now, I recognize where we are from the visions Haida shared with me.

A rolling cloud of gray-brown dust rises up in the distance. I recognize the tumbling plumes as easily as if I'd seen them every day of my life.

From his spot in the back seat, his knees tucked under his chin, Bendegatefran points to the blossoming tufts of desert sand. "It's them, isn't it?"

"Yes. They're the ones Haida showed me. And they're on the move."

"They're the Unsettled," Matholook chuckles over the bounce and grind of the jeep's tires on the rough patches of hard desert ground. "They're *always* on the move."

"Then we need to be, too. Let's go."

"You want us to chase after them?"

I give it a moment's thought. I do my best to patch together what Haida showed me from overhead with what little bit I remember from the special Tracking Seminar Rain taught us a few weeks back in preparation for the upcoming Topography & Navigation class we need to take next term. Combined, I'm able to triangulate what I think will be the point where the crew that captured Gwernna will rendezvous with the rest of their huge, moving army.

"We won't need to chase them," I tell my two companions. "I know where they're going to try to meet up."

"Is that what Haida told you?"

"It's what she *showed* me," I answer with as mysterious a smile as I can manage.

"Maybe you should take the wheel," Matholook suggests.

"Smartest thing you've said all night," I tell him as I scootch up so he can switch places with me and slide behind me into the passenger seat.

I take a second to survey the jeep's controls. Other than getting a chance to drive the Terminus once, I don't have a lot of experience behind the wheel of automated vehicles. We're supposed to be learning how to drive the Academy's fleet of mountain vehicles in War's Transportation & Mechanics class, but he insists on teaching us every tiny detail about them and restricting our not-so-hands-on training to the VR-sims before he lets us take them for a proper spin.

This jeep I'm in now seems pretty straightforward, though, and I instantly launch us into a breakneck sprint of tracking and pursuit.

"You're good at this," Matholook calls out over the rumble. "Do you have vehicles like this at your Academy?"

"Yes," I shout back. "But we haven't been fully trained so we're not allowed to drive them yet."

"Well, when you do, I'm sure you'll get the highest marks in your class!"

I blush at the compliment. Driving *is* fun. But personally, like Haida Gwaii who's easily outpacing us over the rolling desert terrain, I'd rather fly.

Kress said she'd teach me, but whenever I ask her, she says I'm not ready yet. I make a mental note to nag her about it when I go back.

If I go back.

And assuming, when all this is over, I'm alive enough to make that choice.

8

PLANNING

"SHE'S IN THERE," I tell the boys, directing their attention to the white, slow-moving RV surrounded by its escort of dirt-bikes and Skid Steers.

Deeper in the distance—across at least two miles of simmering desert—the huge city of the Army of the Unsettled lies in wait. From here, it looks like a few thousand parked campers, transport rigs, and construction vehicles. But I know from experience that the whole lot of them are actually moving. They may go slow, but they're *always* moving.

According to Kress, the Army of the Unsettled has spent more than a decade roaming the deserts and plains of the west and hasn't stopped once.

Entirely self-sufficient, they migrate over the land, gathering resources for their army, scooping up stragglers to enhance their ranks, wiping out enemies, and decimating any outposts or opponents that might be standing in their way. And, apparently, they've added kidnapping to their long list of activities.

Resting his forearms on the front dashboard of our jeep, Matholook grumbles and shakes his head at the RV and its entourage chugging along up ahead. "It's a moving target heading toward a moving target."

"Then we'd better have pretty accurate aim," I tell him.

The swirl of dust and sand in the distance pushes forward and then pulls back in a pulsing vortex before settling into an eerie stillness.

At first, I think maybe it's my eyes playing tricks on me. But up ahead, the small convoy has definitely stopped. I point this out to Matholook who grins. "They're dumping their waste."

"Really?"

"It's pretty much the only time these little flying squads of theirs ever stop. The big army *never* does."

"Okay, then. This is our window. Chances like this don't happen often, so we need to press our advantage," I say, parroting one of Kress and Brohn's lessons in combat tactics. "Here's what we're going to do. Come with me."

I hop out of the jeep and tell them to come kneel down next to me as I gather a handful of small stones and a bunch of dried twigs.

"These are you," I say, pointing to two dusty red pebbles. Talking fast—the squad we're tracking won't be stationary for long after all—I go on to show them the rest of my makeshift battle plan illustration: "This is me. This is the RV. Here are the Skid Steers. And these are the dirt-bikes. At this point, the caravan will have to slow down to cross this ravine. When they go around this butte, we'll cut them off on the other side where the desert opens up and before they have a chance to rendezvous with the rest of their army."

Bouncing my focus back and forth between Matholook and Bendegatefran, I run through exactly what I'm going to need from them.

"Pay attention," I snap. "If we're off by so much as a second, this won't work, and we'll all be joining your friend Gwernna.

Only, the Unsettled will keep me and her alive. Emergents have value for them. The two of you...well, they'll probably just kill you and eat you."

The difference in their reactions strikes me as really odd at first. Bendegatefran leans in, anxious and eager. He's a stallion champing at the bit, primed and desperate to jump into battle.

Matholook is fidgety. A wrinkle of worry creases deeper and deeper between his eyes. He's not afraid, though. Just concerned.

When I tell him none of us may come out of this alive, he doesn't even blink or seem to give it a second thought. He just insists I make him a promise. "If there's any chance to free Gwernna and get her back to New Harleck, *any* chance, take it."

I start to protest. I don't intend to fail. But he shakes me off. "She's more important than any of us. If your mission really is to save the world—"

"It is."

"Then it's got to start with saving her."

He's trying to hide the tremble in his voice, but he might as well be trying to hide an earthquake.

His nervousness must be contagious because Bendegatefran has a stream of sweat dribbling through the deep creases in his forehead.

I guess their reactions shouldn't surprise me. I already know the Cult of the Devoted are divided into a bunch of different "Guilds," each with its own mission and guiding set of rules they're duty-bound to follow.

Bendegatefran is from a Guild they call their "Vindicators." They're warriors. Tough. Fearless. Charged with the safety of the entire Cult. It's a huge responsibility and an awful lot to ask of a seventeen-year-old, no matter how enormous he is. Matholook is from the "Caretakers" and has just as much weight on his shoulders. He's tasked with looking after the health and well-being of the Devoted.

Right now, I don't know which of them—the gentle-eyed guardian or the freakishly large stonker of a warrior—is most wound up about this mission.

But the intensity of their concern is making *me* nervous.

Is this girl really worth dying for? Even scarier, is she really worth killing for?

Whatever questions or nervousness the boys have got, they swallow it down as I finish outlining my plan.

I keep expecting one or both of them to jump in and challenge me. But they just sit there, nodding.

Am I ever going to feel comfortable being in charge? Is this what Kress feels like? I'm not a leader. I'd rather just be pointed in the direction of battle and cut loose to engage the enemy.

I drag my finger through the warm desert sand and make an "X" by a cluster of pebbles I've stacked into a small pyramid. "They'll take this path," I tell my two new partners. "We'll cut them off here."

"And you really think we can do this?"

"I really think *I* can do this. What the two of you can offer remains to be seen." I hold up my hand to stave off any more questions, objections, or debate. "We don't have time for a discussion. I don't have anything on the line here. This girl is your responsibility. You lost her. If you want her back, you'll need to follow this plan to the letter. What happens to her doesn't matter to me. But I know it matters the world to you. So...are you ready?"

"We're ready," Matholook insists. "But..."

"But what?"

"What happens to her *will* matter to you as well. More than you know."

I can't tell if he's being melodramatic or manipulative. What

I *can* tell is that he's serious and oddly sure of himself. He really thinks this girl we're about to risk our lives to rescue should be important to me.

She's not. Or so I thought. The look in Matholook's eyes tells me she might be, after all.

And now I'm wondering if maybe Haida isn't the only one who can see into the future.

9

RESCUE

PRIMED for battle and with the Unsettled caravan up ahead, grinding back into motion, we skim over the rough terrain on an intercept course.

On my signal, Bendegatefran hops out of the moving jeep and leaps into the middle of the churning, grumbling convoy.

In my experience, whenever someone is surprised like this, they react in one of two ways: they come to a full-on stop or else they run like hell.

Lucky for us, the Unsettled—for all of their constant motion —are fighters at heart. So instead of running, trying to get to their roving army, or waiting for reinforcements, they follow their hearts, they stop, and they fight.

While the RV lumbers on, the escort of Skid Steers and dirt-bikes squeals to a halt, kicking up a red dust storm as they do.

Bendegatefran's monstrous axe carves a glittering silver arc in the early morning air. When it's done, two of the Unsettled are rolling on the ground, clutching their bleeding chests in a hopeless attempt to keep their internal organs from spilling out onto the soft desert sand.

Before the rest of the escort can react, Matholook leaps out from next to Bendegatefran and slides behind the controls of the nearest Skid Steer. Palming it into gear, he sends the studded rubber-coated treads spinning as they kick up more clouds of pebbles and dust.

At the same instant, Haida Gwaii dive-bombs the two lead dirt-bikes. The boy and the girl on the bikes swing their hatchets wildly before they all disappear in a rising, rolling wall of sand and dust.

In the confusion, I slip between the rear escorts. Channeling Haida to a degree I haven't done before (and, honestly, that hurts way more than I expected), I leap fifteen feet onto the top of the slow-moving, white RV. Unholstering one of my deadly Serpent Blades, I easily slice through the steel padlock on the rooftop access panel. Sparks fly as the steel falls apart, and I yank open the panel of aluminum and frosted glass.

Swinging my legs around, I drop down into the belly of the vehicle and land with a plunk in the middle of four scowling, surly teenage boys.

Four guards. That's it?

With my other Serpent Blade out, I feel my "galaxy eyes" gloss over as I pirouette between the four stunned boys.

Kress promised she'd teach me how to stop seeing the Serpent Blades as external weapons.

"Do you want me to think of them as part of myself?" I asked her once.

"No," she replied. "I don't want you to think of them at all."

And right now, I don't. They might as well be my elbows, feet, fists, or knees, some part of me I don't pay any attention to until it's time to unleash them with deadly force.

I take an instant mental snapshot: The four teenaged guards are dressed in a hodgepodge of hockey equipment, leather riding gear, and silver duct tape. Two of them have mesh-less lacrosse sticks with long, rusted nails driven outward through the oval head of the frame.

Nice weapons. They look like the world's deadliest sunflowers.

The other two boys each have an old gun in a leather holster and a machete hanging from a loop of frayed twine strapped across their chests.

The boy with the patchy blond goatee is quick enough to *almost* reach his holster. But that's as far as he gets. And his buddies don't even get that far.

I spring into instant action—no thought, strategy, plan, or contemplation. Jacked up with Haida's predatory instincts, I'm just pure, whirling warrior.

When the boys are down, bleeding and panting their last breaths, I step over them.

The back of the RV has been sectioned off with a floor-to-ceiling steel grate to form a small jail cell. The bars are thick and painted black. A small dome on the ceiling of the cell casts a feeble, yellow glow into the bleak, cordoned-off area.

Inside the dry, metallic chamber is a girl. She can't be more than about nine or ten years old. She's got wide, glinting eyes, spiky hair, and a small red jacket with white cuffs over her blue denim dress.

Oddly enough, she doesn't seem scared. In fact, she's looking at me like she's been expecting me.

"Hi," she says as casually as if we were meeting for afternoon tea. "I'm Gwernna."

I tell her, "I know." And then I tell her my name is Branwynne.

She says, "I know."

Startled for a second but without the time to process her response, I shout for her to stand back.

She complies by hopping back two full steps as I approach the cell.

This lock is three times as thick as the padlock on the rooftop panel. I'm temporarily frozen by its immovable density.

I strike at it anyway with my Serpent Blades.

Nothing.

Sweating and desperate, I try again. I lash out over and over with the blades sending a shower of sparks into the air.

Still...nothing. And I'm out of time. Which means Gwernna is out of time.

She reaches through the bars, tugs at my sleeve, and points toward the interior wall of the RV. "We're going to die."

Great, kid. Thanks for the vote of confidence.

Screams and the sound of revved engines from the Skid Steers outside fill the RV. I don't know if the shouting I'm hearing is from Bendegatefran and Matholook being victorious or if it's from them being overwhelmed by the Unsettled and hacked to pieces.

I even out my breathing, tap into Haida Gwaii, and try to relax myself enough to do something I've never done successfully without Kress standing right next to me.

Bollocks. This is going to hurt.

I concentrate like Kress taught me. In a horrifying moment, I feel every molecule in my body shiver and shift.

The pain rifling through me is unlike anything I've ever experienced. It dizzies up my head and shakes my body to my bones. My skin, muscles, and organs expand and compress and then expand again in an excruciation pulse I pray will end but also hope will last.

The feeling—blasting through me in a microscopic sliver of a split-second—is almost one of...pleasure?

Figure it out later, Branwynne!

Ignoring every rule of physics I've ever learned, I rush forward.

I pass through the iron bars...

I pass through the iron bars! Not between. Through.

I scoop up the girl, and—before I lose my connection or concentration—I pass the two of us straight through the back wall of the RV.

Hitting the hard ground with a concussive thud, we roll, slide, and skid along the desert sand. I do my best to keep my arms around Gwernna to stop her from experiencing the full impact of the sharp rocks mixed in with the soft, warm ground. It would actually be kind of fun if it didn't hurt so much and if we weren't trying to escape with our lives.

Gathering up the girl, I send a mental signal to Haida and run like hell toward the edge of the canyon.

I panic for a second when I feel a grinding rumble tear through the ground, and I hear a pair of Skid Steers closing in on me from behind.

Haida's voice is soft and soothing in my head.

~ *It's okay.*

I realize right away what she means as the two Skid Steers—one driven by Matholook, the other driven by Bendegatefran who has his long legs angled comically in the air—blast up next to me and slam to a grinding halt.

I leap into Matholook's Skid Steer, Bendegatefran scoops Gwernna up and hauls her into his Skid Steer with one hand, and we go tearing off through the canyon with a small fleet of the remaining Unsettled sputtering along in our wake.

"What happened to your jeep?" I cry out over the thrum of the Skid Steer's engine and the grinding impact of its thick black treads on the packed desert sand and the serrated red rocks beneath us. "The plan was to escape in the jeep!"

"We had to trade it in!"

"Not bad!" I confess. "Two for one!"

When the rocky canyon becomes impassable, we cut hard to the side and crash our way through a small, wooded area with

Haida Gwaii gurgle-clacking and guiding us along from overhead.

Her white feathers bristle in the stiff desert air as she soars, banks, and glides her way along ahead of us.

Our two Skid Steers bounce and grind as we cross a rocky-bottomed ravine and finally plunge into a thicker part of the woods at the edge of the desert.

I whip around in my seat, sure the Unsettled will be right behind us, but there's no sign of them anymore.

"We disabled as many of their vehicles as we could," Matholook shouts over the roar of the engine. "Like you told us!"

"Where to now?"

"Back to where we started," he calls out. "In the woods. It'll be safe, and we can decide what to do from there!"

"Can you get us back there?"

"No. I was hoping you could."

Relaxing now, I tell him I think I can manage that.

I don't know if it's my own memory at work or if it's Haida Gwaii's or if it's just a matter of pure dumb luck, but we eventually find ourselves back in the same clearing with the campfire and the cave where we left from not more than an hour ago.

An hour? Did we really just change the course of a war and possibly of the world in sixty minutes?

The campfire is nothing but ashy embers and black flecks rising up into the crisp morning air.

The two boys park the Skid Steers in the spot of flattened woods where they stowed their jeep before we left and saunter back to the dead campfire, striding like conquering heroes with Gwernna looking small but relieved between them.

Gathering up an armful of dried kindling and larger chunks of chipped branches, Matholook goes about reigniting the fire, and we all sit down.

I ask him if that's such a good idea. "The Unsettled could see the smoke," I remind him.

"They won't stray this far from their army," Matholook tells me. "Their unity in that giant, roving community of theirs is a strength. I'll grant you. But it's also a weakness. We'll be okay. Besides, we won't stay here long. Just enough to rest up before moving on to New Harleck."

Bendegatefran shakes his head and beams back and forth between me and Gwernna. "I can't believe we—*you*—got her back. And so fast!"

Matholook beams and slaps Bendegatefran on the shoulder. "I can't believe it was that easy!"

Easy my arse. Tell that to the surly donkey back-kicking its way around my brain.

10

GWERNNA

ALMOST LIKE HE'S forgotten that there's a slightly twitchy, disheveled little girl sitting there next to him, Matholook sputters, "Oh. Sorry. This is Gwernna."

"I know. We met."

I tell her it's nice to meet her...formally. She answers by smiling, raising her eyelids high over her cartoonishly oversized eyes, and scootching over toward Matholook to press her cheek to his arm.

"She's shy," he explains. "We didn't exactly expect to have to go through all of this."

"That makes two of us."

Matholook runs his hand over the little girl's spiky hair.

Her eyes really are huge and darting. Her outfit of worn denim hangs on her like a circus tent on a scarecrow. Everything about her is puppy-like and inquisitive, like she's seeing the outside world for the first time. She even tilts her head back to breathe as she leans into Matholook, her little nostrils flaring with delight.

I glance over the wispy campfire at Gwernna who's listening

to us talk but is nodding her head like she doesn't know it's her we're talking about.

At least she doesn't seem to be scared of Matholook or Bendegatefran, which sets my mind a little more at ease. The fact that she doesn't seem surprised by my ability to *traverse* the two of us through solid matter...well, that confuses, impresses, shocks, and worries the hell out of me. I'm still amazed by my own ability to shuffle my molecules through the molecules of another object. Gwernna's *lack* of amazement makes me wonder what else—maybe even beyond resurrecting the dead—this little girl might be capable of.

I don't know anything about Gwernna or if what Matholook has told me about her is even remotely true. There's a part of me that's on constant alert for signs of betrayal. (Kress says it's the part that's kept me alive this long.)

As we trade stories of our improbable rescue, I can't stop looking back and forth between this odd-ball trio of the Devoted:

Matholook: green-eyed, even-tempered, and able to ooze more simple sincerity and courage into a single moment than almost anyone I've ever met.

Bendegatefran: sitting on a charred log, his knees peaked as high as twin mountain-tops, his head practically touching the canopy of overhanging, leafless branches as he waits for someone to tell him what to do next.

Gwernna: small, sweet, and feral-looking—an Emergent, a pet, a prize, and a lit fuse all at once.

Other than the crackling of our meager morning fire, the clearing is dead quiet, and we're all stuck in a weird moment of sizing each other up. It's a chess match. The pieces are set up for this new game, but nobody wants to make the first move.

Are Matholook and Bendegatefran planning to ask me for even more help than I've already given? Are they about to warn me to stay out of the way? Or are they going to threaten me if I don't? They're Devoted. I don't know how much I could trust them in the best of times. Here in the woods, all of us far from home...well, that's a whole different level of uncertainty.

"What now?" I ask at last. "What's the plan?"

Matholook and the giant exchange another one of those unreadable glances but don't answer.

"You got her back," I press. "You got what you wanted. What happens now?"

When they *still* don't answer, I get nervous and decide maybe it's best to get out of here before things take a turn.

They needed me to help them get Gwernna back, and I did that. So they don't need me anymore. Which could make things between us very easy or else very deadly.

My hand hovers over one of my Serpent Blades.

Clearing his throat as I stand, Matholook asks me why I really came down the mountain.

"I told you. I was hoping to find you."

"But why?" His grin irks me, and I'm kicking myself for giving him the upper hand by revealing so much, especially when I feel like I know so little.

Doing my best impression of a dying fish, I open and close my mouth a few times as I struggle to find the best answer.

Standing there in the mist of the very early morning, I flash back to something Rain taught us in our Puzzles, Codes, & Game Theory class: "When faced with a problem full of unknown variables, the simplest solution is *generally* the correct one. It's called Occam's razor," she explained. "Also known as the Law of Simplicity. It's a problem-solving technique used to shave away the unnecessary, needlessly complicated options. Basically, if you hear hoofbeats, think horses, not zebras."

We all had a good laugh over the obviousness of her example, but I remember thinking, *But what if you live in the grasslands of East Africa?*

Now, I wish I would have asked that out loud.

"I've been feeling a little...off," I say at last, sitting down as a wave of physical and emotional exhaustion passes over me.

It's as close to the truth as I care to come right now. I've been away from the Academy for hours, yet it feels like days. There's something happening inside of me—something potentially dangerous, something foreign I can't pinpoint or control. But until I find out what it is, I figure it's best to stick with the simplest explanation.

"I really should get back to the Academy. I don't know why I left in the first place. It was impulsive and stupid. I guess I'm just tired of feeling...disconnected."

"There's a lot of that going around."

"Were you really expecting me?" I ask.

"I've been expecting you since the day I met you."

"I really shouldn't be here."

"But you are. So let's take it from there."

"Technically, we're enemies, you know."

"Why? Just because your Academy is training you to kill all of us?"

"The Academy is teaching us how to make the most of our abilities as Emergents to help the world to heal."

"Hm. Sounds like the mantra of every fascist regime and super soldier I've ever heard of."

"And every survivor, revolutionary, and freedom fighter," I remind him with a mocking smile, my fingers still hovering over the Serpent Blades in my holster like my hands have got a mind of their own. "Survivor or fighter: I guess you need to figure out for yourself which one I am."

Bendegatefran tenses up, and his eyes swivel over to the

nearby tree where he's rested his monstrous axe, but Matholook shakes his head and holds up a wait-a-minute finger.

"Look. You're an Emergent. We're just two Typics and a little girl. I know you could probably kill all three of us in the blink of an eye..." Matholook begins.

Give me some credit. If I wanted to kill you, you'd never get the chance to blink an eye.

"...but maybe we can all take a deep breath and try trusting each other for a minute," he finishes.

"What do you have in mind?"

"Whatever the reason is, you left the Academy. If you go back now, whatever drove you down here is just going to drive you down here again. You're already here. Might as well make the most of it and do what you came here to do."

"But I don't know what I'm here to do." I hate that I sound so uncertain and whiny, but Matholook lets me off the hook.

He nods his understanding and says, "Come with us."

"Back to New Harleck?"

"Sure. If there's a New Harleck to get back *to*."

"You don't think the Unsettled—?"

"Killed everyone in their raid? No. They weren't waging war. This was a small squad, a tiny team from their army. They weren't genocidal. They were after Gwernna. Either they gave up and left when they couldn't find her..."

"Or else they decided to burn New Harleck to the ground when they couldn't find her."

I'm startled by Haida's voice in my head.

~ It's okay.

What is? New Harleck? Or do you mean it's okay for me to go with them?

~ Both.

What about the Academy?

~ The Academy is a safe place. A place for asking questions.

And New Harleck?

~ It's a dangerous place. A place for finding answers.

So what should I do?'

~ Questions and answers are useless without each other.

I pass my glance one more time at the odd-ball trio. I do a quick calculus in my head:

If I go back to the Academy now, Matholook and Bendegate-fran will take Gwernna back to New Harleck with them where she'll be re-imprisoned as a brainwashed puppet and cultivated as some kind of weapon with the power to reanimate the fighters from the Devoted. Meanwhile, Kress will be furious with me for leaving and will probably plant my severed head on her desk as a warning to the other students.

If I go back to New Harleck with Matholook and Bendegate-fran, maybe I can keep an eye on Gwernna until I can figure out a way to get her away from the Devoted for good. I can sneak her back to the Academy where Kress will still get mad at me for leaving in the first place and will probably plant my severed head on her desk as a warning to the other students.

Either way, my head winds up as a paperweight.

I guess if I'm going to be in trouble, I might as well be in big trouble, right?

In for a penny, in for a pound, as my mother always says.

"Okay," I tell Matholook. "I'll go back with you."

"Great!"

"When do we leave?"

Matholook asks Gwernna how she's feeling.

"All right," she shrugs, her voice as tiny and delicate as Bendegatefran's is low and thunderous.

"Are you ready to go home?"

She looks from me to him and then back again. I get the sense she's confused by the word "home."

But she smiles and asks Bendegatefran if she can have a ride over to the Skid Steers.

The giant slides his hand around her waist and scoops her up as easily and as gently as I'd pick up a brittle-boned kitten. He slides her onto his back where she clamps her hands to the collar of his shirt and squeals with glee.

Like the world's largest student wearing the world's smallest, giggliest backpack, Bendegatefran strides off to the Skid Steers, grabbing his axe along the way.

Matholook stands and brushes off the seat and sides of his pants. "I guess we go back to New Harleck." He kicks piles of dirt onto the campfire with the side of his boot. When he's done, he offers me a hand, which I accept, and he helps me to my feet.

With my hand still in his, our eyes meet, and we size each other up. I know we're curious, suspicious, drawn to each other, and scared of each other at the same time.

We smile at the simultaneous realization and drop our hands to our sides before joining Bendegatefran and Gwernna over at the Skid Steers.

As I duck my head under the roll bar and slide into the passenger seat, I ask Haida if she's sure about this.

~ *No. I'm not sure.*

Then tell me again why I'm doing this?

~ *Spreading your wings to fly into the unknown is always a leap of faith. If you want certainty, stay on the ground.*

11

HOSPITALITY

DRIVING from the cave to New Harleck doesn't take as long as I thought it would.

The Skid Steers—heavily modified and with extra power from small plasma generators riveted to their rear grills—are pretty good at navigating the sloping, uneven terrain.

In the space of an hour, the trees and brambles thin out, the basins fill up, the hills flatten, and the temperature skyrockets.

I push up the sleeves of my red leather jacket, grateful that its nano-variant thermal lining is designed specifically to adjust to temperature fluctuations like this.

I've had this jacket since I lived back in London. I was twelve years old when I found it in a storage locker in the basement ruins of a small, decimated shoe store I was exploring. I cleaned up the jacket and have been wearing it almost every day since. I like it because it's got its advanced temperature-control feature but also because, according to Kress anyway, it makes me look "totally bad-ass."

(It used to have a built-in deodorizer function woven into its lining, but it stopped working a long time ago. Maybe it's because I'm pressed shoulder-to-shoulder with Matholook, but I'm suddenly self-conscious about how bad I must smell.)

Next to me Matholook is currently marinating in his own sweat, which makes me feel oddly better. My mother used to tell me that onion-breath doesn't matter in a relationship as long as you both have it.

Grinning at the memory, I brace myself as our two Skid Steers glide to a stop at the top edge of a rocky cliff overlooking a long stretch of canyons and desert below.

I'm still amazed at the geography of this enormous country and its never-ending stretches of space between its huge, decimated cities. Before I came here, my life was pretty much limited to London: The river. The bridges. The castles. The endless mazes of motorways, streets, alleys, and lanes. (Because the early construction and evolution of the city predates the arrival of the word "road," almost no named thoroughfares in the Square Mile includes the title of "Road.") Then there were the fields of houses and shops and the forests of once-majestic skyscrapers. And of course, the Tower where I lived.

To me and for all I knew, my bleak and beaten city was the entire world, all of it drying out and overbaking under the stifling heat and under a blanket of sinister, churning clouds— all after-effects of years of political corruption, corporate greed, environmental neglect, drone strikes, and, ultimately, a manufactured war.

Here, it's like a bunch of different worlds have all been riffled together. I always thought of mountains, desert, plains, woods, and arctic as different things. Things that lived in their own bands and communities around the world with strict dividing lines between them. Here, they blend together and morph around and into each other.

I can see ripples down below in the desert, struggling scrub brush, towering sand dunes, sharp-ridged cliffs, mesquite trees and ponderosa pines, deep canyons, vertical walls of gray stone and, of course, the snow-capped peaks of the mountains chaperoning it all from high above.

I can totally see why early European explorers once called this the "New World." Although, more accurately, they could have described it as new *worlds*. With all of its various ecosystems of topographies, this entire expanse of land could be a whole solar system by itself.

Right now, Haida's somewhere in the middle of it all.

When I'm finally able to tap into her, I ask if we're okay to keep going.

She says we are and that the kidnapping crew of the Unsettled have returned, empty-handed thanks to us, to their roving city.

~ *But they'll be back*, she adds.

I relay this all to Matholook, who seems torn between appreciating my recon skills and dreading what else I might be capable of as an Emergent.

"If they do come back," he says at last, "we'll be ready for them."

By "we," does he mean him and the Devoted. Or is he including me in that "we"?

In the passenger seat of the other parked Skid Steer, Gwernna remains obsessed with looking around at every rolling cloud in the sky and at each individual speck of dust in the air and doesn't seem to notice the rising temperature.

I'm wondering if maybe she's traumatized from her recent captivity, but she seems happy, so I figure there's no sense in worrying about it.

Matholook and Bendegatefran fire up the Skid Steers and point them down the canyon.

As we continue along, I ask Matholook how long they kept

this little girl locked up in the compound before the Unsettled got to her.

"Most of her life," he admits over the grind of the treads on the rocky ground. "Still, I'm sure it's better than when she was in Sanctum. According to some of the other Emergents who came to us, Epic wasn't exactly concerned with their well-being. At least not beyond what it could do for him. You know. You said as much, yourself."

"This little girl has been imprisoned by Epic, then by the Devoted, and then kidnapped by the Unsettled. And now we're taking her back to New Harleck and returning her into the hands of the Devoted. Do I have that right?"

"It sounds so bleak and evil when you put it like that."

"Maybe that's because tossing a little girl back and forth like she's a human rugby ball *is* bleak and evil."

Matholook clenches his jaw and fixes his eyes on the bumpy surface in front of us.

After a few more minutes, we stop again, this time at the top of a crest covered in long ridges of red rocks and coated in fine grains of crystallized sand.

The charred, half-buried bodies of dozens of old drones lie glinting in a dune of brown, sandy soil.

On the other side of the hill, just past a stretch of empty desert and tucked into a shallow valley, is Matholook's town.

I tell him I'm impressed. "Last time we were out here, we needed Haida Gwaii to get us to New Harleck."

Matholook chuckles and tells me he remembers. "This time was easy. Bendegatefran used to go up to that cave all the time as a kid."

"I liked being alone," Bendegatefran calls out across the small space between our two stopped vehicles. "It can get pretty exhausting being asked to fetch things off the top shelves all the time."

Was that a joke? Who ever heard of a funny giant?

I giggle and hope he doesn't think I'm teasing him.

I may be heading right into the lion's den, but I still have a weird sense of relief. I think maybe being behind enemy lines is still better than being lost.

Trax, my friend and the boy who invited me on the first date I ever had, would find my horrible sense of direction amusing. As an Emergent, he apparently can find his way pretty much anywhere in any conditions. I haven't seen him do it, personally, but I've heard stories about how he helped Kress and her Conspiracy all those years ago when they were still on the run after their escape from the Processor.

Like Trax and unlike me, ravens are expert navigators. Kress keeps promising she'll teach me how to tap into that part of Haida Gwaii's abilities, but we never seem to get around to it.

In fairness to Kress, though, that's probably my fault since I keep begging her to teach me more fighting skills.

Still, I can't wait to tell her about my *traversion* trick back there when I got Gwerna out of that RV jail the Unsettled had her in. We've been working on that one for *years* now, and Kress will never believe how well I managed to finally pull it off. At the moment, I have plenty of good reasons for wanting to stay alive. One of the ones high up on the list is the chance to swagger back to the Academy and brag to Kress.

"Are you ready?" Matholoook asks, tilting his chin toward the circular cluster of weathered wooden buildings up ahead.

I say, "Not really." Bendegatefran says, "Absolutely." Gwerna points at me and squeals, "She walked through a wall!"

I give her a fierce, "stop snitching" glare, and she clamps her lips together and ducks under Bendegatefran's arm.

No sense in letting on about all the weird and impossible things I'm learning how to do. Especially if I might need to do them again.

Matholook gives me a suspicious squint before powering up the Skid Steer.

Palming the vehicles back into gear, the boys drive us down the desert crest and over a series of domed dunes of soft sand, along what's left of an empty desert highway, and then across a field of dead brush, stumpy cactus plants, and copper-red stones.

Stopping under a cloud of kicked-up desert sand, we park the Skid Steers just outside the town.

"We're better off walking from here," Matholook explains. "If the Sentries spot the Skid Steers, they'll think we're the Unsettled."

"Sentries?"

"Guards. The ones responsible for keeping us safe."

"The ones who fought to protect Gwernna," Bendegatefran adds.

I glance over at Gwernna, but she doesn't seem the least bit fazed or surprised by the knowledge that all of this happened because of her.

No, I remind myself. *Not because of her. This little girl never asked to be the rope in some pointless, three-way game of tug-of-war.*

"Is it safe?" she asks into the air. She doesn't seem to be addressing any one of us in particular, and I don't know if she's asking if New Harleck is safe for her or if she's safe from the Unsettled.

Matholook drops a tender hand onto her shoulder and assures her everything is going to be fine.

"Fine" isn't the same as "safe."

"Come on," Matholook says to all three of us with a wave of his hand. "Let's go home."

I've been to New Harleck twice before. Once when I was twelve, I accompanied Kress and her Conspiracy on their quest to locate and start up the Emergents Academy. And then I was there again a few months ago during my mission to find Haida Gwaii and track down the intruder who managed to break into the Academy.

Both times, New Harleck was a quaint, quiet place. It was inviting but with an undercurrent of mystery and danger. Now, we arrive at a place where only the sense of danger remains.

The gloom of defeat hangs over the whole town.

A group of men and women in blood-stained blue jeans and red-trimmed white vests are working in pairs to patch up gaping holes in some of the buildings while other groups are tending to the wounded or lugging bodies out from under wreckage.

"Those are the Shamans," Matholook explains, pointing to a group of men and women in brown capes. "They're healers and advisors."

Frowning, Bendegatefran worries out loud about the lack of security. "The Sentries should be posted. If we can walk into town like this, so can Epic or the Unsettled."

Nodding his agreement, Matholook tells him he's sure the security detail will be back up and running in no time.

We walk deeper into the town, and Matholook and Bendegatefran slam to a stop as sure as if they'd run face-first into a brick wall.

With smiles too inadequate to hide the undercurrent of despair, Justin and Treva—the two leaders of their community —stride out onto the road to welcome them.

Bendegatefran ignores their greeting. Instead, he stares at the ground and says, "We should have stayed."

"Then you would've been killed." Her eyes still locked onto Matholook's, Treva drops to a knee in front of Gwernna. "The only thing that saved us was you saving her."

"How many...?"

"They killed eight of us. Four Sentries. One Negotiator. One Caretaker. Two Historians. We're still sorting out the wounded."

"It was bad," Justin says, his watery eyes flicking from one of us to the other.

"It could have been worse," Treva tells him, her hand on his shoulder. "If they hadn't gotten Gwernna out of here..."

"We fought hard," Justin tells us. "We killed at least four of the Unsettled. And wounded another three." Justin points to a single-story building tucked behind a row of scraggly, leafless trees. "They're over there in the Clinic."

"You're treating them?" Bendegatefran asks.

Matholook puts a hand on the giant's forearm. "We're not animals. We're the good guys, remember?"

Bendegatefran grunts his reluctant acceptance.

"And you," Justin says, turning to me, "you, we remember."

I think maybe he's going to leap over and attack me—after all, the Devoted do have a habit of kidnapping Emergents and a long history of brainwashing people into joining their cult.

But what I think is going to be an attack turns into a warm, slightly crushing hug.

Justin holds me by my shoulders at arm's length and gushes about how much I've grown since they saw me last. "It's been... what? Five years?" he asks.

"Five years," Treva confirms as she loops her arm around my waist and pulls me into hug number two.

And now I feel like I'm being smothered by an elated aunt and uncle, which is—to my surprise—even creepier than when I just thought of them as the enemy.

Stepping back, Justin seems wary when he asks me if I know about Gwernna. I tell him Matholook and Bendegatefran told me a little. "I know she's important."

"She is. But maybe not for the reason the boys may have told you."

"She's an Emergent who can bring the dead back to life," I shrug. "What else is there?"

"That's just her *potential*," Justin says, drawing Gwernna to him and kneeling down in front of her. He licks his thumb and wipes away a smudge of dirt on her cheek. "What she *is*, on the other hand, is a sweet and kind little girl, who deserves to live a life of her own."

"Then why kidnap her from Epic? Aren't you just making her trade one jailor for another?"

Treva scowls at me but then seems embarrassed at her reaction and draws her mouth up into a creased-lipped, gray-toothed smile.

"Epic's focus is always on the future," she explains with a sigh. "He's always trying to figure out what's ahead and how to control what's to come."

"Not us," Justin brags, standing, his fist pressed to his puffed-out chest. "We rely on what's *happened* to guide us. History is our foundation. And the past tells us that no leader—no matter how well-intentioned—can resist the pull of absolute power once it's within reach."

"We're still in a bit of shock," Treva explains. "We've had to fight the Unsettled before. But it's usually out in the desert. They almost never try to breach our perimeter security. Just shows you how much getting their hands on Gwernna means to them. Anyway, we're sorry about the mess."

The mess? She just pointed to a collapsed bungalow and a family sitting outside the ruins with bandages pressed to their bleeding heads like it was all just an embarrassing stain on the carpet.

"We pride ourselves on our hospitality," Justin tells me.

Treva tosses me a long-handled shovel. "So we're especially sorry that our first act of welcoming is to ask you to help us bury our dead."

12

SERVICE

I'm standing alone, a shovel in my hand, and I'm looking down at a dead woman.

Justin and Treva are over at the edge of the fenced-in cemetery with Matholook and Bendegatefran. I can't hear what they're talking about, but I'd be seriously surprised if it was anything other than me. They continue to cast glances back and forth between the cemetery and the rest of the town, occasionally letting their flitting eyes fall on me before quickly looking away.

It's still early in the morning, but the heat is already close to being unbearable. Unlike what I remember from London, this is a dry, all-around heat that seems to sizzle down from the air, rise up from the ground, and simmer around, all at once.

The ground inside the town's limits is mostly rocks and sand. It's going to take a while to dig deep enough to make the graves.

Apparently finished with their little chat, Matholook leaves Bendegatefran behind and joins me inside the fenced-in patch of rough land.

"Are you sure this is okay?" I ask Matholook as we take turns dumping shovelfuls of soil and stones onto a growing pile. "Me being here, I mean."

"You saved Gwernna. You haven't threatened us in any way. And they don't know you're the one who took the other Emergents."

"Let's call it 'rescued,' shall we? Besides, it was *your* idea."

Matholook drags his sleeve across his sweaty forehead and offers me a beaming, cheeky smile. "Fair enough."

"I came here for answers," I tell him. "But I'm not sure I'm ready to die to get them."

"You'll be fine."

"Says you. I'm the enemy, remember?"

"If they found out you're the one who took those Emergents and that I'm the one who let you, I'd be just as much of an enemy as you, and we'd wind up out here digging our *own* graves."

"So maybe we'll just keep those little tidbits to ourselves for now."

"Works for me."

"Were you and Bendegatefran winding me up before? About Gwernna, I mean. If she can bring people back from the dead..."

"If you're asking me to explain how she does what she does..."

"I'm asking you if she really *can* do what you *say* she does."

Matholook makes a vague gesture back in the direction of the main part of the compound. "You'd have to ask them. I'm not the expert. I *can* tell you what I've heard, though."

"Which is?"

"I think maybe she only bring people back who've been killed near her. Like close by. And only if no significant time has passed."

"Really?"

"It's what I've heard. I'm a Caretaker. A protector. If you want those kinds of answers, you're going to have to ask people way above my pay-grade."

"Speaking of which, I notice Justin and Treva didn't exactly ask me a lot of questions."

"Like what?"

"Like where I came from, what I'm doing here, how I managed to help save Gwernna."

Matholook tilts his head back and offers up a throaty laugh. "Don't worry. It'll come. I promise. The rule here is hospitality first, questions later."

And kidnapping and brainwashing after that, with a little light gravedigging thrown in along the way? Seriously, Branwynne, what the frack kind of a shambles are you getting yourself into this time?

The steel blades of our shovels clink together, and we apologize to each other as we continue to dig.

"What ever happened after we left?" I ask.

"When I turned those Emergents over to you?"

"Yeah."

"Not much. I told the Devoted the truth: Six armed Emergents slipped into the compound while our Vindicators were out fighting the Unsettled. The Emergents knocked me out. When I woke up, they were gone, along with our twelve Emergent kids."

"Not exactly the truth."

"But not totally a lie, either." Matholook leans on his shovel and rubs his jaw with his free hand. "You didn't have to hit me quite that hard."

"It was my pleasure," I smirk as we get back to our task.

"In the interest of honesty...," Matholook begins.

"Yeah?"

"You know your friend. The bigger guy? The one with the two sticks."

"His name's Ignacio. And they're called shillelaghs."

"Right."

"What about him?"

"I told Justin and Treva that he's the one who knocked me out."

"How very...*insecure* of you," I laugh.

"It's just that we have certain divisions between men and women in the Devoted."

"Divisions?"

"Historically, male and female roles and responsibilities have always been specialized. We don't judge or discriminate. We're just carrying on some longstanding, well-established, and proven traditions."

I glance over to where Justin and Treva are doling out more clean-up responsibilities. "You have a man and woman running your town."

"Naturally. But when it comes to getting beaten up, it still plays better if I can say I got clocked by a boy."

"That is so bloody stupid," I snap. "All the pointless categories and inequalities." I tap the back of my shovel on the flat bottom of our shallow indentation in the earth. "Everyone comes to this. It's just a shame we don't realize it until it's come to this."

As we get back to our task, the sound of our steel shovel blades against the stone and sand rings out in vibrating, mournful clangs. Down the row from where we're working, Bendegatefran easily digs two more graves with no more than a few strokes of his shovel, which looks like a soup spoon in his gargantuan hands.

"You have an interesting take on things," Matholook says with a respectful nod. "I can see why you'd want to leave the Academy."

"What does that have to do with anything?" I growl.

Matholook must hear the offense in my voice because he stops cold and plants his shovel into a mound of glittering sand.

Resting his folded arms across the tip of the handle, he offers me a glossy-eyed apology. "I know what the Academy means to you. I know they took you in and that they're sincere about helping kids like..."

"Like me?"

"Yes. You're...special. Unique."

"Because I'm an Emergent?"

Matholook shakes his head. "Because you're *you.*"

I'm a little startled by that. I know I should be offended about being feared, scared about being alone inside the Cult of the Devoted, and angry about being recruited to save a girl who might just be imprisoned here for the rest of her life. But I don't feel any of those things. When Matholook gives me that pleading, green-eyed gaze, something happens inside of me, something I've never felt before.

It's not fear, curiosity, or even hope.

It's a feeling of surrender. And I hate it, because I'm a warrior and because I'm not sure if feeling like I want to voluntarily give up a part of myself to someone else means the beginning of me, or the end.

Stripping off his shirt, Matholook continues to shovel in silence on the opposite side of the growing pit. His muscles glisten the color of warm honey under a thin sheen of sweat.

I try not to notice. Instead, I concentrate on processing the crashing waves smashing around in my head.

I'm out here looking for something I'm not sure exists, sweating behind enemy lines, and chatting up a boy I hardly know while we dig desert graves for the newly dead. So why do I feel better now than I've felt in a long time?

AT THE FAR end of the cemetery, Treva cups her hands around her mouth and shouts out to us that it's time for services.

"Services?" I ask.

"You know...ceremonial church services in honor of the dead."

"Oh. Right. Of course."

"You don't have funeral services where you're from?"

I shake my head, and Matholook seems sad. "We think it's important to pay tribute to the dead," he explains.

Where I'm from the dead aren't much more than raven food.

Swept along by Justin and Treva, I'm ushered into the church and am led to a seat in the front pew in between Matholook and Gwernna.

The rest of the citizens of New Harleck begin filing in, their heads down, their boots shuffling along the paths of hard-packed dirt leading from the compound's dozens of long, low buildings to the stone and brick church at the center of town.

Bendegatefran remains standing at the back of the church.

"Otherwise, he blocks everyone's view," Matholook explains through a conspiratorial, leaned-in whisper.

The funeral service is happening in the same church where my Asylum and I—with Matholook's help—rescued those twelve young Emergents and brought them back with us to the Academy.

The last time I was here, it was the middle of the night, we had just escaped with our lives from Epic and then from the Unsettled, and the church had all the gloomy charm of a corpse-filled crypt.

Now, with the exposed wood beams and the intricate crafts-manship of the pews on full display in the natural light, the atmosphere is a lot cozier and more inviting than I remember.

There are input panels built into the walls, but they're camouflaged and barely visible from here.

The window frames have tall panels of glass in place—the kind that get darker and lighter on their own depending on the amount of light and heat needed in the room.

At first, I thought New Harleck was just some primitive, Old West town full of fuzzy-toothed, vacant-eyed hicks. Five years ago, the people came across as a little simple and a bit bland. As I look around, though, I'm starting to think maybe there's more to this place than meets the eye.

I know I shouldn't be here. I should be two and a half miles up the towering mountain, safe with my friends, classmates, and teachers in the Emergents Academy. It's morning, and everyone will be up and about and wondering where the frack I am.

Feeling the trickle of nervous sweat on my neck, I'm tempted to get up and leave. I even start to stand, but Treva steps up to the podium on the small stage right in front of me, so I pretend I was just adjusting my position on the wooden pew to get more comfortable and ease back down.

"First of all," she begins, her words oozing out, solemn and syrupy-slow, "let me introduce our guest."

A buzz fills the room, and I feel a few dozen eyes boring into the back of my head.

"This is Branwynne. She's a guest of Matholook. I understand she's here looking for answers."

The buzz turns into grumbles.

"She's been with us once before. Five years ago when she and her friends joined us and then went on their way." Treva takes two full breaths before adding, "She's an Emergent."

To my surprise—after all, people like me are supposed to be these great and coveted weapons of war—the grumbles morph into gripes.

"But none of that matters. All you need to know is that she's a guest. And being a guest is the first step to becoming a friend."

Or a prisoner.

I'm not tapped into Haida Gwaii, but I don't need to be to hear some of the conversations ping-ponging around the cavernous room behind me.

"...she could be dangerous..."

"...an Unsettled spy..."

"...power-hungry Emergents..."

"...sent from Sanctum by Epic to..."

Treva stops them all with a raised hand. "I think we all know we have enemies in the world. Our clashes with Epic and his Sanctum Civillains, the fact that we're here to pay tribute to our dead after a vicious raid by the Unsettled...But this girl...she saved Gwernna. Which makes her the savior of our savior. This young woman is not our enemy. Whether she becomes a friend or not is up to her."

The grumbling settles down to a dull thrum of echoed whispers and finally disappears completely as Treva begins the service by reciting the names of the six Devoted who were killed. She lists the members of their families going back several generations and highlights all the things—big and small—each of them did on behalf of the community. She runs through a long list of their contributions, from teaching to building bunkers to fighting off drones.

After that, she and Justin take turns reading from two books. Well, not books really. They're two stacks of paper held together with lengths of frayed twine.

I don't know where the text is from, but it's all stuff about adhering to the past, following the lessons of those who've come before, and the importance of "never deviating from the path we're on."

It's not my cup of tea, so I don't give it much thought. But then, after about fifteen minutes or so of listening, I get scared when I find myself nodding in agreement.

13

SAVIOR

AFTER THE SERVICE, everyone files out of the church.

I spend the entire walk from the front pew to the big double doors trying to clear my head from whatever strange haze has tried to slip its way in.

Outside, some of the congregation edge their way over toward me, but with side-stepping, wary-eyed caution, like I'm a kettle about to boil over and scald them all to death.

The ground outside the church is hard and unforgiving. I can feel its heat seeping up through my boots. The air is dry and hot, and parts of the town around us look like they've been hit by a bomb. Other parts look untouched, and I'm reminded about how casually cruel random acts of violence can be.

Towering over all of it is my mountain. Well, not mine, exactly. And it's not a single mountain. The entire range juts up like a mouthful of broken teeth. Caps of white snow cover the very tops of some of the highest peaks, including the one hosting the concealed Academy and the remnants of the Valta. Below that is a band of forest—a patchwork of green life and brown death. And then, the desert. And then, us.

Sandwiched between a mountain range on one side and the

expansive desert on the other, New Harleck—with its worn foot-paths, scraggly clusters of sage brush, and splayed branches from desert ironwood trees—feels weirdly safe.

The people glaring daggers at me...they're another story.

"It's okay," Justin assures them, his arms spread wide as everyone continues to file out of the church. "Branwynne is Matholook's friend, our guest, and Gwernna's savior."

Great. I didn't ask to be all that. Hell, I can barely manage being Branwynne.

An older man—stooped and balding—sizes me up. He grunts a "Thanks" to me and adds, "We all owe you for saving the savior," before turning to the side to spit a glob of yellowish-green phlegm over his shoulder into the low scrub-bushes.

A woman, maybe in her twenties but with gray hair at her temples and deep age lines slicing through the skin around her eyes, clamps a hand to my shoulder. She says, "We're grateful for what you did for us."

To myself, I think, *I didn't save Gwernna for* you. *But if I have to, I'm definitely going to save her* from *you.*

But out loud, I mumble, "No problem," which is both polite and a complete lie.

One by one, the rest of the Devoted sidle by, thanking me as they go. For a second—a *split* second—I feel proud of myself. After all, I personally engineered a daring rescue with little planning and no back-up *and even managed to traverse through a set of bars and a solid wall in the process.* It's exactly what I've been trained to do, and I did it.

But then I remember: All I've really done is return a ten-year-old prisoner back to her captors and deliver myself into the hands of the enemy. If I could have found a way to ditch Math-olook and Bendegatefran, I would have taken off with Gwernna myself and brought her back to the Academy.

Now, I'm thinking maybe I should have risked it.

The thought of the missed opportunity makes my eye twitch, and now I'm all edgy with a weird urge—probably being channeled from Haida Gwaii—to fly out over the desert and kill something and eat it.

As the resident Ravenmaster, Kress has done a great job teaching me how to access my connection with Haida. I've got to remind her to teach me how to make it stop.

Fortunately, Matholook chooses that exact moment to slip his arm into the crook of my own and announce with the grand chivalry of a royal duke that he and I are going to have a stroll around the compound.

"Just be back in time for lunch," Treva says through an unreadable smile. "And for classes."

As Matholook leads me away, I ask him if we're supposed to help with any more of the cleanup, but he tells me there are already crews assigned.

"Everyone has a task around here," he explains.

"I've been hearing about your different teams," I tell him.

"We call them 'Guilds,'" he reminds me. "We have everything from Vindicators and Caretakers to Hunters and Historians. We have our fighters and our healers, our cooks and gardeners, our explorers and our guards, and our teachers and students."

"You have teachers?"

"Of course. We may just be humble Typics and not enhanced, super-powered Emergents. But we know the value of hard work and responsibility. Everyone here is responsible for one task or another."

"And what's your task?"

Matholook gives me an emerald-eyed wink. "Watching over you."

"Seriously?"

"Justin and Treva gave me the assignment, personally."

"I'm sorry you got such a degrading job."

"Honestly, it's the best duty I've ever been assigned."

I turn to the side, pretending to be curious about the strange, laminate-like surface of the long, low building we're passing, but really, I just don't want him to see me blush.

As we stroll along, I start to get more of a sense of the town. Some of the buildings I remember from before. Others look brand new. Mixed in with the older, wonky structures of wood, brick, and stone are some oddly space-age constructions. There's a two-story building of glistening black panels that reflect and distort our images as we pass. There's a mostly white building with a thousand different angles and facets and with deep gray recesses, making it resemble a giant clump of crumpled-up paper. Right after that, we pass a smoky glass dome rising up about ten feet above the ground like a half-buried snow globe. There's a weird randomness to it all. Even the paths we follow through the compound twist, turn, and even double-back on themselves, almost without rhyme or reason.

While I'm taking it all in, Matholook asks me about life in the Academy.

"Classes are hard," I sigh. "I'm basically a walking bundle of bruises and broken bones."

"You're kidding."

"Nope."

"And you get weapons training?"

I draw my perfectly-balanced twin Serpent Blades from their holsters and spin them on the pads of my outstretched index fingers. "We get trained in firearms and alternate weapons. But these are special. One of a kind. And just for me."

Matholook tilts his head toward my Serpent Blades. "Can I try them?"

I tell him, "Sure" and hand them over.

As he takes them from me, I realize how stupid it is to give away my only weapons. Fortunately, he snaps out the retractable blades, snaps them right back in, and returns the Serpent Blades to me with an impressed hum. Breathing a mental sigh of relief, I return them to their holsters.

Out of the corner of my eye, I catch two little boys and a girl nudging each other and pointing my way.

"Don't mind them," Matholook says. "You're something of an oddity around here. Nothing personal."

"You just called me an 'oddity.' It doesn't get much more personal than that."

Matholook chokes back a chuckle and tells me not to worry about it. "I meant 'odd' in the good sense. Like different."

"And 'different' is good?"

"Not usually. We're rooted in the past here. History is our guide. Different usually means scary."

"So those little ankle-biters over there are scared of me?"

"Maybe. But 'different' also means exciting. And they're definitely excited about you."

"And what about you?"

"What do you mean?"

"Are you afraid of me or excited?"

"I guess I'm somewhere in the middle."

"And what, exactly, is in the middle of afraid and excited?"

He scratches his head like he's deep in thought before turning to me with a smile. "Enchanted?"

And for the second time on our little walk, I feel my cheeks go red.

Matholook slips out of his white jacket with the red piping and drapes it over his arm. Tucked into his jeans, the white, short-sleeved t-shirt he has on fits him really well, and I give an impressed mental whistle at the detailed lines of muscle running through his sculpted arms.

Jogging along next to us, the three kids who've been shadowing us are joined by a few more. But we've reached the part of town where the buildings thin out, and there's only open land. With no place to hide, the kids slink back into the confines of the compound.

"Shouldn't they be in school or something?" I ask.

"They will be. First class is after lunch. History. You can visit. If you stay..."

"I don't think so. I came down here on an impulse. Staying any longer than I already have might not be the best idea or especially good for my health. I'm going to get raked over the coals by Kress as it is."

"If you're going to risk so much, then you might as well get as much reward as you can."

"We'll see."

"Okay. So...tell me more about your Academy."

"What's to tell? It's a school to train Emergents."

Matholook's voice quivers a little when he asks what we're *really* being trained for. "If not to wage war and take over."

"Wisp—that's our principal—says we're supposed to save the world."

"From us?"

"Hopefully, *for* you."

"As long as we don't get in your way, right?"

"Or try to keep hoarding us as weapons in your own personal arsenal."

"Hey, I'm the one who got those kids out of here," Matholook reminds me with an unpleasant scowl, and I think he's going to snap back at my cheap shot. Instead, he asks, "Do you have a favorite class?"

"Ha! Is this the part where we pretend like we're normal teenagers living in a normal world?"

"No. But this *is* the part where we try."

I pin my eyes to his, hoping I'll be able to figure out if he's being serious, silly, or sarcastic. But he looks away, and I'm left wondering.

"You've heard the stories, too, haven't you?" I ask him.

"The ones about what life was like?"

"Yeah."

"Of course. It's all we talk about here. For us, the past is God."

"How does that work?"

"We're Devoted. We believe in the purity of older times, before all the violence and corruption. We believe that before the fall into fear, human origins were rooted in peace and harmony."

"Rubbish. I grew up in the Tower of London with no one around but my parents and a bunch of ravens, and even I know there's never been such a time in human history."

"Ah, a cynic."

"No. A person who's lived and who's seen the world."

"You've only seen this version of the world. You haven't seen what it was before or what it could be again."

"We have history classes at the Academy. I know full well what things were like before. And they weren't some kind of utopian paradise like you Devoted seem to think. You talk about getting back, but there's nothing to get back to. Nothing that's not just going to turn into all of this again anyway."

"We have history classes, too. I doubt we're learning the same history."

"Then one of us is definitely hearing the wrong story."

Matholook gives me a playful push to the shoulder and says, "I bet I know which one."

Like Matholook, I've taken off my jacket and am now walking with it slung over my shoulder. Despite the rush of events over the past couple of hours, this particular moment feels slow and nicely casual. The few people we pass give us polite nods. They also throw in a top-to-bottom scan of me for good measure before going on about their business.

I do my best to concentrate on Matholook while keeping my eyes open and my head on a swivel. In my experience, saviors are great at saving everyone...except *themselves*.

14

FRIENDS

MATHOLOOK and I mosey along for a while longer, working our way around the perimeter of the Devoted compound. The town is bigger and better protected than I thought. There's a deep, steep-walled, crescent-shaped canyon running around the back part of it and a barely-visible, fifteen-foot-high laser-link fence curving around the distant edges of the town. Dressed in dusty jeans and blousy white shirts with black Kevlar vests visible underneath, Sentries are taking positions in what look like those old, whitewashed lifeguard stands every few hundred feet along the shimmering perimeter fence.

The Unsettled must've been desperate to come charging in here like they did. Now, I'm wondering if there's even more to their little snatch-and-grab mission than the Devoted are letting on.

Matholook guides us along a narrow walkway next to a rocky overhang that provides a nice bit of shade.

It's scorching hot out, but after a while, I stop noticing.

"It's like being wet," Matholook explains with a laugh. "It's easy to get used to the water once you're fully soaked, and you realize you can't get any wetter than you already are. There's something horrifying but also something comforting about extremes, don't you think?" Matholook makes a grand gesture at the sizzling sky and at the angry, red haze of irradiated clouds somersaulting off in the distance. "The human capacity to get used to giving in to our worst instincts...it's what got us here."

"Great," I sigh with a quick and hopefully inconspicuous sniff under my arm. "It's hot. We're doomed. But at least we stink."

"At least the buzzards won't want to eat us."

"Ha!" I laugh. "Being rejected by the world's least picky scavengers: a sure sign you're having a bad day."

"Come on," Matholook urges. "There's more I want to show you."

Every once in a while, as we walk, I spot another kid or two peeking at us from behind a building or from underneath a cluster of desert shrubs. When I make eye contact with the kids, they run away. Sometimes, just for fun, I glare at them or make mysterious waggly motions with my fingers like I'm a witch casting a spell. When that happens, the kids squeal in terror and delight and go skittering off to get more of their friends to follow us.

"Tell me more about the Academy," Matholook says. "I like hearing about it."

"Why? So you can learn how we work, infiltrate us, and destroy us all before we can destroy you?"

"You know," Matholook drawls, a cheeky grin tugging at the corners of his mouth, "I would never ask you to drop your guard. You *are* behind enemy lines, after all, which means you've already dropped it. At least a little. But do you really need to keep every inch of your armor on? We're having a conversation, not a fight."

"Same thing," I laugh.

"What? How do you figure?"

"Well, we're learning in our Game Theory class about how even simple things like a casual conversation between two people can be a breeding ground for strategic behavior."

"What's Game Theory?"

"Rain teaches it. It's about strategy, rules, logic, choices, and consequences. It basically applies how we play games to how we interact with each other in the real world."

"So...you use games to teach you military strategy?"

"Kind of. But also how to maximize choices in no-win scenarios."

"How do you mean?"

"Well...Okay. Do you know the game of 'Chicken'?"

"You mean like where two people in cars drive at each other to see who'll swerve first?"

"Exactly."

"I've never played it."

"Maybe you have and just didn't realize it."

"I think I'd know if I was driving head-on at someone who was driving head-on to me."

"Don't be so sure. Game Theory teaches about possible outcomes and how we can win at unwinnable games."

"What outcomes?" Matholook asks through a puzzled squint. "In Chicken, you either swerve, or you die."

"Sure. But there are ways to change the choices."

"How so?"

"Well, like you say, in the game of Chicken, your choices are to swerve or die. But if you take away one of your own choices, you also limit the choices of your opponent."

"I don't get it."

"Let's say you and I are driving toward each other."

"Okay. We can both either swerve, or we can both die."

"But what if I rip the steering post off of my car and hold it out the window for you to see?"

"That's insane. You wouldn't be able to swerve."

"But *you* still can, and since you saw what I did, you know I don't have any choice about what happens. But you still have a choice: You can swerve, or you can die. All I can do is die."

While Matholook rubs his hand along his jaw, I ask him, "So...what'll you do?"

"I guess I have no choice, either. I have to swerve."

"And I win."

"Hm. Interesting. And are you playing Game Theory with me right now?"

"I'm having a pleasant conversation with the boy who once risked his own life to save mine, to save the lives of my friends, and to save the lives of twelve young Emergents."

"And I'm having a pleasant conversation with the girl who came down a mountain, saved Gwernna, saved our town, and who might one day accomplish her school's mission and save the world. So...if this is a game," Matholook grins, flicking his thumb between us, "who's winning?"

"We *both* are," I laugh.

We chat for a while longer, and it's like I've lost track of time as we continue our walk through and around the entire town.

At one point, Matholook asks me about the other students in my Cohort.

I tell him all about Libra, Sara, Mattea, Arlo, and Ignacio.

Only, instead of "other students," I refer to the list of my classmates as "friends."

What is it about Matholook that makes me able to see old adversaries as new friends?

Looking over at him and then glancing away before he catches me, I'm thinking very seriously about adding one more name to that list.

15

ENEMIES

LUNCH IS in a giant meeting hall with a peaked, sky-high ceiling held up by long rows of slanted wood beams and a network of vertical support struts lined up throughout the space.

The room is filled with long wooden tables set up in orderly rows with military precision. Fourteen metal folding chairs—six on each side and one at each end—surround each of the tables.

At the far end of the room, a woman and a man in crisp, white aprons are standing behind a cut-out window where they are doling out small piles of protein cubes into the waiting bowls of a slow-moving line of little kids. Queueing up after the kids is a curving line of surly-looking teenagers, each with a nine-inch, wood-handled meat cleaver in a hip holster on one side and one of those *really* old-style, iron-handled six-shooter pistols on the other.

I know guns are in short supply these days, and the Devoted seem to be scraping the bottom of the weapons barrel.

Matholook catches me staring and reminds me how they can't be too careful. "Especially after yesterday's raid."

"So everyone doesn't always walk around armed like that?"

"Only the Sentries. But *everyone* will be on high alert for the next day or two. Just in case."

"And those little weapons are all that's standing between you and the Unsettled's craziness and Epic's actual arsenal?"

"They won't be much good against them. Or against you," he adds, a twitchy grin pulling at the corners of his mouth. "But there's more to waging war than just weapons"

Giving my jacket sleeve a quick tug, he guides me over to the table where Justin and Treva are already seated along with several other adults and a couple of armed teenagers I don't know.

Bendegatefran is down at the end of the table, his legs splayed wide. He's taller sitting down than anyone else in the room is standing up.

"We had a special chair made for him," Matholook whispers in my ear. "But he broke it."

Treva asks me how my morning has been so far.

"Other than the grave-digging, it's been surprisingly pleasant."

"I've been giving her the tour," Matholook brags.

"It's been nicer than I thought," I admit.

"Which part?" Treva asks as Matholook blushes, "The tour or the tour *guide*?"

"Don't pester them," Justin admonishes with a light laugh.

Treva apologizes and tells me she's sorry I had to witness their town at a low like this. "A few things have changed since you were here last. Some new additions to buildings. A new drainage system. Oh, and three new schoolhouses. Maybe after we eat, Matholook can take you to a class or two."

"Sure," I tell her. "We talked about it. That'd be good."

Treva claps her hands together and says, "Great! I'm glad we've got that settled," before turning to ask Justin something about their inventory of medical supplies.

"That's Efnisien," Matholook tells me, pointing to the scowling boy sitting cross-armed next to Bendegatefran and glaring at me through squinty, evil eyes from the far end of the table.

"I remember him. Bendegatefran's brother, right?"

"Half-brother."

"Oh. Right. I remember. He really got his knickers in a twist over that whole 'brother, half-brother' thing, didn't he?"

"I'm pretty sure his 'knickers,' as you call them, are in a permanent knot that he'll never get out."

"He should try using his teeth."

As Matholook laughs, the girl across the table from me leans toward me and extends her hand. When I don't reach out to accept her handshake right away, she winks at me. "I won't bite. I can't speak for everyone in the room, though..."

It takes me a second to realize she's joking. Kind of.

I shake her hand and then the other kids at the table introduce themselves as well. Everyone except for Efnisien.

He's glaring at me, grinding his teeth together with enough force to turn them into powder, and I get the feeling if he clamped his arms any harder across his chest, he'd cut himself clean in half.

I've always had pretty decent instincts. With Haida in my head, they're ramped up nearly to the point of pain.

It's not just Efnisien's glare. That's easy enough to read. There's something else. Something more. Something deadly about him.

Something deadly about everyone here, really.

When Matholook tipped us off five years ago and helped us escape, I never doubted something terrible would have happened if we'd stayed.

A girl with dark brown hair to her knees reaches over my shoulder and sets a small bowl of protein cubes in front of me.

Unlike at the Academy, eating doesn't seem to be a time for socializing. The Devoted eat very little, and they eat very fast. The meeting hall is nearly empty before I even have time to process that fact.

A whimpering cry from the far side of the room catches my attention, and I look over to see a few of the adult members of the Devoted hovering around Gwernna. Dressed in an oversized white t-shirt and baggy denim pants, she looks frail and a little ghostly.

"I'll go see what's wrong," Matholook says, pushing his chair back and standing up. "Sit tight. I'll be right back."

He strides over to where the small group is gathered around the young girl and sits down cross-legged in front of her. I watch from a distance as she wipes her eyes with the tips of her fingers. Matholook reaches over and puts a comforting hand on her arm. It's a simple, charming gesture, and it makes me smile.

He turns over his shoulder to catch my eye and return my smile. Holding up a finger, he mouths, "Just a minute" and returns his attention to Gwernna who is snuffling but also giggling and nodding.

With Matholook tending to Gwernna and with almost everyone else gone, Efnisien walks over and stands across the table from me. He flips the empty folding chair backwards and straddles it, his arms draped over its curved metal back.

"You're awfully brave coming here like this."

"You're awfully brave letting me in like this," I snap right back.

"You just better not do anything to Matholook."

Matholook? That's what his hostility is about?

"I'm not planning on doing anything to Matholook."

"You planned to come here. You planned to find him. You probably even planned to try to get Gwernna from us."

"I didn't plan on any of that. The Unsettled took Gwernna,

and I just happened to run into Matholook and Bendegatefran in the woods."

"Things don't happen for no reason," he hisses, his eyes darting over to make sure Matholook and Bendegatefran are still occupied and out of earshot. "There are no coincidences."

"You seem kind of pointlessly angry," I tell him. "Do you...I don't know...maybe need a hug or something?"

Efnisien shoves his chair away and snaps to his feet.

I'm on my feet just as fast.

Then, as if he's been sucked up into an indoor tornado, Efnisien flies straight up.

Startled, I leap back to see that Bendegatefran has bolted over, grabbed his half-brother by the collar, and is now holding him dangling in midair while Efnisien kicks and thrashes and barks at him to put him down.

"When you learn how to behave yourself around company," the giant bellows, "*that's* when I'll put you down."

Efnisien shoots a dagger-filled glare at Bendegatefran, who lowers him to the floor.

Thinking that's the end of it, I drop my shoulders and take a breath.

That wasn't the end of it.

With a jungle-cat growl, Efnisien hurls himself at Bendegatefran who looks pained—emotionally, not physically—at having to backhand his snarling half-brother clear across the meeting hall.

Efnisien crumbles to a very loud stop in a tangle of overturned tables and chairs.

"She needs to leave," he says, stabbing a finger in my direction. His voice is oddly even and controlled, all things considered.

"She's our guest," Matholook explains.

"She needs to leave."

"She saved Gwernna," Bendegatefran reminds him.

"She needs to leave. Or I'll make sure she's too dead for Gwernna to bring her back."

Without another word, Efnisien storms out of the room. Bendegatefran, his fists balled at his sides, strides out after him.

"There is something seriously wrong with that guy," I tell Matholook.

I expect him to laugh and agree with me, but he does neither.

"Efnisien isn't really wrong, you know. If you don't leave soon, you won't leave at all."

"What," I laugh. "Are you going to brainwash me and kidnap me?"

"Come on," he smiles. "Tour's not over. It's time to go to school."

16

HISTORY

AT THE WORD "SCHOOL," my heart does a little angry tap-dance in my chest, and I get another one of those lovely, full-color images in my head of all the terrible things Kress is going to do to me when I get back to the Academy.

But I'm curious about the Devoted and in too deep to be afraid. Plus, I like being with Matholook, so I tell him, "Sure. Lead the way."

As we leave the big dining hall, I notice some of the adults ushering Gwernna down a nearby laneway and into a white, cube-shaped building with a belt of mirrored glass around its exterior walls.

"What was wrong with her, anyway?" I ask, pointing over to where the group is just disappearing through the building's open doorway.

"She doesn't handle death well," Matholook explains. "She doesn't like it."

"Who does?"

"Good point. I think it's different for her, though. The death of other people seems to affect her personally. And not like it would for you or me." Matholook taps his temple and then plants an open hand on his chest. "For us, death is something we process in our minds and hearts. We think it. We feel it."

"And her?"

"I don't know for sure. But I get the sense she *lives* it."

"She *lives* death?"

"I'm not one of the Shamans," Matholook laughs. "I don't understand gene-sequencing, binary-helix code, or any of the other techno-evolutionary terms they toss around. But lately, they've been saying she has something called 'plethoric empathy.'" When I give him a blank stare, he chuckles an apology. "It means she feels too much."

"I didn't know that was possible."

"Until I met you, I didn't know a lot of things were possible."

"She should come back to the Academy with me," I suggest. "It's a proper school. She can get taught how to handle what's happening to her."

"We have schools here, too," he reminds me, sounding slightly offended, as we walk along. "Because of the way the Cult of the Devoted is structured, we have different needs, and we do our best to match those with the community members whose interests and abilities best address each need. We learn from each other, so everyone here is a student, and everyone here is a teacher."

I stifle a laugh at the way he's explaining things. It's more a recitation than a conversation, and I can tell he's repeating some kind of party line.

It sounds interesting, but these people aren't known as brain-washers for nothing. I've heard stories from Kress and her Conspiracy about run-ins with the Devoted back in Washington, D.C. where they called themselves the "True Blues" and spent their time blowing stuff up. And I've heard about this western branch—the Cult of the Devoted here in New Harleck—and how they somehow manage to draw people in and turn them into hardcore followers with happy smiles and weird, secret plans for coming out on top in the brewing war everyone in this part of the country seems to be preparing for.

Hearing Matholook explain things so casually, like these people and this place are all the most normal things in the world, makes me wonder how long it'll be before they try to get their hooks into me, too.

If they haven't already, that is.

I also wonder if he thinks all the same things about me when I talk about my own life and school.

As Matholook continues, he sounds almost *too* polished, like an actor who's overlearned his lines to the point he doesn't even understand them anymore. It never occurred to me before how you have to brainwash yourself before you can really brainwash someone else. So I listen to every word he says, but inside, I'm reminding myself not to fall into any traps.

Matholook points down a narrow laneway between two long, single-story buildings—one resembling a stretched-out log-cabin, the other a rectangular prism that looks like it's been pieced together with blocks of dried mud. "Down there are the indoor gardens where the Gatherers learn." Dragging his finger along the rough surface of the log cabin as we pass, he tells me it's the brand-new building where the Scouts are taught.

"Scouts?" I ask. "Like my friend Trax at the Academy?"

"Yes. But without the superpowered cheat-code."

"We don't have cheat-codes," I protest. "And we're not super-powered."

"Just techno-genetically enhanced. Aren't you a product of altered digital code and manipulated genetic code? And isn't *that* the definition of a cheat-code?"

"It's the definition of a human being. Which we are."

"I'm human. But I can't do what you can do with that white raven."

"True," I admit, with a playful poke to his shoulder. "But why should *I* have to suffer as a result of *your* incompetence?"

Matholook nearly chokes on his laughter at that and tells me how right I am. "It's funny, isn't it?" he says, wiping his eyes. "You're really good at something, which makes me bad at it by comparison. And that makes me want to bring you down to my level. But not to hurt you. And not because I'm evil. I sure *hope* I'm not evil, anyway! It's because there's something in all of us that wants to connect with each other, and we'll do almost anything—including acting on our worst instincts—to help make those connections happen."

That's not funny at all.

"Maybe instead of bringing me down to your level," I suggest, "you could try bringing yourself up to mine."

"You know, you're pretty smart...for a superpowered Emergent."

"I'm *not* superpowered."

I really want to be mad at Matholook right now. I know he's winding me up, but there doesn't seem to be any edge or malice to him. He seems willing to argue when he disagrees with me, but then he turns around and is just as quick to agree when I've said something that could change his mind.

What kind of game is this guy playing at?

From everything he's told me so far, unlike the Academy, their school is more about adherence to the past and to traditions. I make a mental note about that. It could be a weakness of theirs when it comes to entering the war. When you keep looking backward, it's a lot easier to stumble and fall.

"Here," Matholook says, leading me through an open doorway and into the narrow hallway of the mud-brick building. "I'll show you one of our classes."

I follow him into one of the rooms where a class is being taught by a woman with straight gray hair and impossibly wide hips. She introduces herself as "Marm Vitarria" and welcomes me with a clamp-toothed smile and an invitation to stand at the front of the class in front of the rows of desks.

Unlike the desks in the Academy, which are clean and ergonomically sleek, these are the definition of "old school." Made of wood and tubes of steel, they creak and groan under the weight of the students, who squirm around before sitting up at straight-backed attention.

Marm Vitarria scrawls my name on a scratched-up green chalkboard that covers the entire wall behind her. The board must be a hundred years old.

Like her blue denim dress, Marm Vitarria's fingers are coated in streaks of powdery white dust.

She brushes her chalky hands on her dress and calls the class's attention to me and Matholook.

"We have one of our Caretakers with us today. And his special guest..."

A young girl with long, scraggly blond hair launches her hand into the air. Without waiting to be called on, she blurts out, "Are you the one who saved our savior?"

I laugh at her over-the-top enthusiasm, but then I slam on the brakes when I realize she's totally serious.

"Yes," Marm Vitarria answers on my behalf. "This is Branwynne. She saved Gwernna."

News travels fast around here. I wonder how much else the students know about me.

A tall boy with sunken cheeks and a single, thick eyebrow drawn down into a V-shape clamps his hands to the side edges of his desk. "She's an Emergent."

He says it like he's accusing me of being a murderer.

"She's a *guest*," Marm Vitarria scolds. "Hospitality is one of our core values," she explains, turning to me. "We've inherited that tradition from the Ancient Greeks."

"You never know when a guest might be a god in disguise," Matholook explains to me out of the side of his mouth.

I ask, "Really?" but he doesn't have time to answer.

Marm Vitarria clears her throat and addresses the class. "We'll ask our Caretaker and our guest to take their seats..."

On cue, Matholook leads me to two empty seats at the back of the room and off to the side where I can get a good view of most of the students.

I scan the class and see a few faces I recognize from the dining hall, a few from the church, a few more from when Matholook and I were being stalked while out on our stroll around town. And then there's one face I definitely remember: Efnisien. Usually, he stares daggers at me. This time, it's more like machine guns, and I actually press back in my seat when he locks his eyes onto mine.

"Is every kid in your compound here?" I whisper to Matholook as I struggle to maintain my composure.

"We don't separate students based on age," Matholook whispers back with a shake of his head. "Students are grouped mainly by their abilities and by their interests. This class is made up of those who have shown a unique interest or talent for recalling the past. A couple of them even come close to having eidetic memories."

"Eidetic...?"

"They remember pretty much everything. They absorb what they hear, read, and see. They internalize it. And then they're able to reproduce it for the good of the community."

"Sounds like they're pretty superpowered to me."

"It's hardly the same thing as being able to link minds with a raven."

"Maybe not. But it's not that far off, either, is it?"

"That's an interesting point."

"And these kids here will become members of one of your Guilds?"

"Exactly. These will be our next group of Historians. After this class, I'll take you outside to where the future Vindicators will be in training."

"And those are your warriors?"

"Like Bendegatefran, yes."

"And now it's time for review," Marm Vitarria announces. She scans the rows of students in front of her, her eyes landing on a small boy with a bowl haircut and pock-marked skin. "James, what was Lord Acton's famous line about power?"

"Power tends to corrupt, and absolute power corrupts absolutely."

"And what does that mean?"

"It means once people get even a small amount of power, they tend to use all of it all the time."

"Even when its use could hurt those who are less powerful?"

"Especially then."

Marm Vitarria turns her attention to another boy. "Daveed, historically-speaking, is there a correlation between having power and being bad?"

Daveed's asymmetrical eyes narrow and then get equally wide. "Definitely. Lord Acton also said that great men are almost always bad men."

Marm Vitarria suppresses a smile and asks, "Was he right?"

"History says he was."

"And should history always be believed?"

A small girl sitting just behind Daveed rises half out of her seat and starts waving her hand like she's being electrocuted. "Lord Acton said that 'history is the arbiter of controversy, the monarch of all she surveys.'"

"And?"

Sitting back in her seat, the girl bites her lip and stares at the

ceiling. "History is ... not a burden on the memory but an illumi-
nation of the soul."

"Very good, Izzy," Marm Vitarria beams. "Now, back to what
James remembered about the relationship between power and
corruption. What can people like us do against Emergents and
the other new rulers of the world?"

*Rulers of the world? Is that really what they think of us? I have
certain abilities. That doesn't automatically make me some sort of
tyrant...does it?*

I clear my throat and am about to raise my hand to object to
this nonsense, but Matholook reaches over and places his hand
on my forearm. Not hard. I could shake him off. But his eyes tell
me he knows what I'm about to say but that this isn't the time or
the place to say it.

The girl called Izzy says, "Joseph Stalin teaches us that
there's no such thing as 'invincible armies.'"

"Meaning?"

"Meaning that no matter how powerful the enemy, there's
always a weakness, always a flaw."

Izzy goes on to rattle off a dozen examples of triumphant
underdog stories. The tortoise and the hare. David and Goliath.
Moses and the Pharaoh. Odysseus and the Trojan Horse. Her
recitation is impressive—I don't know half of the examples she
gives—but it sounds almost...robotic?

When she's finished, she leans back in her seat with a smug
smile.

I'm tempted to raise my hand again. Those are *stories*. In real life
—in places like London or right here in the Divided States—giants
like Goliath kill people like David all the time. God doesn't always
swoop down and help people like he did with Moses. Trojan armies
burn suspicious gift horses to the ground along with all the soldiers
hiding inside. And no tortoise has ever outrun a hare.

But a second subtle and clear headshake from Matholook stops me from saying anything.

Bollocks. How does he always know what I'm thinking and what I'm about to do?

Marm Vitarria carries on with the class while I listen, squirm, and resist the impulse to shout, "Bollocks!" after nearly everything she says.

It doesn't make sense. A lot of what they're on about is based in fiction and mythology. Sure, they talk a lot about historical events, too. But they keep talking in absolutes. There are canyon-sized holes in every argument and contorted logic at every turn. I'm hardly the smartest student in the Academy, but even I could dismantle half of what they're saying.

So why do I keep feeling like I want to believe?

In this moment, I can feel that pull again. It's in my body and in my head. It's warm and comforting. It's tugging at me—not in an annoying way—more like it's trying to get my attention. It's a soothing pull. It's calling to me. It's also scaring the hell out of me.

Time seems to drift after that, and before I know it, class is over.

Marm Vitarria calls on Efnisien to have the last word of the day.

Efnisien stands, presses the tips of his fingers to his desk, and clears his throat. His voice is a raspy snarl, peppered with an extra sprinkle of unprovoked hostility just for good measure, in case I'm not picking up on how much he hates me. "People with power will *always* abuse it. People with special skills wind up sacrificing empathy in favor of ability. But history teaches us that even these mighty will fall. Abraham Lincoln said it himself: 'You cannot escape history.'"

He swings away from Marm Vitarria and directly toward me,

looks right into my eyes, and stresses the "You" when he says this.

My mouth hangs open, but Matholook—for the third time since we came in here—puts his hand on my arm. His fingers slide down and curl around my wrist, and he gives the tiniest shake of his head.

He doesn't have to worry. I'm not shocked at being called out as a potential tyrant. I'm not offended at being feared as an Emergent. And I'm not angry at Efnisien's confrontational posturing.

I'm confused about why so much of what I'm hearing today suddenly makes so much sense. Why should I care what Efnisien or any of these other slaves to history thinks about me? Why should I feel guilty for being specially selected and trained to salvage what's left of the world?

No. Efnisien doesn't have to be worried. But now, with my head foggy, I'm wondering if maybe *I* should be.

17

JUNIPER

WORRYING about Efnisien is one of the smarter things I've decided to do.

After our little dust-up in the dining hall, I figured he'd lie low, maybe lick his wounds, and wait for me to return to the Academy so he could get back to his full-time job of being a psycho.

Why do I have a nagging feeling that I figured wrong?

After Marm Vitarria dismisses the class, Matholook leads me outside and into a dry, dirt-packed courtyard with a single, thick-trunked tree in the middle. Maybe fifteen feet high and surrounded by a decorative ring of polished orange stones as big and round as basketballs, the tree's limbs are a horror show of gnarled branches peppered with a mangy assortment of dead and dying brownish-green, needle-like leaves. Everything about the tree—from its scabby bark to its crooked fan of spindly arms —comes across as a deformed mess of an organism.

If Hell had its own Garden of Eden, the tree of life would look like this.

A few students start straggling into the courtyard. They give me the usual barrage of curious stares or disapproving glares before queuing up in the shade against the walls of one of the long, single-story buildings surrounding the open terrace.

I recognize a couple of the kids. There's the girl Izzy from the History class that just let out. There's Bendegatefran, who's hard to miss since his head's as high as the edge of the building's shingled roof, and he has to scrunch down to stay in the shade. And there's Efnisien, arms crossed tight across his chest, his creepy, beady eyes fixed on me.

"It's a juniper tree," Matholook tells me when he catches me swinging around to stare at the tree's twisted trunk and its tangled mess of exposed roots.

"What?"

"The tree. I saw you looking at it. It's a juniper tree."

"It's ugly."

"Or beautiful," Matholook grins. "I guess it just depends on how you look at it."

"Yeah," I say, tilting my head and squinting. "Maybe if I look at it like this...Nope. It's still ugly."

Matholook chuckles and points to a spot far off in the distance, out beyond the cluster of buildings in this part of their compound. "There are more juniper trees in an orchard out that way. I'll show it to you on our next tour. We sometimes use the wood to make weapons. It's especially good for making bows. And the bark is soft enough for us to pulp it, dry it, and turn it into toilet paper. Oh, and the berries are tasty. We use them to make sauces and gin."

"Gin? You mean, like the alcoholic drink?"

"Yes. 'Juniper' is where the word 'gin' comes from. In Dutch, the name for the tree is 'jenever.'"

"Great. I left school and now here I am...in school."

"It could be worse."

"It was," I laugh, reminding him of what we've been through

in the last few hours. "But I still enjoy a good fight with the Unsettled from time to time."

"You'd make a great Vindicator," Matholook says. "No wonder Bendegatefran likes you."

"How did that guy get so tall, anyway?"

"I don't know. How does anyone get to the height they are? I guess someone just forgot to tell him to stop growing."

"He makes War and Terk look like you and me."

"Speaking of your school, aren't they going to be looking for you?"

"Probably. But they won't find me here."

"Why's that?"

"First of all, they'd never know I was headed here. I didn't know it myself until the *pull*."

"The pull?"

"Just a feeling," I shrug. "Something told me to visit the Valta. And then it told me to...keep going down the mountain."

"To find me."

"I guess," I sigh. "I just said it was a pull. I didn't say it made sense."

"So how come your teachers won't find you?"

"I'm hiding."

Matholook glances up at the clear, open sky over New Harleck. "Not exactly the best place in the world to hide. Won't Kress's raven be able to track you down or something?"

"Normally, yes. Render *is* our expert tracker. But no, he won't be able to track me down."

"And why is that, exactly?"

"I sort of have the ability to control my body temperature, metabolic rate, heat signature, my physical disruption of the ripples in the earth's magnetic field...things like that."

"You're kidding, right?"

"Nope. I'm not great at it yet. But I'm okay."

"Does it...?"

"Hurt? Yes. That's why I'm still in training."

Matholook stares at me for a second. Then, he stares off into the distance and lets out an impressed whistle before shaking his head. "Really amazing. The things you can do."

"Hey, that was quite the class," I tell him, flicking my thumb back toward the building we were just in and hoping he doesn't press me anymore about my abilities.

"It's pretty basic stuff," he says. "We've all taken Marm Vitarria's class."

"So...I still don't get it. Why the big emphasis on history?"

"You're kidding, right?"

"No. Seriously." I gesture around at the bleak compound. The dirt paths. The scorch marks—clear signs of old drone strikes—on the tops and sides of the nearby buildings. The men, women, and children still skittering around in the laneways, cleaning up after the attack by the Unsettled. "How does learning about the past make any difference to surviving in the present? It seems like there are more important things to worry about."

"History gives us perspective," Matholook explains. "It *stops* us from worrying. After all, everything you see here will be a part of someone's history one day. So all the stress you feel, all the worry, fear, and anxiety...it doesn't really accomplish very much, does it?"

"We learn about history, too, you know."

Matholook tosses me a condescending grin. "Oh, really? You said your teachers aren't much older than us."

"War and Mayla are older. And Granden. Kind of."

"So what can the rest of these not-much-older, so-called elders of yours possibly have to teach you that's better than what we learn here?"

"Well, in one of our assignments, we read about a man named George Santayana."

"I know all about him."

"Then you know he said that history is 'a pack of lies about events that never happened told by people who weren't there.'"

"There are only three problems with that."

"Only three?"

"History may be filled with distortions and misinterpretations. Those last. Lies don't. All events happened. Maybe not in the exact order or with the exact details we're told, but there's more than one world and an infinite number of ways of experiencing them."

"That sounds like something Kress would say. Or Haida."

"Your white raven?"

"Yes."

"I'm still not used to the idea that she *says* anything."

"There are more ways to talk than with just our mouths," I tease.

"Fair enough."

"And the third thing?"

"What third thing?"

I hold up my thumb and my first two fingers. "You said there were *three* problems with Santayana's quote."

"Oh, right. The last part. The part about history being told by people who weren't there. You see, for us—for the Cult of the Devoted—we *were* there. We *are* there. History is a living, growing thing, an all-encompassing entity. It's a mother's arms wrapped around us. A writer named James Baldwin said, 'People are trapped in history. And history is trapped in them.' We take that to heart. It's because of what's happened in the past that we know what might or might not happen in the future. We're taught to see the world as a long line, a timeline, with each point on the line being a chance to learn how to get to the next point. Think of it like a series of stones in a river. Knowing how to balance on one can help you balance even better on the next."

"Or you can slip off, crack your head open, and drown."

Standing next to me, Matholook has his hands plunged into his pockets, and he gives me a playful nudge with his elbow. "You know, for an optimist, you have a pretty bleak view of the world."

"It's a pretty bleak world. And who said I'm an optimist, anyway?"

"You wouldn't be here if you weren't hoping for the best."

Now, it's my turn to nudge him. "I'm still waiting to see if the 'best' is yet to come."

We chat for another minute or two while the courtyard continues to fill up with kids straggling in. We're interrupted by a tall woman with olive skin and a long, black ponytail, who comes striding out from the shadows of a laneway and into the light of the courtyard. She summons the kids over to her, and they gather in a loose cluster under the scraggly canopy formed by the branches of the juniper tree.

Except for Bendegatefran. He stands outside the cluster with his head invisible somewhere in the tree's knotty branches.

"What class is this, anyway?" I whisper to Matholook.

"Olympics."

"Olympics? You mean like the old games people used to compete in?"

"Exactly. Except 'games' might not be the most accurate term for what you're about to see. There's wrestling, foot races, and archery. Pater Gentry usually teaches those. He teaches fitness and boxing classes, too. You won't get to meet him, though."

"Why not?"

"He's running a nutrition seminar on the other side of the compound right now. So today, you get to see brawling."

"Brawling?"

"Yep. Once a week, the kids in Olympics Class are treated to a no-holds-barred, unarmed combat. Same as you take." Math-olook pats my arm and starts walking toward the tall teacher and the class.

"Wait. Really?" I call after him.

"It used to be to the death," he tells me from over his shoulder. "But then we started running into the little problem of a shrinking population."

I'm trying to see if he's kidding, but the cheeky beggar's already turned away.

18

OLYMPICS

MATHOLOOK IS JUST ABOUT to introduce me to the instructor, but she beats him to it.

"You're Branwynne," she says, her hand extended in greeting. "Our savior's savior."

I swear. If one more person—

"She's a little uncomfortable with that," Matholook explains on my behalf.

"It's the truth, though," the woman practically purrs. "This young lady here risked her life for a cause other than her own. Thanks to her, Gwernna is home. Thanks to her, we may survive a little longer. That rescue...it happened. Branwynne's discomfort won't change that, will it?"

Looking like a chastised eight-year-old, Matholook drops his eyes and shakes his head. I half expect him to go all the way and plunge his hands into his pockets and draw circles in the ground with his toe. But he stops at the head shake.

"My name is Marm Pintada," the woman says, swinging her gaze from Matholook to me. "Welcome to my class. I'll be your instructor today. We're all looking forward to seeing what you can do."

I put my hands up and shake them back and forth like I'm polishing a giant pane of glass while I take a Bendegatefran-sized step back. "I'm just having a look around before I head back."

Marm Pintada seems to freeze in place. She doesn't move, doesn't blink, and doesn't change her expression for what feels like twenty minutes, but it's probably more like a fraction of a second.

Finally, she blinks her mud-brown eyes, runs her hands over her slick hair, draws her ponytail over the front of her shoulder, and gives me a broad smile that would be quite lovely except for the chapped lips and the dark black holes on either side created by at least four or five missing teeth.

I glance over at Matholook, then at the students in the class, and finally at the buildings surrounding the courtyard before letting my eyes settle back on Marm Pintada.

When my eyes meet hers, her smile widens, and she gives me what comes across as kind of an angry wink.

"There. You've had a look around. I hope you enjoyed what you saw. Now, unless you have any more excuses, it's time for class to start."

She gives a shrill, wet whistle through the gap in the side of her mouth, and the students—all sixteen of them—shuffle out to the edge of the circle at the perimeter of the courtyard.

She gives another whistle—longer and higher-pitched this time—and a dozen of the Devoted Sentries step out from in between the buildings around us and take up rigid positions at the outermost edges of the courtyard.

She steps away and turns her attention to her class, while I ask Matholook what's going on.

"*They're* going to brawl," he says, his eyes skimming along the ring of students. "And *they,*" he adds, gesturing with his thumb at the statue-like Sentries, each gripping what looks like a butcher knife attached to a long wooden handle, "are there to ensure everyone's full participation."

Nudging me forward, he tells me I need to queue up with the others.

"You really expect me to join in this thing?"

"When in Rome…"

"I've never been to Rome."

"Me, neither. But I hear its Coliseum was once the hub of entertainment."

"Yeah," I grunt. "Nothing like tossing slaves into a fighting pit to entertain the Wealthies."

"You don't have to do it. I can talk to Marm Pintada."

I'm about to take him up on the offer, but then I feel that pull inside of me again. "No. I'll give it a shot."

"Don't worry. She won't let it get out of hand. After all, you're our savior's—"

I cut him off with a sharp elbow to the arm.

He says, "Ow," and grimaces like I just hit him with the business end of a cricket bat.

Marm Pintada strides out to the middle of the courtyard in front of us, calling out instructions as she goes.

"Most of you have participated in the Brawl before. But I see some new faces as well. Some scared faces."

She better not be talking about me.

"And I see some angry faces," she continues. "You'll lose that anger soon enough. There's no place for it in battle. You think it will spur you on, but it won't. It will only weigh you down."

She points to two of the students a few spots down from where I'm standing. The girl is stocky, rosy-cheeked, and soaked in sweat with rice-paddy-sized pit stains under the arms of her blousy white shirt. The boy is angular with knobby elbows and knees and a quivering look of terror carved into his face.

Marm Pintada sweeps her hand from me to the two nervous

kids. "Allizabet and Elexander are both new to the Brawl. So a reminder of the rules. You can't step outside of the circle. If you do, you lose, but you'll be sent back in anyway as a reminder that quitting is just another form of failure. You may choose to go it alone. Or you may choose to partner up. I will be assessing each of you for your strengths, weaknesses, and for how close you get to an optimal strategy selection. And please try not to damage the tree."

Marm Pintada puts her hand on one of the tree's weirdly misshapen branches and presses her cheek to it like it's a sheet of rare, Egyptian cotton.

As if she's just been startled by some unseen specter, she pivots in a quick circle and surveys her class. "And don't even think about snapping off one its branches to use as a weapon. If you do that, you'll fail the class. Plus, I'll kill you."

I catch Matholook's eyes. "Um, maybe I have the wrong idea of what the Olympics were about..."

"The Olympics had games, competition, fights, races, and battles. But that's not what they were about."

"Then what—?"

"They were about connections, especially the forbidden ones like the attraction between men."

"Wait. What?"

"Combat is the ultimate connection. The Olympics, like all sports and like all wars, gave men the chance to be intimate with each other outside of the confines of a restrictive society."

I stare at Matholook.

His eyes wide, he asks, "What?"

"I'm waiting for you to tell me you're joking."

"And why should I do that?"

"Because you're talking like you're stark raving, off-your-trolley bonkers."

"Is it that crazy to think human beings will find ways—

subtle, underhanded, obvious, and even violent—to be themselves?"

"Okay," I confess after a pause to soak that in. "That's a good point. I never thought about it that way before."

Marm Pintada snaps at him to step away to the outer edge of the courtyard.

That's when it occurs to me: I've been training in all kinds of armed and unarmed combat. Hell, I've even fought blindfolded, one-on-one in a pit with spiked walls and a moving floor.

But never, not once, have I been jam-lucky enough to fight sixteen other people all at once.

Marm Pintada raises her thin arm high into the air and snaps her long, knot-knuckled fingers three times. When she drops her hand to her side, all sixteen of the students— including Bendegatefran and his evil-eyed half-brother—step over the ring of perimeter stones and into the courtyard.

"You seriously expect me to do this?" I ask Matholook out of the corner of my mouth.

From somewhere overhead, Haida Gwaii gurgle-clacks a chuckling laugh.

Thanks for the vote of confidence.

"I expect you to do as your history dictates," Matholook says. "I'm guessing that means taking the path of *most* resistance and leaping headfirst into a long-odds fight because you know you could die if you do, and you know just as well that your *soul* will definitely die if you don't."

"I'm guessing you're right."

Either I've become ridiculously transparent, Matholook has turned somehow psychic, or...Could it be that the vague connection I came here looking for is real?

Handing my jacket to Matholook and dropping the holster for my Serpent Blades on the ground, I step over the ring of rocks and into the fray.

In for a penny, in for a pound.

Now, I just have to hope I'm the one who'll be doing most of the pounding.

19

BRAWL

KRESS HAS BEEN TEACHING me how to relax myself into my telempathic bond with Haida Gwaii. Lately, we've been working how to maximize what the bond can do for me.

Ravens have evolved in lockstep with human social evolution. They've adapted to rapidly changing environments and radical temperature fluctuations. Their respiratory and circulatory systems are highly specialized and advanced with incredible cardiac output and oxygen diffusion. On top of that, they're expert tricksters who've been known to plant false clues to lead competitors away from places where they've hidden food. They will even "play dead" to keep other ravens and rival predators away. And they use their uncanny ability as mimics to confuse, disorient, or distract prey and potential enemies. With their speed, reflexes, gymnastic agility, and physical endurance, they are deadly hunters and natural survivors.

So...Basically, Kress has been teaching me how to be a raven.

And Kress, as I'm discovering, is a *really* good teacher.

I fly into the crowd of circling, shuffling, and swinging kids. I zip, dart, juke, and even throw in a couple of zigs and zags as I feel out the melee.

The fist flying at my head slows to a crawl. I can make out every hair on the boy's ropey-muscled arm. I duck his attack and pivot at the same time to slip out of the path of an orange-haired girl, whose attempt to lunge at me ends with her sprawling to the ground and getting trampled by four boys locked in a rat-king clutch.

A different boy thinks he has the drop on me. I wonder if he realizes how wrong he was as I throw a vicious elbow to his jaw and watch a mist of blood spray from his mouth along with two of his teeth.

As a girl and a boy go tumbling by, a brawny, lantern-jawed girl manages to latch a hand onto my shoulder. A half-spin later, and I've got her arm pinned behind her back and am snow-plowing her into the chest of a shaggy-haired boy. The air woomphs out of him as he and the girl land in a heap on the hard, heavily-trampled ground.

The girl is down but not out. I help her cross over into unconsciousness with the sharp front kick I snap to the side of her head.

As the scuffle continues, I realize something's missing...

It's anger.

There's no snarling. No taunts. No warrior battle-cries. There's not even the tension, stress, or uncertainty I've seen in combat situations. In fact, a lot of the kids are laughing as we go. Even the boy whose teeth I just knocked out is practically glowing with glee as he slings a smaller girl—the new one named Allizabet—around by her ponytail, sending her pinwheeling to the ground.

She grins at him as she scrambles to her feet and leaps onto the back of a disoriented, lanky boy, locking her arms around his neck in what looks like an excruciating chokehold.

Grabbing at her forearms, he launches himself backward, pinning her to the ground underneath him. As he clambers to get to his feet, she answers his attack with a tight-fisted uppercut to his plum-nuggets.

His eyes roll back, and he staggers into a bald, hulking boy who punches him in the side of the head. Mr. Plum-Nuggets hits the ground and disappears under a cloud of dust.

One by one, kids get knocked down only to pick themselves back up.

Their will to win never falters. Their bodies, on the other hand, eventually succumb to the punishment, and the brawlers start dropping out one by one.

As they fall, the Sentries leap into the courtyard to drag them out or hoist them onto their shoulders and carry the injured and the unconscious to safety.

What started out as a sixteen-person brawl has turned into a three-person stand-off.

It's all come down to me, Bendegatefran, and Efnisien.

Looming over me, Bendegatefran is literally blocking out the sun. The coolness of his shadow hovers over me, and I feel like I'm squaring off against the broad side of a barn.

Don't get me wrong. I'm not afraid of him. Sure, he's taller than some buildings and trees I've come across, but he's not very fast and not especially ruthless. At least not for someone on the Vindicators who's been tasked with front-line battle duties. Besides, I beat him just a few hours ago out in the woods. And that's when it was still dark out, and he had an axe.

Efnisien is another story. There's something about him I just don't understand and definitely don't trust.

I'm figuring that it'll be those two against me. After all, they're brothers. Well, half-brothers, as Efnisien likes to remind anyone who'll listen.

Bendegatefran looks downright apologetic as he squares off to face me and raises the twin boulders he calls "fists."

I smile, but it's not meant to be teasing or goading or anything. It's a smile of respect.

I once told Kress how strange it is that warriors come in all shapes and sizes.

She told me, "That's because being a warrior has less to do with the shape and size of *you* and more to do with the shape and size of the goal you're fighting *for* and the enemy you're fighting *against*. And..." she added, "the first enemy is always the one inside of yourself."

As much as I always want to believe everything that comes out of Kress's mouth, right now, it's pretty clear that whatever enemy is inside of me is a lot smaller than Bendegatefran and a lot less openly hostile than Efnisien.

What was it I was saying a minute ago about no anger?

Efnisien seems content to scuttle his way around the perimeter of the ring, leaving me and Bendegatefran to close our tight, two-person circle.

With one eye on Efnisien and fully anticipating some kind of underhanded sneak attack, I do my best to focus on not getting killed by the giant in front of me.

Bendegatefran throws a feeble jab. He's tentative. Hesitant. He's seen my speed in action, and he's smart enough to know there's more to me than meets the eye.

I give him credit for giving me credit.

He throws another punch, this time with more power behind it.

I dodge it easily, and it's a good thing I've got these enhanced reflexes. Even a half-hearted strike by this giant would be enough to turn most people's heads from a solid into a liquid.

I can tell by the way he moves that he's been almost exclusively trained to fight with weapons, probably with his enormous axe.

The cheers (or are they jeers?) of the crowd of kids outside the ring of perimeter stones distracts me for a second.

Focus, Branwynne. You've been in training for years now. So what if you never trained to fight a human-shaped battleship...

Bendegatefran takes an aggressive step toward me, and I scurry around to the far side of the juniper tree.

I bet some gin would taste really nice right about now...

Ducking down, he easily reaches around the tree and comes an inch away from latching onto my shoulder with those giant-salami fingers of his.

With his enormous reach, there's no legitimate place to hide, so I don't bother trying. Stepping out from behind the tree, I drop my guard and practically beg him to take a clean shot at me.

He complies, and the wind generated by his swinging fist is enough to stagger me for a second.

His follow-up, backhand swat tags me on the shoulder. It's a glancing blow, but it's enough to send me reeling on a ten-foot slide that ends with me on my backside.

Springing to my feet before he can launch a follow-up, I slip under his arm and slide right up to him.

With my feet in between his and my nose nearly at his navel, I've negated his reach advantage and locked him into a close-quarters combat situation.

As I suspected, he's caught completely off guard. And why shouldn't he be? When you've spent your fighting life being conditioned to have people desperately trying to give you a wide berth, the last thing you're prepared for is a five-foot-four-inch girl standing too close for you to hit.

He tries to back up, but I press forward.

It's got to be infuriating for him. The more he wants to put distance between us, the closer I get to him.

Clearly rattled now, he makes the mistake I've been waiting for.

With his irritation clouding his judgement, he starts hammering wildly down at me, which is all the opening I need.

Dodging his chaotic strikes, I drop down and scramble between his tree-trunk legs until I'm behind him. As he pivots, I catch him with a sharp kick. The edge of my boot meets the soft spot behind his knee, and his leg buckles.

Flailing to keep his balance, he's now completely exposed, and I'm a little embarrassed for him. I'm also feeling a little guilty. After all, there are so many good targets to hit, and I don't know which one to go after first.

So I decide to strike bottom-to-top. After the spot behind his knee, I throw three quick lightning jabs to his kidneys followed by three quick hacks with the blade of my hand to the carotid artery at the side of his neck. Clamping onto his shoulder, I vault myself around to deliver a flying knee to the bridge of his nose.

That all happens in the space of about two seconds. It takes half that long for him to drop to one knee and hold his hand up.

"I'm out," he groans.

I'm almost too distracted by my second victory over the giant to notice the flash of movement behind me.

Efnisien charges at me. I sidestep him and then realize he's not going for me at all.

With a whoosh of wind and the ferocity of a jungle cat, he leaps onto Bendegatefran's back.

It's only now that I realize Efnisien has claws.

Not Talons like the blades Kress has been known to bring into battle. No. These are his actual fingernails. Each one is curved, yellowed, and filed to a needle-sharp point.

With frantic, unrelenting speed, he claws over and over at the giant's face and eyes as Bendegatefran bellows out a horrifying moan and tries to roll his attacker off of him.

But Efnisien seems locked onto his half-brother with super-human strength and with his knees clamped to the giant's waist in a stubborn refusal to be thrown off.

Lumbering to his feet and reaching behind his back, Bende-gatefran scrambles to get a grip on Efnisien, but Efnisien slips upward and latches his arms around the giant's neck.

It's the same move I used on Bendegatefran in the woods. Except that I had my Serpent Blades, and I was just looking to win, not to kill.

Efnisien seems to have different plans.

He rakes his nails across Bendegatefran's face, drawing long red marks into the giant's skin.

Marm Pintada gives her shrill wet whistle, but the attack continues.

She whistles again and snaps her fingers, and Efnisien whips his head around to give her a death glare. For a second, I think he might be going after her next.

She snaps her fingers again, harder this time, and stomps her boot to the ground like a woman disciplining a disobedient dog.

Efnisien doesn't let go of his half-brother right away. Instead, he leans in close and whispers something in his ear I can't hear. And then, as he's finally releasing his grip, he drags his pointed nails in a quick slash—one more time as a parting shot—across Bendegatefran's throat.

The giant howls and clutches his hands to his bleeding neck as Efnisien stalks away, shouldering past me on his way to the outer edge of the courtyard.

Tearing themselves away from the Sentries, the kids from the class who aren't too wounded limp as fast as they can until they're swarming in a worried cluster around Bendegatefran.

In a rage, he swats at them, and they scatter.

"Sorry," he grumbles as he tries and fails to lurch himself to his feet. Collapsing back down, he presses his fingertips to the open, bleeding cuts on his face and neck. The concerned kids gather in closer with some of them calling off to the side for someone to bring a stretcher for Bendegatefran whose eyes are unfocused and who still can't get to his feet.

As for me, I'm standing there, sweaty, shaking, and shocked.

Matholook snaps me out of my daze with an arm around my shoulders. "Come sit over here. I'll get us some water."

He guides me to the outer edge of the courtyard, tells me he'll be right back, and then disappears into an open doorway in one of the buildings, leaving me alone to wonder if Bendegate-fran is going to die, if Efnisien is going to come after me next, or if things will settle down and Matholook will return with some water as he's promised.

That is three *very* different outcomes, and I smile to myself, wondering which one of those options will someday be known as the historical truth.

20

SUPERMAN

SITTING with my back to the warm wood of the building's exterior wall, I wrap my arms around my knees and try to process what just happened.

It's hard to believe it's the same reddish sun up there I see almost every day from the rooftop of the Academy. Hell, it's hard to believe this is even the same world.

It's still pretty early in the afternoon, but it's already hot enough to dry out my eyes.

The fact that Kress and the others haven't tracked me down tells me my plan to camouflage myself is working.

Either that, or they just don't care and haven't been looking for me at all.

While I watch the aftermath of the Brawl, Efnisien storms out of the courtyard alone. No one looks at him or talks to him. I don't know if that's out of respect or fear. Or maybe they're the same thing.

Bendegatefran gets carried out on a boat-sized stretcher by half the class. Standing five-by-five on either side of the wood and canvas litter, they look like some kind of old school funeral procession. Only, in this case, the "deceased" is squirming and moaning while the panting, straining pall-bearers limp and wobble their way past the juniper tree and over the ring of rocks.

Flanked, herself, by two of the Sentries, Marm Pintada ushers the procession along, and the whole whack of them disappears around the corner.

Carrying two small vials of turquoise water, Matholook returns with a smile and plops down next to me.

Water. Way better than some of the alternatives I've been imagining.

Handing one of the vials to me, he scans the courtyard as the last of the straggling students files out.

Once everyone is gone and the courtyard is quiet, Matholook leans back against the shingled wall, his shoulder pressed lightly to mine.

"That was...insane," I mutter.

"That was the Brawl."

"Do they always end like that?"

"You mean with people getting hurt?"

"I mean with a raving nutter going bonker-town banana pants."

"Efnisien has...issues."

"I don't see why Bendegatefran doesn't fight back against him. He's a Vindicator and five times his size."

"They're brothers."

"Half-brothers."

"Bendegatefran doesn't see the difference. All Efnisien sees is the difference."

"Must be a challenge," I say with a dry chuckle, "seeing eye to eye with someone that tall."

"We do our best. I love the way we live, but I won't pretend it's perfect. But for all of us to survive, everyone has to have a role."

"And what's Efnisien's role? Is there a special Guild for Devoted who are stark raving mad as a bag of ferrets?"

"Actually, Efnisien is unique here."

"Blatantly."

"He doesn't belong to a Guild."

"I though everyone here had to."

"Technically, yes. But Efnisien was one of the ones who escaped from Epic down in Sanctum. I don't know what happened to him there or why he is how he is. But, for whatever reason, he just never really found a place here. Never felt...connected."

"And you think he's an Emergent, don't you? A defective one."

"I don't know what he is. But whatever it is, I'm glad he's on our side." Matholook hands me one of the two vials and invites me to drink-up. "You sound like you've been chewing on sandpaper. Here. This'll help."

I swirl the liquid around in the glass, test-tube shaped container. The drink turns milky-white with tiny crystal flecks dancing around inside.

"What *is* this stuff?"

Matholook twists the cork-top off of his vial and sips from its round lip. "It's water. With some low-grade alkaline tabs and anti-radiation purifiers mixed in."

I sniff at the cloudy concoction and wrinkle my nose.

"Here," he says, taking a tiny sip from his and then reaching over and taking an even smaller sip from mine. "I didn't invite you here to poison you."

I sniff the top of the vial again and nod. He's right. Thanks to my symbiotic relationship with my keen-nosed raven, I can make out the exact odor of each ingredient he listed as well as some he left out. None of it's toxic.

I start to tilt the whole tube back toward my mouth, but

Matholook laughs and plants a firm hand on the crook of my arm. "Easy. That's got to last the whole day."

"The whole day?"

"At least. Why? What do you drink up there in your Academy?"

"Um...Water."

"Big difference between the water up there and the water down here. Not that much of it makes its way this far. What *does* make it usually winds up too toxic to be any good. There's a lot of bad stuff for it to pick up from way up there to way down here." Matholook raises his vial to the air in a mock toast. "Thank you, Krug and the Atomic Wars."

I raise mine, too, to say, "Cheers," and we clink the thin glass tubes together. "I won't lie. We have some pretty decent amenities and resources in the Academy. Maybe my people and your people can come to some sort of agreement. Maybe a sharing arrangement or something. I can't speak for the Unsettled, but if Epic wants a war so bad, wouldn't it be better if at least two of our factions were united against him?"

I blush when Matholook laughs, and I ask him what's so funny about that.

"We're historians."

"So?"

"So, we know history. And history tells us that human beings are incapable of the kind of sharing you're describing. Human beings get territorial, jealous, greedy, scared, and dangerously insecure, especially in times of uncertainty or stress." Matholook points out into the empty courtyard. "You saw what just happened here. Every two groups of human beings in the world have said they'd set up an arrangement.' But the empathetic will always suffer. The ruthless will always prevail." Matholook shrugs. "It's the historical nature of human beings."

"As you're fond of reminding me, I'm an Emergent, not a human being."

"Exactly. You have power. All the more reason an 'arrangement' won't work. How much of your own power are you willing to sacrifice for someone else? What happens when it gets to be too much? What happens when you give up so much of being powerful that you join the ranks of the weak?"

"I don't see that happening."

"On the contrary, can you think of a time when that *didn't* eventually happen?"

My mind flashes to Krug and his Patriot Army, the Deenays, the En-Gene-eers, the Royal Fort Knights of Buckingham Palace, the Banters of Kensington Palace, Epic and the Sanctum Civil-lains...And I'm *almost* ready to agree with Matholook. But then I say, "The Academy."

"The Academy? What about it?"

"We have different degrees of power like you say. But no one person tries to dominate the others. Kress and her Conspiracy have given up everything and have literally put their lives on the line for us."

"And all of the students are happy with this arrangement? No one is sneaking around using their Emergent abilities for their own gain?"

"No."

"You're sure?"

"Yes."

"Don't be."

"What do you know about it?" I ask in a huff.

"I know enough."

I doubt that. And where do you get off criticizing my people, my mentors, my school?

Tense and annoyed, I lean away from Matholook, who stretches his legs out and crosses them at the ankle. Without turning to look at me, he asks, "Have you ever heard of the *übermensch*?"

"No. Is that another warring faction like the Unsettled?"

"No. The *übermensch* is a term used by a philosopher named Friedrich Nietzsche. It means something like, 'the superior human...the one who transcends all the baser parts of human nature.'"

"Let me guess. You think Emergents are that and we're going to use our abilities to crush everyone and take over."

He pauses for a pretty long time before he finally says, "No. I don't think that."

Before I can object, he raises his hand to stop me. "*I* don't think that. But yes—a lot of people do."

"A lot of the Devoted?"

"And the Unsettled. And Epic and his Sanctum Civillains. And can you blame them? Can you blame any of us? Krug came to power based on the idea of the *übermensch*."

"That doesn't mean Emergents are going to follow his same, bloody loony of an example."

"Some people would say that's exactly what it means."

"Some people are idiots."

"Ha! I'll grant you that. But the idea of the *übermensch* should never be taken lightly. No matter how well-intentioned, the idea has been interpreted, reinterpreted, and misinterpreted over the years. Despots have latched onto it as the idea of the super man, the one who rules over everyone else."

"That *is* what it sounds like."

"It's not supposed to."

"Then what's it supposed to mean?"

"It's *supposed* to mean the one who transcends the worst parts of themselves in order to become what we're each capable of being. It doesn't mean the person with the most power rules the world. More like, the person with the most empathy, self-discipline, and introspection can rule themselves."

"To thine own self be true."

"Kind of like that. Only I think of it as more like, 'for your own self, be better so your best self can inspire the best in others.'"

"You know an awful lot for a kid from an isolated desert cult."

Matholook laughs. "You have your training. We have ours. You're in training to save the world. We're in training to understand how we got to where we are."

"So you can stop history from repeating?"

"No. So we can be prepared for it when it does."

"It's going to happen, isn't it?" I ask.

"The war?"

"Yeah."

Matholook is quiet for a long time before he finally nods. "It's closer than any of us thought. The way the Unsettled risked so much to get Gwernna from us, the way Epic caught you and what he was trying to get from you and Haida...sooner rather than later, things are going to get a lot worse."

"I've lived in my own country, and I've driven across yours," I sigh. "There's so little left worth fighting over."

"That's what makes it worth fighting over."

I wince and rub my backside. I don't have Arlo's rapid-fire healing power, and it still hurts from where Bendegatefran knocked me down.

I'm trying to be subtle about it, but Matholook notices and asks if I'm okay.

I give him a squint and a scowl before telling him I'm fine. "That was nothing," I half-joke, pointing to the empty courtyard with its lone juniper tree, its ring of orange stones, and its glistening surface of blood-soaked rocks and sand. "Our training is way more intense than that."

"So what's the problem?"

"That, out there...that was just...cold."

"You mean the way Efnisien fights?"

"What's with that guy, anyway?"

"We all have something tugging at us from inside. It's why you're here. You have questions. He has hate."

"Would he really have killed his brother if Marm Pintada hadn't stepped in?"

"Half-brother."

"Right. Would he have killed him?"

Matholook leans his head back and shrugs as if I've just asked him for the time of day. "He's killed members of the Devoted before," he says at last.

"He's killed other students in the Brawl?"

"In the Brawl. Over breakfast. Any time he's felt ignored, slighted, disrespected."

"So what happens to him? Does he get punished?"

Matholook seems genuinely confused for a second when he asks, "Punished? For what? For surviving?"

"For killing."

"What's the difference? Everything in the world kills to survive. It's historical. It's inevitable."

"What about squirrels? They don't kill anything."

"They eat acorns, berries, figs, and bugs. Those are all living, growing organisms."

"I have to admit, sometimes your logic is really infuriating."

"That doesn't make it any less logical."

"I suppose. Look, I know it's combat. But there are still rules you don't break, right? There are still lines you don't cross."

Matholook throws his head back and laughs. When he sees my frown, he puts his hand up and apologizes.

"Seriously," he asks, "what rules are there anymore? Look around us. Look at the world. You've seen it. You said it yourself. What lines can't be crossed that haven't been crossed already?"

"But that kind of underhanded coldness..."

"There's no place for emotion in history."

"Maybe if there were more emotion, history wouldn't keep repeating itself."

Matholook doesn't answer, and I'm feeling that pull again.

It's a desire to stay here, but not just because of Matholook. It's more like my brain is trying to convince itself that something it knows is bad for me really isn't.

My eyes spring wide open when I realize where I've felt it before.

In the Academy. There've been times when I've felt it happen to me and seen it happen to others. I've seen my friends make arguments in class they'd never make outside of it. I've seen them swear to things I know they don't really believe.

I always figured they were just doing what we're taught: questioning everything, including our own points of view.

But now the stuff that was happening in class is happening inside of me.

Is that the pull I've been feeling? Is it desire? Instinct? Is it even real? If I'm feeling a pull, doesn't that mean something, or someone, is out there doing the pulling?

How do I know if what I want is *really* what I want and not something I'm being tricked into wanting?

For all their isolated weirdness and tragic habit of kidnapping children, the Devoted are pretty nice people. They're into hospitality, history, and nostalgia. They're open to outsiders, and they're forgiving of those who've hurt them. They don't even have a lot of bad things to say about the Unsettled. Overall, they're intense, fun, caring, and kind.

Now that I've seen the extremes they go to, they may also be the most dangerous people I've ever met.

Whatever is pulling at me eases up and gives me some slack as Matholook invites me to walk around with him some more.

We heave ourselves to our feet, brush the dust and sand from our pants, and make our way out of the courtyard.

When I was here before, we were just kids. We walked side by side just like this, two twelve-year-olds in their own little bubble while the rest of the world burned.

This time, he slips his hand into mine. This time, I don't pull away.

You could be the rule I break. You might just be the line I'm willing to cross.

21

KISS

BEFORE LONG, we're standing on a cliff looking out over the valley and down into the town of Sanctum.

Like New Harleck, it's a small town with only a few roads visible from here. There are scattered people moving around, walking down laneways and in and out of the dozen or so weathered wooden buildings and some of the weirdly glossy contorted ones.

I know first-hand that there's more to the town than meets the eye.

The Emergents and I have our half-castle, half-college up in the mountains. The Unsettled have their monstrously large army roving around in the desert. The Devoted have their hodgepodge town of low and high-tech. And Epic and the Civillains have Sanctum, a little nothing of a ghost town on the surface but with an entire, complex of a science-city underground.

I get a chill as I flash back to being held captive there just a few months ago. I was only there for a few hours before my friends from the Academy rescued me and Haida. But it felt like a lot longer, and, if Epic had had his way, it definitely would have ended a lot worse.

"Hey," I ask Matholook. "What did you mean about Epic? You said he was trying to get something from me and Haida."

"It's no secret. Epic has been looking for the secret of you for a long time."

"I figured that much. He wants to know what makes us tick."

"I didn't mean the secret of Emergents. I mean I think he's looking for the secret of *you*, specifically."

"Bollocks," I scoff. If he wanted to know the secret of anyone, it should be of Kress and Render. With those bio-tech tattoos in her forearms, she can do things I can't even come close to. And she and Render have been doing it way better and for a lot longer.

Matholook shrugs. "I don't know Kress. But I know you. And I can see why..."

"What?"

Matholook clears his throat and blushes. "I can see why he'd want what you have."

"And what do I have, exactly?"

"I think maybe you have the ability to make connections."

"Like with Haida?"

"Yes. But also with other things. Things like the earth and the air. Maybe even things *beyond* the earth and the air."

Overhead, Haida gurgle-clacks to get my attention.

As I look up, scanning the skies to find her, her voice slips into my head.

~ *He's looking for you.*

Who is?

~ *Render.*

Oh, bugger and blast. Does he know I'm down here?

~ *No.*

Good. Let's keep it that way.

Haida's voice—louder this time, more insistent—nudges its way deeper into my head.

~ *You came here for answers. Now you have them.*

I do?

~ *Having something and knowing what to do with it are two different things.*

What do I do now?

~ *You need to learn the difference.*

And how am I supposed to do that, exactly?

~ *The same way you learn anything. You need to get back to school.*

"I need to get back to the Academy," I say out loud and with an abruptness I didn't even expect, myself.

Matholook doesn't seem too surprised by my weird non sequitur. In fact, he gives me a look of pure understanding and tells me he knows. I'm surprised by his lack of surprise because it feels like there's a whole palette of fear, doubt, worry, and regret slathered all over my face.

"I wish you didn't have to go," he confesses.

"I don't *have* to," I correct him. "I *want* to."

"You've barely been with us. You could always stay longer, you know."

"I know."

"Are you going to at least come back to the compound tonight? You could have dinner with us. You could say goodbye to Justin and Treva and all the others."

"I'm not big on goodbyes," I confess. "I'd rather just get going."

Matholook gazes out over the valley and the cluster of buildings below. From here, it's possible to see the spiky line of rocks surrounding the town of Sanctum. It's weird to think that there's literally an evil mastermind down there and the beginnings of a war brewing beneath its surface.

"I'll pass along your gratitude," Matholook says without looking at me.

"Thanks."

"The next time we see each other—," I begin.

"We could be enemies."

"It depends. If the Devoted, the Unsettled, and the Civillains can find a way to get along..."

"Easy for you to say," Matholook snorts. "You're not down here fighting over resources and supplies."

"We're not going to spend our last few minutes together arguing, are we?"

"I'd rather not."

"When the war comes," I begin, working hard to talk past the tightness in my chest and throat, "I hope we can find a way to be on the same side."

"I hope so, too. Unfortunately, hope isn't a strategy, and it definitely doesn't win wars."

"I guess that's true. But without hope, wars would never end."

Matholook and I chit-chat for a few more minutes as the sun continues its slow downward crawl behind the mountains in the west.

When I finally manage to pull myself away, I feel that pull again. It's worse this time, though. Not because it's tugging me to do something I might not have otherwise done. It's worse because this time it feels like the pull is making me leave a part of myself behind.

Matholook gives his lips a little lick and clears his throat. I can tell he wants to kiss me.

(I can also tell he knows leaning in like that toward someone with my training, instincts, and Emergent connection to a predatory raven could end up with what's left of him being buried in three different graves.)

I've got no problem diving into combat.

Diving into a kiss like this—one that means giving up a part of myself—is a new experience for me. But, like battle, I set the fear aside and leap.

It's only the second time I've ever kissed a boy, but it's the first time I felt connected while I did it.

"I'll see you on the other side of the battlefield," I say when we pull away at last.

I can feel his eyes on me as I turn to clamber up the steep, rocky grade. I'm happy when I break through the foliage at the top. It means I can look back and see him without having to worry about him seeing me cry.

22

CONNECTED

I KNOW the hike back up the mountain will take a long time, so I steel myself for the trip.

I could take the mine shafts for a good chunk of the way, but I want to be outside right now.

With no real sense of direction other than "Up," I scamper and climb the hills and slopes toward what I hope will be the Valta and then the Academy.

I know it'll take hours, but I'm not in a hurry. It's nice to leave the heat behind and feel the air get colder and fresher as I trudge along uphill.

The truth is, I enjoyed my brief time in New Harleck. But after spending the whole day with the Devoted, I'm eager to get home.

Funny. I've been thinking about the Academy as my *school* for a good chunk of the last year. This is one of the first times I've thought about it as *home*.

I just have to hope they didn't change the locks.

As I pick and scamper my way up, I tap into Haida, who shares her vision of the mountain with me. She lets me access the navigational centers of her brain, which I follow as easily as a leaf being carried along in the current of a gently-flowing river.

I stop a few times along the way. Sometimes there's a cliff or an outcropping I just can't resist. I stand with the toes of my boots over the edge and suck in gulps of fresh air. (I learned from Kress that Walt Whitman called moments like this, "the exquisite realization of health.") After a lot of deep, even breaths, I look out over the forests, deserts, and valleys far below and feel a wave of guilt wash over me.

Why do I get to breathe fresh air up here and feel exquisitely healthy when so many people down there are living in what's left of a toxic wasteland? Was Matholook right? Am I on the wrong side of things? When the time comes, will I be on the wrong side of the war?

It's too much for my brain to handle at the moment, so I step back from the edge and continue on my way. It's slow going at this point. After feeling perfectly fine for the first part of the ascent, the blood in my legs and the air in my lungs has now gone stinging and acidic.

I really hope Kress will give me some flying lessons.

After a couple more hours, I arrive at the old military guard-station at the bottom of the overgrown road leading up to the Valta.

This is where Kress and her Conspiracy crossed over. This is where the course of their lives diverged from the path they were placed on to the path they were meant to follow. It's where they went from being driven away from home to learning how to take the wheel and find a new home of their own.

Shaking off the thirst and fatigue, I make my way up to the Valta. Unlike last time, I don't pause to reminisce. Besides, they're Kress's memories, not mine.

At the far edge of town, I reach the warped and rusted metal guardrail forming the barrier between the town and the hidden footpath leading the rest of the way up to the Academy.

I'm just thinking how lucky I am to be taught by Kress and her Conspiracy when a noise from behind startles me, and a dark figure steps out from the deep shadows cast by the light of the rising, blood-red moon.

The figure steps forward, his emerald-green eyes nearly bright enough to light the gloomy air around us.

"Matholook? How...?"

"Well, to be honest, I kind of cheated."

"Cheated?"

"I drove part of the way up in one of our Rovers. When I couldn't go any farther, I ran."

That explains the red cheeks, the thumping chest, the matted hair, and the sweat-soaked clothes.

Matholook holds up a wait-a-second finger while he pauses to gather his breath. "There's no way I was letting you trek all the way down the mountain to find me without returning the favor. After all, being connected with someone works a lot better if they're together."

I tell him how sweet that is. "Sweet and very *very* stupid." I point up the steep, winding, ice-coated footpath leading up to the front door of the Academy. "That isn't day camp up there. The people on the other side of that door are Emergents. They're powerful people. Good people. But still very powerful."

"Maybe this'll be the first time someone with power manages to be good."

"I've heard your History class. I remember what you told me about the *übermensch*. I know you don't believe that's possible."

"I didn't think you and me meeting again was possible. But here we are."

"Trust me. You don't want to have anything to do with me or

the Academy or any of the Emergents. We're the reason why Epic is two seconds away from waging a full-on war."

"And I'm willing to risk it. You saw how I live. I'd like to see how you live. As for all the teachers and the students being Emergents, I can live with that."

"Or you can die from it."

"If you can spend a day inside our lion's den, I can spend a day inside yours, right? Look, we're all just doing what we can to survive. How many billions of people have died in the Atomic Wars, the drone attacks, the Eastern Order assaults, the climate crisis, and in all the fallout? And we're still here. That's got to mean something, right? Besides, what's the worst that could happen?"

"I'll remember to include those last words when I deliver the eulogy at your funeral."

"If you're the one delivering my eulogy, I'll know one thing at least."

"Yeah? What's that?"

"I lived a good life."

I try so hard not to smile and even harder not to blush, but I fail miserably at both.

"Okay," I tell him. "If you're sure. If you think you have any idea of what you're getting into..."

"I'm sure. I wouldn't be here if I weren't."

I point to the steep path in front of us. It's coated in rough, chunky slabs of ice and a slippery dusting of snow. There's a flat, monstrous wall of rock on one side of the path and a bottomless abyss on the other.

Even though the Academy is still concealed by the Veiled Refractor, I know that "home" is just a few hundred yards away.

I'm glad I'm walking ahead of Matholook. I'm embarrassed by my big, stupid smile I can't seem to get rid of.

I don't know what will happen after this. And, right now, I

don't care. My teachers can yell at me. My fellow students can ply me with questions.

For now, at this particular second, at this particular time, and in this particular place—as I navigate the long footpath from the lifelessness of the Valta to the robust energy of the Academy— I've got Matholook right behind me, and I feel connected.

PART 2

BACK TO SCHOOL

23

RAKED

IT FEELS like it's been months. But the reality is, I was gone for a less than twenty-four hours.

The biometric ID scanners posted above the front doors of the Academy scan me and signal the security system to deactivate.

The big double doors swing open. I really want to *stroll* into the Academy. I want to stride in hand-in-hand with Matholook, regale everyone with tales of running into him and the giant, rescuing Gwernna, and attending a Devoted memorial service for the dead. I want to find Kress, pull her aside, and tell her about my *traversion*. I want to brag about my victory in the Brawl and announce my triumphant return to the Academy, where I'm fully prepared to jump right back into the swing of things like I'd never left.

But my feet won't move.

Matholook asks me what's wrong. I lie and tell him, "Nothing."

There's no way I'm going to admit to him that I'm frozen in fear.

Why is coming home so much scarier than leaving?

At last, with Matholook following just behind me, I suck in a breath, and then I take the world's most hesitant step across the Academy's threshold.

The doors shut behind us, locking out the cold, the whipping wind, and any chance of escape or hope of turning back.

Above us, the mezzanine level is quiet. Feeble wisps of moonlight trickle down into the towering, open space from the slanted skylights in the roof. The synth-steel, chrome, glass, and light pine making up the stairs, banisters, and interior doors and floors glisten in the quiet darkness with a fresh, clean sparkle.

The white-tiled lobby is empty and polished, as always, to a high shine.

Although it definitely continues to shine, it doesn't stay empty for long.

My enhanced senses don't register the feel, sound, or smell of people approaching until it's too late.

(I guess Haida Gwaii's abandoned me. I don't blame her. I wouldn't want to be me right now, either.)

Matholook isn't greeted with the same hospitality the Devoted showed me. In fact, he winds up hovering a full foot off the floor when Terk, in a single motion, snatches him up, locks his pronged, Modified clamp onto the front of his jacket, and slams him against the wall.

Startled, I shriek and try to grab onto Terk.

Shouldering me aside—and nearly knocking me down in the process—Kress and Brohn flank Terk and start grilling Matholook about who he is and what the frack he thinks he's doing here.

Before I can react, I've got Rain latched onto my left arm and Kella locked onto my right.

Dressed in their black combat gear—like they were expecting battle in our front lobby this late at night—the two teachers haul me clean off my feet. They drag me back like I'm nothing more than a sack of feathery down, and I'm amazed, as ever, by how bloody strong they are.

Everyone parts like the Red Sea for Wisp who strides across the lobby, her thick-soled military boots banging out in angry echoes, with Granden thundering along just behind her.

Matholook is now face to face with seven of the Academy's battle-tested teachers. Only War and Mayla are missing. I'm guessing they're probably assigned to keep an eye on the rest of the students upstairs in the Dorm. Ever since Micah managed to infiltrate the Academy on Epic's orders, our teachers have been hyper focused on keeping us safe and protecting the holy hell out of us.

I have to give Matholook credit. Pinned up against the wall, his feet dangling, he's the exact right amount of innocent, poised, and scared.

Terk is a really nice man and a great teacher. With his junk-yard mess of a Modified arm, shoulder, neck, and ribcage—all clear as day under his stretched-to-the-breaking-point tank top —he's also kind of a horror-show to look at.

Anyone else would be quivering in their urine-soaked pants by now. But Matholook takes the grilling in stride and promises he's not a spy and that all he wanted to do was spend a little more time with me.

On the one hand, that's very sweet of him to credit me for his loony impulsivity. On the other hand, does he really need to throw me under the bus in the process?

Kress whips me a nasty look over her shoulder, but all I can do is shrug. It's not my fault the guy's dumb enough to sneak away from the safety of his own home and into an enemy camp on some fool's errand to meet up with someone he barely knows...

Oh...wait. Bloody hell. I did that, too.

Wisp surges forward, slamming to a stop next to Terk.

She tells him to let Matholook go, but Terk doesn't seem to hear her.

Instead, he leans in close and growls something into Matholook's ear. I only catch part of it, but it definitely involves something about tearing Matholook's arms off and shoving them up...

I can't make out the rest. But the spirit of the warning is pretty clear. Not a lot of gray area there.

He shoves Matholook back once more, and the sound of Matholook's head hitting the wall makes me queasy. (I can't imagine how it must feel to *him*.)

"Matholook, right?" Wisp asks, as Matholook's feet hit the floor, and his knees do a wobbly, buckling little dance.

He blinks hard, nods, and tries to peer past Wisp to meet my eyes, but we've got Terk looming between us. I want to dash over to stick up for him, but Rain and Kella still have me locked in an unbreakable vice-grip, and I can't budge.

Kella, I understand. Ripped and toned, she's the definition of pure, physical strength. Rain, on the other hand...well, I don't know where the frack *her* strength comes from. She's at least half-a-head shorter than me, but she's about one pound of pressure away from snapping every bone in my wrist.

"You're that boy we met in New Harleck," Brohn says to Matholook. "One of the Cult of the Devoted. You helped us. But your people were planning something a lot less friendly." It's not a question.

Matholook tries two times to say, "Yes," but the tiny word seems to catch in his throat, and he has to sputter-cough twice more to get it out.

Without taking her eyes from Matholook, Wisp tells Rain and Kella to turn me over to Kress. "Get Branwynne upstairs, Kress. I'll take care of our guest."

She says, "take care" in a weird way, and I can't tell if she means she'll show him all the politeness and hospitality of a welcome visitor, or else she'll let Terk shred him bit by bit like a hunk of pulled pork and toss what's left of him into the deep abyss outside the front doors of the Academy.

Rain and Kella shove me toward Kress who grabs me by my jacket collar and marches me up the stairs and down the hall to the office she and Brohn share on the Academy's second floor.

It all happens so fast that don't even have a chance to have a last look back at Matholook or call out to him that everything is going to be okay.

Too bad. I was just starting to like him, too.

With Terk-like strength, Kress slings me into the mag-chair in front of her desk. I bounce down with a "whoomph," happy at least that the chair's mag-stabilizers are working. Otherwise, the chair and I would be halfway through the far wall right about now.

When she finally starts to dig into me, Kress stays in her own high-backed mag-chair behind her desk and talks quietly. That's when I know she's serious. I'd be okay if she paced and yelled. Hell, I'd prefer it. This quiet, controlled, even-toned lecture...this is *way* worse.

Kress tells me if I ever pull a stunt like that again, I'll be gone for good. I don't think she's talking about expulsion. I'm pretty sure she means she'll kill me. It's not a theory I'm eager to test out.

I spin my head around hard enough to give myself whiplash when Brohn storms into the room. He stops just behind my chair and stands over my shoulder, and I say a silent "Thanks" that he hasn't punched me in the back of the head.

Yet.

Too afraid to turn around, I glance up at him out of the corner of my eye. He's got an active volcano going on behind his own eyes, and I force myself to sit up straight and keep my shaking to a minimum.

"What were you thinking?" he thunders.

For all his fury and strength, Kress manages to cut him off with a simple look. She goes about counting off on her fingers a ten-item list of how stupid I am. And then, just for good measure, she adds a few more items to her long list of reprimands. "You put us at risk. You gave away our location. You may have inadvertently given an enemy a tactical advantage."

"On top of that," Brohn adds with a growl that sends the hairs on the back of my neck standing up at stiff attention, "you made us worry." He clamps his hand onto my shoulder. *Hard.* "And I do *not* worry."

"What you need to understand," Kress says, her eyes on mine, her voice barely above a whisper, "is just how much you don't understand."

I must look positively muddled because Kress sighs and says she'll explain. "The Devoted are not what they appear to be."

I start to object, but she cuts me off with a raised hand. "We've had other encounters with them over the past five years. Encounters you don't know about."

Other encounters?

I know Kress and her Conspiracy have gone on missions to places outside the Academy. I guess I just never figured New Harleck was one of them.

What could they possibly have been doing there? What could they possibly have discovered?

"The details aren't important," Kress continues. "There's more to the Devoted than meets the eye. That's really all you need to know. They're dangerous, and they have more power in their innocent-looking little compound than you can imagine."

"They're just trying to prepare so they can survive Epic's war," I manage, embarrassed at how squeaky my voice sounds in my own ears and, honestly, a little annoyed that Matholook is somewhere in the Academy at this very moment getting interrogated. "He's not a spy," I insist. "And he's definitely not a soldier."

I expect Kress to snap at me or cut me off, but she doesn't. Instead, she gives Brohn a nod, and he leans over me, his fingers curled around the back of my chair. "They're not preparing to survive Epic's war, Branwynne," he says into my ear. "They're preparing to *win* it."

Great. I've got Kress—my hero and mentor—in front of me and her bulletproof boyfriend snarling at me from behind. And both of them seem to have more information than I knew about and are clearly mad as a bag of ferrets at my cock-up.

So, Branwynne. This is how it ends. After seventeen years of surviving the bloody apocalypse, you're going to get killed by two of your teachers right here in their very own office.

Thankfully, a knock at the door distracts Kress and Brohn from the horrible hellfire I'm sure they're about to rain down on me.

Without waiting for a response, Chace sticks her head into the office. She pushes her round, oversized glasses up onto the bridge of her nose and apologizes for the interruption.

She's pretty small for a *deus ex machina*, but she'll have to do. She's delayed my execution, and I breathe a sigh of relief as Kress and Brohn turn their attention to her and away from me.

"I heard we might have a visitor," Chace says through an eager grin, her slender fingers curled around the edge of the doorframe.

Kress's voice is somehow soft *and* steely when she snaps, "Not now!" at Chace.

Chace's happy little face goes rose-red, and she disappears as quickly as she came.

(If this were a cartoon, I swear she would have left a puff of smoke in her wake.)

Swinging his glowering attention back to me, Brohn plants

his hand over my shoulder one more time before easing off and stepping around me to half-sit on the edge of Kress's desk.

"Let's hear it," he growls.

"Let's hear what?" I squeak.

"Why? Why did you leave the Academy?"

"And I swear...," Kress begins, loading up what I'm sure is going to be an epic eyeroll, "if you tell us it was because of that boy..."

"It wasn't. Not really. Not exactly."

"Then why?"

"I—I felt...wrong."

"And you thought a little jaunt down the mountain with about a million chances to get killed along the way would make you feel right?"

"Honestly, I didn't really think about it."

"No shit."

Kress's voice goes soft, like when she's giving me my Apprenticeship lessons, and I know she doesn't want to discourage me when I'm struggling. "We're trying to do something important here, Branwynne. This isn't one of those myths you've heard about." She takes a second to pivot toward the window that looks out over the steep drop-off below. "The world is on the brink right now. For real. It's about to be as bad as it's ever been. The Atomic Wars are over. Krug is over. We're still doing our best to get the word out about the truth behind the Eastern Order. But we're doing it in a power vacuum, which Epic is dead set on filling. We're not guessing here. The Unsettled, the Devoted, and the Sanctum Civillains are about to collide. Epic is nearly ready to make sure they do. And when he makes his move, there's going to be an explosion."

"A big one," Brohn adds.

"These are precarious times," Kress continues. "We don't get a second chance to put things right. And we can't sit this out. The stakes are just too high."

"We *are* the stakes, after all," Brohn adds.

Kress nods her agreement. "You, especially, Branwynne. And in this war—the one we know is not much more than days, maybe *hours* away—we either succeed, or we die."

With Kress's permission, I take my turn, telling her and Brohn about everything that's happened to me outside of the Academy over the past twenty-four hours. When I'm done, Kress and Brohn start reminding me again—just in case I've forgotten already—about how dumb I am and how much danger I may have brought into our school. It takes about ten minutes. (If feels like two weeks.)

I don't even know where to let my eyes land as the two of them finally finish laying into me.

After they're done, I'm pretty sure I know how it must feel to be pig guts in a sausage press.

Once they're finished squashing and bashing me around and I've got a nose and a throat full of tears I refuse to let fall, they tell me to get upstairs to the Dorm.

I've been on some dangerous adventures in my young life. I usually think of myself as a pretty bad-ass, deadly assassin. So how come right now I feel like a puppy that just got spanked for peeing on the carpet?

With my chin tucked into my chest, I plod upstairs to the Lounge where the school's five Cohorts—all twenty-nine students—are wide awake and waiting for me.

There are six students per Cohort, and every one of them has apparently decided that my life is suddenly way more important than anything else in the world.

Brace yourself, Branwynne. Kress and Brohn may have been salty-bitter with you back in their office, but these kids are going to be curious. Which means they're going to ask a lot of questions, Which means you're going to have to talk to them. Which is going to be way worse than getting raked over the coals by Kress and Brohn.

Entering the Lounge, I do my best to prepare myself for the million questions I know I'm about to receive, all the while hoping to find an answer to the two burning questions of my own:

What missions have Kress and Brohn been on? And what the frack do they know about Matholook and the Cult of the Devoted that I don't?

24

CHRONICLE

As EXPECTED, I climb the stairs, enter the Lounge, and am instantly bombarded with wave after crashing wave of questions.

Libra nearly dislocates my shoulder dragging me into the big room with its sleek collection of couches, loveseats, armchairs, ottomans, billiards and ping-pong tables, dart boards, and pinball machines.

As if Libra's assault isn't enough, Ignacio slings me around and practically launches me into one of the room's plush orange couches while the rest of the Emergents press together in a huddle in front, behind, and all over me.

One thing's for sure: We're a motley assortment.

Kress and her Conspiracy rescued Libra, Sara, Mattea, Arlo, and Ignacio from a Processor in Valencia, Spain.

Roxane was a stowaway from Bordeaux, France.

Chace and Trax are from a group of kids who Kress and her friends met in these very mountains after escaping their own Processor in the Emiquon National Wildlife Refuge in Illinois.

We picked up Lucid and Reverie from St. Paul's Cathedral in

London where they were being held by a group of En-Gene-eers in the same facility I escaped from.

There are the twelve kids Matholook turned over to me and my Asylum.

And there are the seven kids Kress rescued earlier this year from a military base somewhere west of here.

I know there are just twenty-nine kids in front of me, but right now, it feels like the entire barmy world.

Some people like having the world focused on them. For me, being the center of attention is like being the center of a target in a sniper range.

I'd much rather be the one doing the shooting than the thing getting shot at.

Unfortunately, with this gang of Nosy Parkers, no such luck.

Sitting down on the mocha leather footstool in front of me, her hands draped over my knees, Libra launches a salvo of rapid-fire questions fast enough to make my head spin:

"Wherewereyou?Whydyouleave?Whathappenedoutthere?"

When she's done and way before I have time to answer, Mattea, her chocolate-brown eyes sparkling, hops up onto the back of the couch, takes a turn:

"IsWispmad?WhatdidKressandBrohnsay?Areyougoingtoget-expelled?"

Not to be outdone, Arlo—his face with its eerie patchwork of scars and shadows—nudges Mattea to the side and leans over my shoulder from behind the couch. Dark and slow, his voice might as well be coming from the bowels of a grave. "Was it really for a boy?"

"It was for...a connection," I correct him with a playful swat.

Libra turns and winks at the cluster of students. "It was for a boy."

After everyone has a nice, hearty laugh at my expense, I hold my hands up and promise to explain.

Chace inches over and sits down on the floor with her back to the big armchair across from me.

Pushing her glasses up onto her nose and with her holo-pad out, she taps the stylus on the glass panel and starts scrawling notes in the air an inch above the receiving pad as I rehash the glorious tales of my amazing adventures.

I start by answering their first salvo of questions.

"I went back down to New Harleck," I begin.

Libra sticks her tongue out at Ignacio. "See! I told you!"

"But no, I didn't leave specifically to see a boy."

"See?" Ignacio snarks back at Libra. "*I* told *you!*"

"The fact that I ran into Matholook was a..."

"Coincidence?" Mattea asks.

"I'm starting to think maybe there's no such thing," I answer. "As for the rest of what happened down there, it's a long story. A lot happened in a short time." I turn to Mattea and confirm that, yes, Kress is mad. "*Really* mad," I add for emphasis. "Kress and Brohn gutted me pretty good. As for whether or not I'm going to get expelled..."

"They won't kick her out," an almond-eyed boy named Dolon from the Committee of Vultures assures everyone in the Lounge. He's barely thirteen, but he's already got a deep voice and the beginnings of a pretty solid moustache. "Branwynne was the first Emergent at the Academy."

"And Kress's favorite," a younger boy named Gleeson snickers, his wild, curly hair framing his angular face like a lion's mane.

"I'm definitely not her favorite at the moment," I assure him. "In fact, I'm lucky we're not having this conversation in the Infirmary with me hooked up to life-support system and breathing through a tube."

"Tell us more," Reverie pleads, sliding her fingers through

her long black hair as she steps in front of her zombie eyed twin brother. "We want to hear *everything*!"

So I tell them about leaving the Academy in the middle of the night. I tell them about Matholook and the giant. They shake their heads in admiration (or is it disbelief?) when I tell them about rescuing Gwernna. I leave out the part about my *traversion*. It's only the third time in my life I've actually managed it and the first time I did it without Kress standing next to me. Either way, it's never been an especially pleasant experience, and this is a developing ability I'd rather keep between me and Kress for the moment.

I go on to recount my experiences with the Devoted: the classes, the Brawl...everything.

I tell my fellow Emergents about how much worse the air and water are down there than they are up here. A lot of them kind of know, but it's mostly theory. They've lived most of their lives in Processors, after all. But the twelve Emergents who came here from New Harleck, they know firsthand what life is like down there. I don't know what their actual experiences were— they're all oddly tight-lipped about it—but they must have some idea, right?

My reminder about the conditions in the world outside of the Academy is met with an overlapping, muttering chorus of contradictory groans, sympathetic sighs, hopeful decrees, and pessimistic proclamations:

"It's their own fault..."

"We should help..."

"It's too late..."

"Got what they deserve..."

"We have a responsibility..."

"It's our world, too..."

Chace takes it all in—my stories and the reactions of our fellow students—scrawling along on her holo-pad. I don't know if her abilities as an Emergent make her a weirdly good listener, a talented artist, or an obsessed historian. But I see why everyone refers to her as the Chronicler.

So I go through it all again, just like I did with Kress and Brohn.

(Recounting my adventures is a lot easier without two teachers hovering over me and scowling at me from across a desk.)

Along the way, my fellow students continue to bombard me with questions.

Ampah, the ebony-skinned boy with the flashing eyes and deep dimples, raises his hand like we're in class. Smiling to myself, I call on him. He says I seem really brave and asks if I was ever afraid while I was gone.

"Except for a few minutes here or there on the mountain," I tell him with total sincerity, "*frack* yeah. Pretty much all the time!"

That gets a round of appreciative laughter, and a spate of elbow nudges passes around the crowd.

Anderton, pale as a ghost and freckled as a robin's egg, thrusts his hand into the air next. He wants to know how I got out of the Academy in the first place. "And how'd you bypass the motion sensors and heat detectors?"

Everyone leans in for this part, but I have to disappoint them. "I can't say," I apologize with a combination smile, wink, and a shake of my head. "A magician never reveals her secrets."

With her bottom lip protruding in a pout, a very tall girl named Jia Li from the Committee of Vultures slumps her entire spine into a question mark and mumbles, "Not fair."

"Sorry," I explain with a shrug. "I'm lucky I escaped from Kress's office with my life. If she finds out I told the rest of you how to get around the school's security...well, I'm not quite *that* brave!"

The questions keep flying, along with round after round of appreciative "Oohs" and "Aahs."

I'm not a great storyteller by any stretch. I ramble. I exaggerate. I stutter, stammer, and leave stuff out and have to go back again and explain.

It doesn't matter. After about twenty minutes of stories, all my audience seems to care about—all they want to ask about now—is Matholook.

And then it occurs to me...

Most of us in the room have dealt with fear, confinement, and even outright captivity. Most of the kids in front of me have been experimented on to the point of torture. Some of us have seen combat, fought for our own lives or helped to save the lives of others.

But the one thing I keep forgetting is the thing we all have in common: All of us have been disconnected from the world at one time or another. I lived in isolation in the Tower of London with only my parents and the Tower's ravens as company. Except for Roxane, I think almost everyone else in the Academy has been a prisoner, in some cases for most of their lives. Our chances for interactions, connections, affection, and attraction have been severely limited. Which is to say that we've all been severely deprived of one of the basic foundations of what it means to be human. Or Emergent, for that matter.

So I sigh and agree to tell my fellow deprived students a bit more about Matholook.

"Do you think Wisp is going to let him stay?" Mattea asks.

"I doubt it."

But I sure hope so.

As the night dwindles, so do the Academy's Cohorts. In a slow, one-by-one trickle, the Exaltation files out of the Lounge and plods back to their Dorm. Then, the Descent follow suit, shaking their heads and muttering about all of my crazy adventures and how they can't wait to get out of the Academy and have crazy adventures of their own. After them, the Committee stands up, stretches, enjoys a group yawn, and shuffles out. And then the kids from the Battery follow right after, leaving me alone with my Asylum.

We talk a bit more. Mattea tells me about how the school went into lockdown when Wisp and the other teachers realized I was gone. "But it wasn't like you might think," she elaborates. "There weren't any blaring sirens. People weren't screaming and scrambling around."

"Well, *some* people kind of were," Libra clarifies.

"Right," Mattea giggles with a tilt of her head toward the multiple doorways around the Lounge where the other Cohorts just filed out on their way to their Dorms. "Some of the younger students *were* kind of freaking out."

"Especially Nalessia and Davenex," Libra laughs.

I don't know Nalessia very well other than the fact that she's a girl from the Exaltation of Larks and that she has really long black hair, which she refuses, whether she's in class or in combat training, to braid or even put into a ponytail. Davenex I know a little better. He's from the Exaltation, too. Most Emergents display at least some hints of a future ability at or around the time they turn sixteen or seventeen. For some of us, we develop our abilities quite a bit earlier. (I was about eight the first time I heard Haida Gwaii's voice in my head and twelve the first time I walked through a wall.) In some cases, Emergents don't develop any abilities at all. Instead, techno-geneticists working in secret labs all around the world identify them by certain genetic markers. Then, if the kid demonstrates Emergent abilities, they get recruited. If they don't demonstrate Emergent abilities, they get killed.

I'm not sure why we can't just be left alone.

Davenex is my age, but he doesn't have any special abilities, so he's made it a habit for the past few weeks of asking me about mine. Unfortunately, we don't have any classes together, so his opportunity to interrogate me has been limited to a few minutes in the Tavern and to the occasional breaks when we find ourselves walking up or down the stairs of the Academy at the same time.

"I'm glad at least somebody around here was worried enough to go arse over elbow for me," I grumble through a pretend pout.

"Don't listen to them," Arlo advises. He slides down from the arm of the couch and squeezes in next to me. "You're our friend. We were worried. Honestly, we were all in a *bit* of a panic."

"But not Wisp," Mattea says, her voice soft with reverential awe. "She was cool as frost on a polar bear's butt."

Everyone nods and hums their absolute agreement at this.

"And what about Trax?" Libra asks.

"What about him?"

"Well, with Matholook here, there's the whole chance of a love triangle happening." Libra claps her hands together. "It can be like a soap opera."

"You've never seen a soap opera *or* a love triangle, so how would you know?"

"A cute girl and two cute guys? It's not exactly rocket science now, is it?"

No. Rocket science would be a whole heckuva lot easier.

Surprisingly, now that the crowd has thinned out, it's Sara who's the most interested in my experiences with the Devoted. She and I don't always get along, so at first, I'm flattered by her curiosity. Then, I realize she's asking an awful lot of questions about Matholook. And not just the ones everyone else has been on about.

Focusing for the moment on Sara, I tell her about my fears and anxieties. I tell her how sad it was to be back in the world of death and suffering and about how much I missed the Academy. Finally, I launch into a massive, rambling rant about the weirdness and the unexplainable intensity of my feelings for Matholook.

She asks if I'm attracted to him. I laugh and tell her, "No," and I hope to hell she doesn't see my burning cheeks screaming, "Yes!"

When I get to the part about the "pull"—the undefinable tugging that got me out of the Academy in the first place—she's the only one of my Asylum who doesn't seem surprised.

But her eyes light up every single time I say Matholook's name.

Wait. What is this tight, fiery fist in my chest?

From somewhere outside of the Academy—I think she's in her roost on the roof with Render—Haida's voice, soft and sad, slips into my mind:

~ Jealousy.

Wait. Is she jealous about my connection with Matholook? Or am I jealous about her weird, inappropriate interest in him?

~ I just experience your mind. I can't read it.

You know, for a wise, shared consciousness, sometimes you're not very helpful.

The fading ring of Haida's gurgly laughter in my head is the last thing I hear before she slips back out of my mind.

Libra slaps a hand to my knee and rises up off the couch with a groan and with her other hand pressed to her lower back. "Well, this has been fun! But we've got a test in Coordination and Reflex skills in the morning. We'd better get to bed."

Everyone agrees and heads into our Dorm. Except for me.

My cheeks are flushed hot, and I'm feeling oddly embarrassed. I hate being so open. I just spilled my guts to Sara in front of the rest of our Asylum about a boy I hardly know after an adventure I'm lucky to have survived and shouldn't have been on anyway. So why did I just let my guard down like that?

I mean it as a rhetorical question, but from inside my head, Haida answers me anyway:

~ *You have to disconnect from yourself before you can connect with someone else.*

I don't know what you mean.

~ *Sara does.*

25

DECISION

Lying in bed and with the rest of my Asylum deeply asleep in their own beds, all I can think about is Matholook.

And not for the reason Libra keeps winding me up about. Kress took me from London because my parents asked her to. She brought me to the Academy because she needed to.

But Matholook...he followed me because he *wanted* to.

And now, the boy who just laid his life on the line to follow me up here is downstairs with my teachers, who are deciding—as I'm lying here helpless and useless—what to do with him.

We're Emergents. This Academy was literally built for us. It was designed to be a home, a school, and, most important, a haven where we could do our best to make sense of who and what we are and figure out our place in the world.

Most important, it was designed to be a safe space where we wouldn't have to worry about Typics trying to get their hands on us, experiment on us, figure us out, and eventually (and there's *always* an eventually) weaponize us.

Matholook is a Typic.

That makes him dangerous. He's a Devoted. That makes him dodgy. He trailed me here. That makes him foolish.

Or does it make him romantic?

It doesn't seem right that a little thing like a microscopic blip in our genetic code or the ways our brains and bodies behave due to some techno-evolutionary hiccup should be a reason for so much bloody resistance, distance, and turmoil.

It's not fair to be forced away from someone I feel connected to.

It's not like I haven't been around Typics. I've known others. Granden. War. Mayla. My parents. They're all good people, educated, open-minded, and unafraid.

But they're turning out to be in the minority. It was Typics who started the wars.

And, from what I understand, they did it to get control over us. We were just the latest in a long line of tools rich and powerful people tried to use to stay rich and powerful. I can handle most anything. Being a student. A fighter. An Emergent. Even a target. What I hate is being a pawn.

I'm just drifting off to sleep when the door to our room slides open. On light feet and without making a sound (I don't think she even displaces the air in front of her when she moves), Kress glides over to stand next to my bed.

"We want to see you in Wisp's office first thing in the morning."

"Before classes?" I ask in a tremulous whisper. "Before Morning Address?"

"First thing," she repeats.

And then she glides out the door and is gone as quickly and as quietly as she came.

IN THE MORNING, I'm the first one up. It's easy when you're the only one who didn't fall asleep.

The blue morning holo-lights flash like they do every morning to signal the start to another day. In about five seconds, I'm in and out of the sonic shower, dressed, and bounding downstairs to Wisp's office.

I step inside where I'm told to sit down in front of an angry-faced semi-circle of Wisp, Granden, Kress, and Brohn.

As if yesterday wasn't bad enough...

Wisp pushes up the sleeves of her oversized, multi-pocketed military jacket. Anyone else her size would get lost in a jacket that big. But Wisp somehow manages to exude a Bendegatefran-sized aura despite her small frame. "Branwynne, normally we'd make this decision entirely on our own. But you're invested in this, so we want you in on it."

Granden, dressed in his khakis and his own olive-green military jacket with all the pockets, drums his fingers on the table. "You've given us a bit of a dilemma here."

"Dilemma?" I stammer.

"You see," Wisp says, "we can send your friend back to New Harleck. Or else we can keep him here with us."

"For how long?"

"Well, forever."

"Really? Why?"

"Because the one thing we can't afford to do is have him here where he can gather intel and then ship him back to the Devoted where he can—and almost certainly will—use that intel against us. There's no middle ground. That's the dilemma."

"This is a high risk, low reward situation we have here," Granden explains. "On the one hand, Matholook can tell us more about the Cult's plans, goals, and strategies."

"And maybe even about the plans, goals, and strategies of Epic and the Unsettled and the upcoming war," Wisp adds. "On the other hand, he could be here for the same reason: to gather intel on *us*."

"He wouldn't do that."

"How do you know?"

"I don't know," I shrug. "I just feel it."

Kress pauses for an uncomfortably long time before jumping in to respond. "Feelings are one thing, Branwynne. I've been training you to trust your instincts."

"Then how come—?"

Kress cuts me off with a raised hand. "You're in training. You've come a long way. But you still have a long way to go."

I reach back to rub my neck where a trickle of sweat is threatening to turn into a river of rapids. "So...what's going to happen to him?"

Please don't tell me you're going to kill him.

"We're going to let him stay."

I start to say, "Thanks," but Wisp cuts me off.

"We're going to let him stay. But not for any of the reasons you probably think."

"He's not a guest," Brohn explains. "He's an asset."

"An asset? So...you're going to *use* him?"

"That's exactly what we're going to do," Wisp says. "His people will be looking for him. We're not worried about that. The Academy is tucked away and too well hidden."

"Then what—?"

"We're worried about what we don't know about him," Kress explains, sounding oddly apologetic.

"And," Brohn drawls, "we don't know what he'll do if...no, *when* it comes time for him to make a decision, when he'll have to choose between you and the Devoted."

"They don't call themselves 'the *Cult* of the Devoted' for nothing," Wisp explains, nodding her agreement.

Curious now, I clear my throat. "You said you've had other encounters with them over the past five years?"

Brohn nods. "We have."

"The missions we've been training you for..." Kress explains, "we've already been on a lot of them. That's why we know what to expect and what exactly to train you for."

"It's an unusual situation," Granden says, his voice even and measured with military control. "And these are unusual times. Things could go very well from here. We could continue to gather and train Emergents, and those trained Emergents could bring stability and order to a world on the brink."

"Or," Wisp adds, her small hands planted firmly on her desk, "we could get drawn into the war before we're...before *you're* ready and lose everything we've fought for and believed in."

My eyes do a little hummingbird flit from Wisp and Granden to Kress and Brohn. "And you think one seventeen-year-old can make all the difference in the world?"

Kress holds up her fingers in a "V." "No. We think *two* seventeen-year-olds can make all the difference in the world."

"Me and Matholook?" In all the time I've known her, I've never known Kress to look helpless. Until now. "You think the two of us have something to do with stopping Epic?"

"Not exactly. We don't know how things are going to play out," she confesses. She runs the backs of her fingers along the network of lines, curves, swooshes, dots, and dashes that make up her techno-genetically implanted forearm tattoos. "These enhance my abilities. They may also hold the key to understanding a lot of things: Who we are as Emergents. Where we come from. What our purpose and potential might be. The encounter you had with Epic before...your connection with Matholook now...these may be pieces in a much larger puzzle."

"But for now," Brohn says, "we need to tread lightly."

Wisp runs her fingers over the small holographic display projected above the desk in front of her. She scrolls along, tapping icons and inputting data. "That means being careful with how we handle your new friend."

"Listen, Branwynne," Kress says, leaning back in her mag-chair. "Matholook is a Devoted. Their motives are never what they appear to be. For us, being on the losing side of Epic's war could mean an end to our chance to find a lot of answers. And way worse...it could mean an end to us."

Great. So Kress thinks the first deep psychic connection I've had with someone other than a bird could be what causes us to lose a war? But that's not what scares me. What scares me is for the first time, I think three words I've never thought before: *Kress is wrong.*

"So what's he supposed to do now?" I ask.

"He's supposed to do what everyone your age is supposed to do. He'll go to school."

"With us?"

"With you. Consider him your shadow for the day."

"And after today?"

"Let us handle that. For now, we'll let him stay. *For the day.* But with a few restrictions in place. We can't exactly have a member of the Devoted running loose in the Academy."

"And you'll send him home when he wants to go?"

"We'll send him home when *we* want him to go."

"Don't worry," Wisp says softly. "We're not going to do to him what his people might want to do to us. He's our guest. And your responsibility. And we'll let him stay."

"For now, at least," Kress adds.

Wisp dismisses me, and, with that heavy thought weighing me down, I trudge on legs of lead back upstairs to the Lounge and to my waiting Asylum.

26

ENROLLED

STEPPING INTO THE LOUNGE, I'm greeted by the inquisitive, wide-eyed stares of my Asylum, who are gathered around Matholook. His face is tense and vaguely blue, and I think he might be holding his breath.

"So what did they decide?" Libra asks.

"He can stay."

Arlo pushes up the sleeve of his hoodie and reaches across the glass coffee table in front of the couch to offer Matholook a congratulatory handshake. "Nice to have you on board."

Matholook stares at the offered hand for a second and then over at me, like I'm supposed to give him permission or something. Just to humor him, I nod, and Matholook, releasing the breath I suspect he's been holding for most of the morning, reaches back over the table to accept the handshake.

I notice him noticing the thick, rubbery scars running along Arlo's forearm and the crags and calloused skin on the back of his hand.

"Matholook's not exactly on board," I tell Arlo. "He's allowed to stay. But in a limited capacity."

"How limited?"

"He can be part of our Cohort but only for observational purposes. He can't be part of competitions or testing or training or anything like that."

Sara props her chin in her cupped hands and locks eyes with Matholook. "How long are you staying?"

"Um...I'm not sure?"

"They haven't figured that part out yet," I tell her. "For now, it's supposed to just be for the day."

"I hope it's for a while," Sara coos. "It'd be nice to have someone around who's actually lived in the world instead of being cooped up in a Processor." Sara makes an exaggerated show of looking all around the Lounge. "Or in a place like this."

"Listen," Mattea says, plopping down on the armchair across from Matholook. "I just wanted to say thanks for setting those Emergents free. They're doing really well here."

"I'm glad to hear it."

"Are you?" Ignacio asks through gritted teeth.

"Hey," I snap at him with a backhand smack to his arm. "He's our guest."

"He also kidnapped and tortured kids like us."

"I didn't—"

"*He* did no such thing," I remind Ignacio. "It was the Cult of the Devoted."

Ignacio flicks a thumb in Matholook's direction. "And where's he from again?"

"Being a part of something isn't the same as *being* that something."

"You're splitting hairs," Ignacio growls.

"Keep it up," I warn him with a clamped-up fist in his face, "and I'll split your lip."

"Whoa!" Mattea says, stretching her arms out between us. "We're on the same team."

"Are we?" Ignacio smiles, without taking his eyes from Matholook.

Bouncing forward and planting herself on the couch next to Matholook, Libra draws her thick hair back into a ponytail and asks him what it's like being a Typic with all these Emergents around.

"Honestly?"

"Of course."

His green eyes glinting with that warm emerald glimmer, Matholook scans the six members of my Asylum before offering up a pleasant smile to Libra. "It's terrifying."

We all have a laugh—even Ignacio—and Libra asks if he's serious.

"I'm assuming you can all do something special, something I can't."

"It doesn't really work like that," Arlo explains. "It's not like in comic books."

"He's right," Mattea agrees. "Some of us can do weird little things—"

"With proper training," I elaborate.

"Right. With proper training," Mattea continues. "But our abilities don't always work, they're not always consistent, they sometimes hurt, and there are plenty of kids here in the Academy who've been identified as Emergents based on digital identification and DNA sequencing, but they haven't exhibited any extraordinary abilities at all."

"Yet," Libra stresses.

"Either way," Matholook says, "at least some of you have abilities beyond anything I've ever seen, right out of the stories we learn about in History. It's amazing. Inspirational. And also, yes, terrifying to know what you could do to me if I got on your bad side."

"Then definitely stay away from Sara," Libra beams. "*All* her sides are bad."

Sliding a lock of her short blond hair behind her ear, Sara doesn't seem the least bit fazed by Libra's warning-slash-insult. "We're all just so glad to have you on board," she coos, her voice trilling and baby bird soft.

Pushing his hoodie back and exposing his face full of raised, patchy scars, Arlo points out to Matholook that being an Emergent isn't all that glorious. "As you can see, my friend, sometimes it comes with its downsides."

Arlo's scars seem to throb and pulse in the stark white light of the Lounge.

Clearly shaken and unsure how to respond, Matholook makes a weird laugh-grunt noise, so I come to his rescue.

"Being alive on the planet comes with its downsides," I remind Arlo. "We're *all* talented, and we're *all* flawed. Typic or Emergent, that's what makes us vulnerable and responsible for each other. That's what connects us."

Libra flashes a wide smile and claps her hands together. "That is *so* true!" Turning to Matholook, she throws an arm around his shoulders and points to me. "Listen to Branwynne. She's a lot smarter than she looks!"

Scowling at her, I tell her to leave poor Matholook alone and stop bugging him.

"It's all right," he insists. "You guys are a lot different than we are."

"How's that?" Mattea asks.

"Well, for starters, we don't really do this whole 'clever banter' thing you all seem so good at."

Mattea crosses her legs and rests her dark, slender arms over her knees. "What *do* you do down there?"

Matholook's shoulders rise up to meet his ears. "I don't know. We learn. We train."

You brainwash, kidnap, recruit, and lie about it.

"Tell us more," Sara implores, leaning in, her hands folded under her chin.

"Like what?"

"Oh, I don't know. How many members do you have down there in your compound? What kind of weapons? What training do you do? I mean besides the big brawl Branwynne told us about."

"Um..."

"And what about Epic's war? You've got to be worried, right?"

Matholook looks to me, but I don't have any answers to give him. Sara seems interested in grilling him about everything from what he eats for breakfast to the politics of the impending war.

Maybe a little too interested?

From her seat on the ottoman in front of the couch, she gives me a little wink. It's a wink that says, "Don't worry about it. I'm just getting some intel we can use later." I'm sure it's supposed to be a reassuring wink.

So why do I feel so nervous?

27

PERFECTION

BECAUSE OF ALL THE EXCITEMENT, Wisp has canceled morning classes. Which is fine with me. There's no way I'd be able to keep my mind on any of the lessons today, anyway.

With the rest of the students either gathering upstairs in the Lounge, getting caught up with schoolwork in one of the fifth floor reading nooks, watching movies in the Screening Room, or working out in the Fitness Center, I find myself alone downstairs in the Tavern.

I don't even hear Kress when she walks in, so I'm startled when she pulls out the seat next to mine and sits down.

"About earlier..." she begins. "We only came down on you so hard because of how important you are."

Slumping in my seat, I fold my arms heavily across my chest. "The Devoted think I'm their 'savior's savior.' And now I've got the weight of a war on my shoulders. I refuse to believe that everyone's relying on me to play some important part in taking down Epic."

Kress shakes her head and says that's not what she meant.

"What then?" I ask, sitting up a little and letting my arms drop to my sides.

"I meant how important you are to *me*." When I don't answer (because I'm too stunned to form words), Kress laughs and reminds me about the promise she made to my parents. "I said I'd take care of you. I promised I'd protect you. They told me your future was tied to mine..."

"And...?"

Kress takes a breath and drums her fingers on the table. "They told me your future was tied to mine *and to Manthy's*."

"Manthy? But Manthy's—"

"I know. But maybe not forever."

"I don't understand."

"That makes two of us. But in my experience, with good friends around and with everyone connected and working together, figuring out the impossible isn't all that hard."

Kress stands up and pats my shoulder.

I reach up and catch her hand before she can turn to leave. "Can I ask you a question?"

"Sure."

"What's the hardest part about...?" I begin, struggling to gather my thoughts.

"The hardest part about what?" Kress asks with a twinkly-eyed smile.

"I don't know. You're my teacher. And my trainer. And my mentor. And my advisor."

"That's a lot of hats to wear," she agrees. "I'm surprised my head doesn't collapse under the weight."

"I'm pretty sure nothing could collapse you," I assure her. "I guess I want to know what's the hardest part about being you? After all, you're training me to be a better version of you, right?"

"I don't know about that. I think of myself as training you to turn your survival instinct and abilities into something contagious, something that can help others to survive when they otherwise wouldn't."

"So...?"

I think maybe Kress will do her usual thing and change the subject or else chastise me for taking my mind off of more important things. But she doesn't do any of that. Instead, she's quiet for a long time. When she finally clears her throat to speak, she says, "I guess the hardest part about being me is being a perfectionist who's afraid of perfection and who has no desire to be perfect in the first place."

And with that, she turns to leave.

ALONE AGAIN IN THE TAVERN, I only have a minute to process our conversation when Matholook straggles in, looking downcast and exhausted. He straightens up and beams a big smile at me, though, and makes his way through the large, empty room to my table.

I pat the seat next to me, and he collapses down with a heavy exhalation.

"They assigned me a room for the day in East Tower," he says. "Top floor."

"You'll be just down the hall from our indoor gardens."

"I guess it's better than getting tossed out of a window."

"Aren't the Devoted going to be worried about you?" I ask.

He plops his face down into his folded arms on the table. "I didn't sneak out. They know where I went."

"You told them you were going up the mountain to try to find the Academy?"

"They know Epic found you. They know he got someone inside. They figured maybe we could take a shot at it, too."

"We?"

"Me and Bendegatefran. He came with me for part of the way."

"Where is he now?"

"Back at the campsite. He's going to wait for me there."

"How does he know you'll even be back? I mean, what if Kress and Wisp decide...you know..."

"Not to let me go?"

"Yeah."

"If he hasn't heard from me by the end of tomorrow, he's going to go back to New Harleck."

"He'll tell them he lost you along the way?"

"Yes."

"He'll tell them you were killed?"

"Yes."

"By Emergents?"

"Yes."

"And that'll add another reason for the Devoted to hate us and eventually jump into Epic's war against us?"

Matholook raises his head and slides his eyes over to meet mine, but he doesn't say anything.

"It's okay," I assure him. "I know the answer."

Annoyed now, I start to stand up. Pushing my seat back, I turn away so he can't see the pain and disappointment I know must be written with crystal clarity on my face. "Is it really worth it?"

"It's not," he says, standing up too and taking my hand in his. "But *you* are."

28

BEDROOM

WE STAND THERE for a second until the moment morphs from surprising to sweet to kind of awkward.

When he breaks the silence and invites me upstairs to show me his quarters in East Tower, I say, "Sure!" way too fast and with a lot more gleeful enthusiasm than I intended.

Bloody hell. Rein it in, Branwynne. You're starting to sound like Libra.

After clearing my throat and pretending like his invitation is no big deal, I tell him I'll go—but only because I'm curious to see how Kress has the room set up for him.

"It's not bad," he assures me as we walk down the long hall and toward the thick wooden doorway leading to the tower. "A little like a jail cell, but I guess that's kind of appropriate."

"You're *not* a prisoner."

"Sure. I just can't leave. I'm suspected of being a spy. My movements are restricted. Oh, and I'm from an enemy faction you're being trained to defeat. Why on earth would I think I was a prisoner?"

I glare at him, and he glares back. But then he breaks into a hearty laugh.

"You're taking the piss?" I ask, letting go of the tense knot in my chest.

"Taking the—?"

"Having me on," I giggle. "Winding me up. Yanking my chain."

"I wouldn't dare yank anything around here."

"You're a wise man."

Matholook tugs my sleeve. "Come on."

We start to climb the narrow, circular stairway leading up to the gardens at the top of East Tower.

Where the main building of the Academy is all lightness, openness, and clean lines, the East and West Towers are cramped, dark spaces with natural rock walls, narrow passageways, and thick shadows.

The stairs leading up the tower are unforgiving, cold, gray stone. It's dark, like something out of an old fairy tale. I've been up this way before, but it still gives me the creeps. The more holo-lights Wisp and Granden have put up over the years, the darker it seems to have gotten.

Halfway up, Matholook and I have to slam our backs up against the wall as three of the kids from the Committee of Vultures come tearing down the stairs.

Cackling their apologies as they pass, they scurry down into the darkness to continue with whatever mischief they've got going on.

"Some of the younger kids like to hang out in the gardens," I explain.

"You really have gardens up there?"

"It's not as elaborate as you might think. It's a hydroponics lab Mayla started up when we first got here. You haven't seen them?"

"No. Kress and Brohn showed me my room, but that's about it."

"Well, the gardens are just down the hall from you. They're not much, but they're getting bigger and more elaborate all the time. Anyway, there's lots of lab stations, suspended grow-pods, exposed irrigation piping, storage closets for the harvesting equipment...and lots of fun places to hide, gad about, and make general mischief when the teachers aren't around."

"Never a dull moment around here, is there?" Matholook observes as the kids and the echoes of their chuffed-up laughter disappear down the tower stairs.

"They're cute as kittens," I admit. "And almost as smart."

"Where are those ones from? I don't recognize them."

"Those are three of the Emergents Kress and her Conspiracy rescued from a Processor somewhere west of here."

Matholook starts heading up the stairs again. As we walk, he turns over his shoulder to ask me if that's really what the Academy is for. "To rescue Emergents?"

"Yes," I tell him. "And to bring them back here where we can all be safe and get trained."

"Training in how to control your abilities?"

"Yes. But that's turning out to be just one part of it. We're being taught to control ourselves first."

At the top of the stairs, Matholook takes a deep breath before leading me down the hall to his room.

It's a small room with not much more in it than a bed, a chair, a dresser, and a frayed area rug with a pattern of overlapping circles of different sizes printed on it. The door to an attached washroom sits open. The meager, low-intensity holobulb recessed in the ceiling is barely enough to light up the windowless room.

Because it's just down the hall from the gardens, his makeshift bedroom—it used to be a storage room—smells like basil, mint, thyme, and tomatoes.

He plops down on the bed—which is more of a sad-looking

military cot—and the springs squeak under his weight. He pats the space next to him, but I decline, deciding instead to sit in the rickety wooden armchair by the door.

Matholook crosses his legs and sits with his back pressed to the slatted iron headboard of his narrow bed. (They *do* resemble prison bars.) "We seem to keep finding each other, don't we?"

"It's not an accident," I remind him. "I left the Academy to go find you. Kind of."

"You never really explained why."

"That's because I'm not a hundred percent sure, myself. Something inside was pulling at me, and Kress has been teaching me how to channel Haida's instincts to enhance my own."

"So you followed your gut."

"Not exactly."

"Then what—?"

"I don't feel like I was 'following' anything. It's more like something was tugging at me, drawing me into action."

"Something?"

"Or someone."

Matholook laughs. "You think you were hypnotized into coming to find me?"

I try to laugh, too, but it comes out as more of a whimper. I cover it up with a shrug.

Matholook pauses to set his smile into a tight, serious line. "You might be the toughest, stubbornest, and most determined person I know. I can't imagine you getting *hypnotized* into doing anything,"

I make a mental note of the compliment and tell him he's probably right. "But there've been some strange things going on," I add.

"Strange? Like what?"

"I don't know. Weird things. People right here in the

Academy saying things I know they don't believe. People not thinking for themselves."

"People being brainwashed?"

"I'm not ready to go that far."

"Not everything is explainable."

"I guess not," I concede. "But what about us? What are the chances that we'd meet five years ago? Or that you'd wind up helping us and those kids like you did a few months ago? Or that Kress and her raven would find me and my raven on opposite sides of the Atlantic Ocean and that I'd even wind up here at all?"

"And then we practically ran into each other in the woods."

"Technically, I ran into Bendegatefran. *Literally*." I shake my head. "I don't know. What if it's all just coincidence?"

"What if *coincidence* is just a word someone made up to describe those rare times when we can see the connections that are around us all the time?"

"That sounds like something Lucid and Reverie would say to explain the *Lyfelyte*."

Matholook gives me a head-tilt of curiosity and seems suddenly alert. Nodding and leaning forward, his arms draped across his knees, he prods me to go on.

"The twins say the *Lyfelyte* is kind of a middle dimension where our reality connects with every other reality," I explain. "They say the places where they intersect, where one dimension is visible from another...they say it's where we experience what we call dreams."

"That sounds...interesting."

"I guess," I shrug. "I don't totally understand it."

Matholook's eyes have gotten humorously big, so I figure I owe him at least something of an explanation. I reach over and pat the wall next to me with my hand. "Everything we think of as solid is actually made up of mostly space and only a little bit of matter. It's inside of here where you can access the *Lyfelyte*. Well, not *you*," I laugh. "But Kress, the twins, and..."

I almost tell him about my growing ability of *traversion*, but I hold back. There's no telling how he might react to something like that, and I'm enjoying our conversation too much to risk running it off the rails.

"And the twins think there's a connection between dreams and the *Lyfelyte* in that wall?" he asks.

"So they say."

"Maybe they have a point."

"How do you mean?"

"Obviously, you remember when you ran into Bendegatefran in the woods, right?"

I rub my rear end and tell him, "I can still feel it in my Queen mum. Sorry. My bum."

Matholook grins and blushes a little. "He was out there because he was keeping watch while I tried to get a little sleep before we made our next move in our search for Gwernna. We'd had a *very* long day."

"I don't doubt it."

Matholook swings his legs over the side of the bed and swivels around to face me. "I fell asleep. Just for a few minutes, mind you. But I had a dream. It should have been about the Unsettled. Or Gwernna. Or a million other things. But it wasn't. It was about you. And then you were there."

"I was where?"

"In my dream. But also in my reality. I heard Bendegatefran going at it with someone in the woods. Before I was even all the way awake, I knew it would be you out there. I think I summoned you somehow from inside of my dream."

"Maybe it was the *Lyfelyte*," I agree. "On the other hand, maybe it was a coincidence." I lean forward and give Matholook a conspiratorial wink and a spooky, waggle-fingered, "Oooo...

Maybe it was destiny." When he frowns, I grin and clap my hands, "Oh! Maybe there's some Emergent or a Hypnagogic working behind the scenes and making it all happen!"

Instead of laughing along with me, he gets serious. "Or... maybe those very different explanations are really all the same."

I shift in my chair and pretend to buckle my boot even though it's already buckled. I can feel Matholook's eyes on me, and I know he'll be looking straight at me when I raise my head.

Sure enough, his green eyes are glinting along with his cheeky smile, and I wonder if he's having me on again.

"Listen," I say at last, "about all that stuff they were asking you about downstairs..."

"About being a Typic in an Academy of Emergents?"

"Yeah."

"What about it?"

"I don't believe you."

"You don't believe me about what?"

"About being terrified. I don't think you're scared of us at all."

Matholook grins out of one side of his mouth. "Can I tell you a secret?"

"Sure."

"I'm *not* scared of you. You can do some amazing things. The talking to birds and such. But you're hardly the first."

"I know. You've been around us before."

"Not just you. Remember, in the Devoted, we're all about history."

"What does that have to do with it?"

Matholook nods like he's agreeing with me about something I never said and reminds me that all of life's answers—according to the Cult of the Devoted, anyway—can be found in our own history. "If you know where to look and how to keep your eyes and mind open," he adds.

Sitting up straight and counting off on his fingers, he proceeds to regale me with a litany of people he's learned about.

"There was once an actor we read about who had *hyperthymesia*. She could remember every detail about her own life. What she did on which day. What she wore. Everything. There was a baseball relief pitcher who had *polydactyly*. That's an extra finger on his throwing hand. A boy in England could draw anything he saw in exact detail after only a few minutes of examination. He was called 'the living camera.'"

"I heard about him!" I exclaim with another unfortunate outburst of enthusiasm. "From my parents," I explain, settling down and giving myself a mental slap in the face for sounding like such a daft-bloody naffer.

Matholook laughs and goes on. "Another man had a photographic memory. The two lobes of his brain—the corpus callosum—had almost no separation, which may have given him his superhuman ability to read the left page of a book with his left eye and the right page with his right eye and the even more superhuman ability to remember nearly all of it. There was this unexplained blind piano prodigy. He could play anything after only hearing it once. And another guy experienced *synesthesia* where he saw numbers as colors and patterns and could remember them all. And he could learn a brand-new language in less than a week."

"So...there've been some talented people in the world. You're saying Emergents aren't new?"

"There have been countless people like you, people with unexplained resistance to disease or who've exhibited extraordinary feats of endurance or athleticism. People who could part the seas or walk on water."

"And you think they were all Emergents?"

"Not officially. No one ever called them that. But the truth is, Emergents—whether they were called savants, witches, prophets, goblins, gods, saviors, or sorcerers, have been around for as long as there've been people." Matholook takes a deep breath, like he's debating whether or not to keep going, like he's got a secret he may not want to reveal.

"Go on," I urge.

After a sigh, he does. "Twenty years ago, a man with a techno-genetic signature no one ever saw before volunteered to help President Krug build a drone army designed to identify and control Emergents as a first step toward enslaving the world." Matholook makes a sweeping general gesture at the walls. "What happened out there, the poverty, the suffering, the disease, the ruined cities, the wars, and all the death...it started with him."

"Him?"

"He was obsessed with unlocking the mysteries of human evolution, especially the part where it merges with digital technology in the event known as the *Singularity*. He didn't want power or control, just answers. But that made him just as dangerous as any genocidal warlord. He was also rumored to be immortal. You know him as 'Epic.'"

With my mind swirling, the word barely registers, so I repeat it once to myself before repeating it out loud. "Epic."

"I know you've met him. I know you escaped from him. I know what he would have done with you if you hadn't. You need to know that he's not the first Emergent. But he might just want to be the last."

"And that's what his war is all about? Finishing what he started with Krug?"

"Yes."

"And you think *he* thinks I can help him do that somehow?"

"Yes."

A thick, heavy silence hangs between us. We lock eyes, two

chess players sizing each other up from opposite sides of the board.

I move first. Standing up, I shimmy over and sit down on the edge of his bed. He inches closer until we're shoulder to shoulder.

"If you know all this," I say, staring at the floor, "we should tell Kress. She and her Conspiracy—all my teachers—have been searching for the answer to us for years."

"They're smart. They've been at this for a long time. You said it yourself. I doubt I could tell them anything they don't already know."

"You've already told me more than *I* knew."

"That's the power of history." He puts his hand above my knee but doesn't bring it down. I watch as it hovers there for a second, and then he tucks it under his leg. "History will know what to do. History brought us here. Everything that's happened has led to this."

I know he said, "...has led to *this*," but for a second—just for a second—in my mind, it sounded like he said that everything that's happened has led to *us*.

29

HOST

By THE TIME I say goodnight to Matholook, it's not even night anymore.

In a single second, a few dozen thoughts flash through my very tired brain:

We talked through the whole night? How'd that happen? Other than Kress, I usually can't stand being in the same room with anyone for more than about two minutes before I want to leap out of the nearest window. And now I'll have to hear from Libra about me not spending the night with my Asylum in our Dorm. That's going to mean all kinds of prying and probing questions. Urgh. Why doesn't this room have a window?

The blue light from the flashing indicators in the hallway pulses under the door, and I stand up to stretch. I get a little offended when the springs in Matholook's cot sound like they're breathing a metallic sigh of relief.

Awake now but still tired from talking all night, I drop down into the chair by the door where I sit with my arms draped over my knees as I stare at the circles in the faded area rug. Right now, I'm supposed to be downstairs in the Tavern having breakfast with my Asylum. Instead, I'm squirreled away up here in East Tower with my mind going a mile-a-minute.

I left the Academy to find answers. No. That's a lie. I left to feel a sense of connectedness I'd never felt before. Nope. Another lie.

The truth is that I left because I felt like I didn't have a choice. Honestly, I didn't even really leave. Something *pulled* me out of the Academy. Something *pulled* me down the mountain. Something is still hard at work *pulling* me and Matholook together. I thought I knew what it was, but now I'm not so sure. In fact, I'm less sure about a lot of things: The feelings in me that don't really feel like mine. The desire I have to connect with someone else. The equally powerful fear I have that doing so will mean killing off a part of myself. The role I played in retrieving a little girl who could also be a weapon of war. Matholook and the Devoted possibly being something more sinister than they seem.

And on top of that, Kress seems to be full of intel and living a whole other life I don't know anything about. I feel like I've been assembling pieces to a very important puzzle, but the more I squint at the image, the blurrier it becomes.

Realizing how long I've been sitting here, I call out Matholook's name to get his attention. "We missed breakfast. But I've got to get to class," I say to his reclined, curved back. "What are you going to do all day?"

He rolls toward me and props his chin in his palm. "Apparently, right after the Morning Address, your mentor and her friends are going to grill me some more. Should be fun."

"Don't sound so nervous," I laugh.

Matholook swings his legs over the side of the cot and starts sliding his blue, Academy-issued compression top over his head. "What's to be nervous about? I'm just trapped in a hidden school with a dozen super-powered people who want to kill me."

Doing my best to ignore how the shirt accentuates his muscles, I tell him, "There are way more than a dozen of us," and I drop my gaze before he has time to figure out if I'm winding him up or not.

I buckle my boots on and head toward the door.

"Hey!" Matholook calls out, hopping on one foot as he scrambles to get his own boots on. "Wait up. I'm supposed to stay with you."

"Says who?"

"Says Kress. And I hate to admit, but she really *is* terrifying."

"Come on, then," I laugh. Let's get to Morning Address. Kress'll be there."

"Great."

"You're supposed to face your fears, right?"

I lead Matholook down the spiral stairs of East Tower. From there I tell him to follow me the rest of the way downstairs by one of the rear service staircases, so we don't run into anyone. I try to time our walk so we get to the Assembly Hall after everyone else has already filed in.

My plan *almost* works.

Everyone from the other Cohorts is already inside except for the one person I was most hoping to avoid.

"Running a little late, are we?" Sara asks, her voice full of snark. She's leaning against the wall by the Assembly Hall door, her arms folded across her chest. Giving her head a little toss, she flicks aside the strands of blond hair hanging over her eye. Her smile is warm, pretty, and fake.

"I was keeping our guest company," I tell her.

Why am I explaining myself to her?

"Wow, Branwynne," she says, clapping her hands to her cheeks and pretending to be beyond impressed. "You're a *really* good host."

"And you're a really good pain in my—"

"Good morning!" Matholook exclaims, his hand extended to Sara in greeting. "I'm looking forward to your Morning Address."

Without accepting the handshake, Sara scans him up and down. Twice. "Probably won't be nearly as exciting as your Morning *Un*-dress was."

While Matholook's face goes cranberry-red, I growl at Sara to knock it off.

"Just being a good host," she sneers.

Then, she slips her arm into the crook of Matholook's and escorts him ahead of me into the Assembly Hall.

MORNING ADDRESS IS the usual inspirational speech by Wisp about how we need to focus and redouble our efforts in class.

She tears through a long list of activities either going on already or about to take place at the Academy.

She's got an urgency in her voice, which is strange because Wisp is probably about the most composed person under pressure I've ever known. She's the smallest and youngest of all of our teachers in the Academy, but she magically commands a room like she's a seasoned, seven-foot-tall field general.

Even though communication is sketchy, Wisp explains how —with Kress and Render's leadership, along with "a network of ravens and Survivalists in various outposts"—they've been able to start connecting the Academy more effectively with the country's East and West Coasts.

She launches into a whole explanation about atmospheric ionization, magnetic radioscopic radiation detectors, compromised high-orbit satellite telemetries, and a dozen other things I'm struggling to pay attention to.

I get why she wants us to know these things. We're in a

school, after all. But I've got the fate of a war and of the world on my mind and Sara sitting as smug as a bug between me and Matholook, so it's kind of hard to focus at the moment.

"We're getting reports from Washington and from San Francisco," Wisp goes on to explain. "Not consistently yet. But it's a start."

I perk up when Granden adds a bit about some upcoming missions Kress and her Conspiracy will be going on, including a possible search and rescue mission in some place called Nevada's Great Basin National Park. "Don't worry," Granden assures us. "It's nothing dangerous, and we'll make sure your classes are covered."

Forget about safety and covering classes. I want to go with them!

After the rest of her pep talk, Wisp rattles off a list of minor changes to the schedule.

"The Exaltation will take Communication Skills with Mayla for the next two weeks before switching to a special lab with me and Kella to learn about the rooftop Sensor Array. That seminar will include operation and routine maintenance. The Battery of Quail Cohort has been assigned to inventory the weapons and rations supplies. That will start this afternoon under Rain's supervision and shouldn't take more than a day or two. Mayla will be asking for volunteers to help run some of the produce from the hydroponics lab downstairs to the protein-inducer engine."

She rattles off a few more duties, changes, and assignments, which I tune out since none of it has to do with me.

After Morning Address, Wisp sends us off to class while Kress—looking stern and determined—comes over to escort Matholook to her office on the second floor.

30

FLEET

Standing just outside of the Assembly Room doors, I watch Matholook disappear down the stairwell at the end of the hall. As if he's being led to the gallows, he hangs his head the whole way.

As I sigh and send him mental hopes for a quick and painless second round of interrogation, the five Cohorts of the Academy part ways, each group heading off to its own class or assignment.

The rest of my Asylum gathers around me with Libra poking me in the arm with her finger.

"So...?" she drawls.

Three months ago, I would've gotten annoyed. But Libra—despite her constant cheeriness and endless prattling—has actually turned out to be a pretty decent listener and a good friend. So instead of getting annoyed, I just whack her hand away.

It's replaced immediately by Ignacio's. "Someone didn't come to bed last night," he accuses, his voice an obnoxious singsong.

We'd been getting along so well. Why does everyone seem to want to provoke me into punching them in the face this morning?

It's Arlo who comes to my aid and tells the others to back off and leave me alone.

"Come on," Mattea grins at him, "aren't you even a little curious where our little Miss AWOL was last night?"

"Or what she was doing?" Sara teases.

"Or who she was doing it with?" Ignacio adds.

"Okay, okay," I bark. "You all know full well I was upstairs with Matholook."

"Yeah, but the whole night?" Libra prods.

"We just talked."

"You left the Academy for him," she reminds me.

"No. I left because I needed to feel connected."

"Same thing."

"Hardly."

"Come on," Ignacio calls out with a gleeful clap of his hands. "Enough gossip. We're finally getting the class we've been waiting for!"

He sprints down the hall. He's the biggest one in our Cohort, but right now, he's darting ahead with the goofy glee of a six-year-old sugar addict.

The rest of us hustle along after him, scampering all the way downstairs to the Sub-Basement. I'm thankful when the silver pedestrian door slides open, and we enter the vehicle hangar. At least now we'll have something to talk about other than my relationship with Matholook.

We step across the threshold, and the rest of my Asylum is practically shaking with excitement. I have to admit, I'm a little keen, myself. Today, we get to start the supplemental training session of War's Transportation and Mechanics class.

For the past few weeks, we've been learning all about the Academy's fleet of motorized vehicles. War's been grilling us on fuel-type consumption, maintenance logs, repair protocols, safety requirements...basically, all the most boring stuff in the world.

But today, we finally get to take the vehicles out for a spin.

With Libra bouncing along in front of us now, we make our way across the bright, high-ceilinged hangar to where War is waiting for us by the parking pads.

"Good to have you back," War says to me.

"I was only gone for a day—," I start to explain, but he cuts me off with a grunt.

"I'm guessing Kress already had a chat with you."

"Yes. If by 'chat' you mean, 'screamed at me for an hour and a half.'"

War laughs. "She snapped at me once in D.C. I don't even remember what for. Maybe I was moving into the wrong position in our final fight against the Patriots. Whatever it was for, it felt like she'd kicked me in the gut. That is one tough lady." War grins down at me and pats his stomach. "She made me forget that I'm twice her age and four times her size."

"She has that power," I laugh.

"Well, since you've been appropriately chastised, how about if we get back to learning about our various options for transportation?"

"Absolutely!"

War herds us the rest of the way across the room to the far end of the hangar.

The air is sterile but with hints of oil, smoke and heat from the numerous tools on the service tables and in the glass-topped workstations in front of each stall.

For the next hour, War reviews what we've learned so far. Standing in front of us and our workstations, he runs us through all the riding protocols again, gives us a preview of what it'll be like cruising around the mountain, and even speckles in some more stories about his experiences driving out in the world before Krug and the Atomic Wars.

"Cars as far as the eye could see," he reminisces, his voice its usual elephant-low rumble, an uncharacteristically cute sparkle in his eyes. "Gas cars. Electric cars. Mag-cars. Trains. Subways. Buses. Cabs. Motorcycles. Scooters. Gyro-transporters. The works."

He's told us dozens of stories before. Stories about driving kids to school. Taking the little league football team he coached to practices and games all around Chicago. He always stops right before the good part, though, the part where he went from teaching night classes and coaching football to becoming the Survivalist warlord of some Chicago gang called "the Garfield Boulevard Syndicate." (We know what happened afterwards—about how he joined Kress and her Conspiracy and helped them take down Krug in D.C. Someday, I've got to get him to tell us the juicy stories about his days as an evil kingpin.)

"Looks like we're about ready," War announces, checking a vehicle status holo-display projected just above his teacher's workstation.

My Asylum launches into an excited twitter.

Normally, I'd be clam-happy myself about *finally* getting to go out on an actual motorized adventure. But something's missing.

I don't realize what it is until it...I mean *he*...comes walking through the door at the far end of the hangar.

Escorted by Kress on one side and Brohn on the other, Matholook walks his way over to War.

"Kress says I can join you."

War turns to Kress and opens his mouth, but he doesn't say anything.

"It's okay," Kress assures him. "Matholook's driven before. He knows the basics. What he doesn't know, he'll learn as you go."

"Give him a crash course," Brohn says with a wink that seems to amuse War and shock Matholook. "Seriously, though. Take care of him. Show him a good time."

"I'll look after him like he's one of our own," War promises.

Kress and Brohn say, "Thanks" to War and wish the rest of us luck on our first outdoor excursion before they turn on their heels and head back out of the hangar.

"The Asylum's already familiar with the fleet," War explains to Matholook. "But come on. I'll give them a refresher and you an introduction before we head out."

Queuing up like a waddling line of baby ducks, we follow War over to the fleet.

Compared to the bulky, powerful vehicles of the Devoted, the Unsettled, and even Epic's Civillains, our little collection of one and two-rider motorized bikes and mountain rovers isn't all that impressive.

I've been in the Terminus, of course. It's what got me here. Now, *that's* an impressive vehicle. The other members of my Asylum came here with Granden in the older truck—nearly as big but half the power and twice as ugly—sitting next to it.

In addition to those two beasts, there are the special mountain-rigs and the small assemblage of surveillance, transportation, and combat vehicles.

War walks us past the *Treadchairs*, single-seat mag-propelled mini-snowmobiles. Very sleek. Very fast. And, according to War, very prone to tipping over if not handled with absolute care and the utmost control.

After that, we move along to the wide-track *Grip-bikes*. They're powerful, beefy monsters, like motorcycles on steroids. Built low to the ground, powered by a calibrated magnetic converter-coil and running on a single, studded tank tread, they can handle pretty much any terrain—from clustered woods to icy slopes to nearly-vertical cliffs—the mountain might throw at us.

Ignacio rubs his hands together and claims dibs on the red one.

Matholook and I exchange a smile and an eyeroll at Ignacio's drooling enthusiasm.

War laughs, too, and confirms that these are the vehicles we'll be taking outside today. "And yes, Ignacio...I'll save the red one for you."

Ignacio throws up a celebratory fist pump like he's just won some major sports championship or something.

"You've worked on the *Magni Tri-blades* before," War reminds my Asylum, patting one of the skeletal-looking, wide-footed snow trikes in the next stall. "They may not look that impressive," he explains to Matholook, "but wait until you see these little guys in action. Nothing's better for navigating deep snow or for keeping ahead of an avalanche."

From under his hoodie, Arlo asks if they're really as fast and reliable in blizzard conditions as War's told us.

War gives him a little wink and says, "You have no idea," before moving on.

I get a knot in my gut when he walks us past the modified *Skid Steers* like the kind the Unsettled use. I elbow Matholook, and he nods at our shared memory. It wasn't much than a day ago that he and Bendegatefran nicked a pair of Skid Steers just like these from the Unsettled to get us and Gwernna back to New Harleck.

"Not as fast as some of the others," War reminds us, his eyes fixed on the small, two-seated front-loaders, "but they're armed to the teeth and coated in a lighter version of synth-steel. Great combo of speed and lethality."

As he walks along, his huge boots bang out on the glossy white floor.

"We're missing parts for some of the Mountain-walkers," he explains sadly to Matholook. "But we were able to cannibalize parts from a few of them to get these three up and running." Like a caring parent fretting over his sick child, he gives the four-footed, spider-like vehicles a sad sigh before moving on.

"These aren't for the faint of heart," he cautions Matholook, pointing us all in the direction of the grav-charged *Wing-gliders*.

"Have you ever flown one?" Matholook asks, gazing at the wide-winged contraption with its assemblage of thin struts, leather harnesses, and metal buckles.

War slaps a hand to his own bulging shoulder. "They have a size and weight capacity. Wisp has flown one. Me? I'd fly about as good as a petrified penguin."

Doubling back, War returns us to the Grip-bikes. There are eight of them in all: four black ones, a blue one, a yellow one, a green one, and yes, one red one for Ignacio.

We've been learning about these impressive, slightly intimidating bikes for weeks. We've done maintenance on them, and War had us in the VR-sim a dozen times. But the idea of actually riding one, of being outside on the mountain...

"Get geared up," War instructs, sliding open the long steel locker containing helmets, gloves, and full-bodied, armored riding gear with the Emergents Academy crest on the chest. The large locker also holds our individual weapons, which we collect and strap on.

"I'll be in the *Timberland Chopsaw*," War tells us after we've slipped into our kits and got ourselves zipped and buckled up.

I pat my hip to ensure I've got my Serpent Blades safely stowed in their holsters.

With everyone geared up, we all gather around to take in the Chopsaw, an impressive beast of a treaded tank. Built solid, as if carved out of the world's largest engine block, it seats five and has a synth-steel body over a carbonized chassis. It's shiny as wet glass, and we all know War thinks of it as his baby. (Not that we've ever had to guess. He polishes the bloody thing practically every day, freaks out if any of us dares to fanny around with it, and I'm pretty sure he sings to it after class.)

War deactivates the mag-pads with the green master override switch on the wall, and all of the Grip-bikes in their glass-walled stalls ease down to the floor one by one.

Dragging his finger along the silver pads of one of the bike's thick handlebars, War turns to us with a thunderous clap of his huge hands and a wide, cheeky grin. "Okay! Time to power up. Let's see what you little monsters can do on *these* little monsters."

31

ADVENTURE

WAR CLIMBS into the Chopsaw and activates its mag-powered engine, which revs to life with a hypnotic hum.

The beast of a machine vibrates fully to life, and War eases it out of its dock and glides it to a stop in front of the large silver door leading to the exit tunnel.

Leaning out of its open driver's side window, he calls out for us to keep up.

"You've learned about every one of these machines. Time to turn theory into practice."

I hop onto the yellow Grip-bike and invite Matholook to climb on behind me. He takes a deep breath like he's about to swan dive into an ocean of razor blades, but he puts on his helmet and swings up onto the bike, his arms locked around my waist.

Libra takes the blue one, Mattea claims the green one, and Sara and Arlo each hop onto one of the black ones.

Ignacio, of course, throws his leg over the seat of the red one and clamps his hands onto the wide handles.

Almost in unison, we all press our thumbs to our bikes' ignition pads and light them to life. Their front headlights throw an overlapping, crisscross pattern of blazing light and crisp shadows through the hangar.

War smiles and snaps the clear visor of his helmet down and bellows for us to follow him.

His voice shifts from being thirty feet ahead to being right inside my ear.

"The comm-links built into your helmets will let me stay in touch with you," his voice crackles. "The range is limited, and the tech is sketchy, so don't get too far out of my sight. One wrong turn on this mountain and you'll know what it feels like to be a pebble in an avalanche."

In single file and with War in the lead in his monster Chop-saw, we motor through the hangar's double doors and into the dimly lit access tunnel.

After a few hundred yards, War opens one of the tunnel's exit doors, and we barrel out into the crisp mountain air.

With his Chopsaw tearing a deep path into the snow and mud, War leads the seven of us on an exploration of the steepest, snowiest parts of the mountain range. We fly down treacherous, snow-covered embankments and leap our Grip-bikes over deep fissures in the ground.

Way up ahead now, Ignacio is clearly having a blast dodging between trees and exposed boulders.

Bouncing, flying, and skirting along, the thrill is more than enough to kick my heart and adrenaline levels into overdrive.

Matholook lets out a triumphant "Yahoo!" and we laugh like crazy as we catch air over a whole field of snow dunes.

With his hands cinched around my waist and his legs pressed tightly against mine, we zip down into a bowl-shaped expanse of ice and snow, weaving and dodging in a high-speed game of chase with Libra and Mattea.

That game morphs into follow-the-leader with Sara flying ahead of the rest of us, banking between trees, plunging into steep gullies, and grinding her Grip-bike up ice and mud-crusted slopes. She's a fearless and creative rider, who shows us no mercy as she takes on impossibly steep cliffs and weaves at dangerous, breakneck speeds through mazes of deep pits, along slanted snowbanks, and even over towering precipices, leaving us, one by one, puttering along in her wake.

"She's good," Matholook pants in my ear. "Crazy. But good."

"Sara would need ten years of intense psychotherapy just to advance to 'crazy.'"

At the top of one of the ridges, we finally catch up with her just as War grinds his Chopsaw to a stop in a spray of ice.

We rearrange our Grip-bikes to form a semi-circle around our instructor.

Sliding out of the Chopsaw, War beams at us while we slide off our helmets and tuck them under our arms. "So...what do you think so far?"

Ignacio slaps a gloved hand to the side of his red Grip-bike. "This thing is amazing. How come we can't ride them all the time?"

"Not many places to ride them *to*," War guesses. "As you've seen, it won't be much longer until even the mountains won't have snow on them anymore."

"We could always use them in the desert," I remind him.

War seems to ponder this for a weirdly long time. I ask him, "What is it?" but he just shakes his head and seems sad.

"They *do* work in the desert, right?" Libra asks over a sudden howl of wind that sweeps over us like a wave of water.

"They do," War concedes. "It's not that, though."

"Then what?" Mattea asks, her face a wrinkle of worry.

"The six of you—sorry, Matholook—the *seven* of you...you've never seen snow until the Academy, right?"

Sara raises a defiant hand and points back and forth between herself and Libra. "We were born in the U.S. I lived with my parents in Denver until I got taken to Spain. I've seen snow."

"And you remember it?"

Sara says, "Of course," but in a weird way that makes me not believe her.

Why would she lie about something like that?

Ignoring Sara for the moment, War swings back around to face Libra. "The reason I have a problem with using these vehicles in the desert has nothing to do with their functionality."

"Then what...?"

"You're being trained to win a war and then end all the fighting, right?"

"And to save the world," Libra beams with pride.

"Right. And to do that...to do any of it, you need to break existing cycles. What you're suggesting—taking these things down into the desert—is the opposite."

Libra is red-cheeked, but I don't know if it's from the cold, the whipping wind, or if she's annoyed by War putting her on the spot like this.

We're all looking back and forth at each other until I put up a hand and ask War what he means.

"We have excellent vehicles in the Academy," he says, his voice even and steady and nothing like the boast I first thought he was offering up. "They're designed for certain conditions. When conditions change, it's in our nature to adapt."

"Isn't that a good thing?" I ask.

"Sometimes. But other times, it's a shortcut. Instead of addressing how much damage we've done to the environment and then doing something significant to fix it—and *ourselves*— we acclimate to the new conditions as if they were natural and normal, and we pat ourselves on the back for our amazing adaptability. We look out over the desert wasteland we've created, and our response isn't, 'What can we do better?' It's

'Now we can just ride our marvie vehicles in the sand instead of in the snow.'"

War must suspect we're not really following his train of thought because he sighs and rubs the red line on his bald head from where the front edge of his helmet had been pressing in. "All I'm suggesting," he tells us as he slips back into the driver's seat of his waiting Chopsaw, "is that we all need to think about fixing things first and adapting to them being broken only when all else has failed."

In my ear, Matholook says, "I see his point."

"I do, too," I admit. "But we can ponder the self-destructive hypocrisy of humanity when we get back. For now, let's have some more fun, shall we?"

Matholook and I put our helmets on, and he taps me on the shoulder to indicate he's ready to go.

Powering up our vehicles, we cruise along, gliding over lakes of ice and hurtling over cliffs and across long stretches of deep, red-hued snow.

War's Chopsaw isn't as fast as our Grip-bikes, and it's not long before everyone in my Asylum has gone tearing off in their own direction.

As for me, I've got War's words—no, his *warning*—still skittering around inside my head when I nearly collide with Libra who's ground her Grip-bike to a dead stop at the edge of a cliff lined with a scraggly assortment of scaly lodgepole pines.

I stop too and am just about to tease her for being too scared to make the jump when she raises a hand and waves us all over.

The rest of our Asylum brings their vehicles to a quiet, thrumming stop in a cluster around Libra.

Behind us, War brings his Chopsaw to a chugging stop. He clambers out of the vehicle and stomps across the field of snow and exposed rocks to where the rest of us have gathered.

"What is it?" he asks, sliding his helmet off and tucking it under his arm.

Libra points down into the valley. "I think it's...a village?"

War steps closer to the edge and looks out over the valley toward the cluster of steep-peaked snow-topped wooden buildings.

"That's not a village. It's a ski resort."

32

RESORT

FROM UP HERE, most of the smaller buildings and sheds look like they were destroyed a long time ago.

All the signs of drone strikes are there: caved-in rooftops, collapsed walls, splintered support beams, black-rimmed craters scorched into the ground, skeletally leafless trees, buckled roadways, and piles and piles of bones.

I saw it back in London. Even as a little girl, I could tell which weapons had been deployed by which type of drone, even after the drones themselves were long gone. There were drones used to knock out a neighborhood's electrical systems and power supplies. There were drones used for crowd control, dispersal, and relocation. There were drones that fired concussive grenades, gelatinous flame missiles, and speckly-green napalm bombs. It didn't take more than a few hours before the bodies left after those strikes were picked clean by scavengers: dogs, feral cats, foxes, badgers, rats, and ravens.

But then a follow-up fleet of drones would swoop in and drop radioactive plasma pellets. Those left bodies no animal would touch.

This is like that.

The only thing worse than corpses on a battlefield is the undisturbed, flesh-crusted bones too distasteful to tempt even the most desperate scavenger.

This bone-filled valley is patchy, with bald-spots of rock and a leopard pattern of dried grass cutting through the drifting mounds of soft white snow.

And it has even more heaps of bones and bodies than I first realized. There must be hundreds of them. Some are lying out on the ground, fully exposed. Others look like they've been dragged and dropped between the cluster of lodges and the giant, overflowing pit on the far end of the resort.

Parked now and with our helmets off, Matholook asks in my ear, "What happened here?"

A helpless head shake is the most I can manage.

Of the entire complex of wrecked buildings, only the larger lodge—the main building among the smaller, flattened ones —remains.

Tucked into a deep natural basin in front of a ring of towering mountain peaks, it pokes up from the ground in a clump of cracked rooftops, collapsed walls, and boarded-up windows.

Even though it must have been years—maybe decades— since anyone used this place as an actual resort, the trenches of old ski slopes are still visible behind it. Like the rest of the area, the curving hills are disfigured with rocks and littered with dead, fallen trees. They start out at the lodge and extend up and out, winding and bending their way to the top of the mountain.

All together, the lodge and the slopes behind it resemble an open hand reaching up from a grave.

The chill I get isn't from the cold.

War calls out for the seven of us to put our helmets on and "saddle up."

Sara squints and points into the valley. "You really want us to go down there?"

"You wanted an adventure," War reminds all of us. "This is your chance to make this outing more than just a joy ride."

Libra's eyes are wide as she stands frozen, her gaze riveted to the horrifying carnage below.

I ask if she's okay, and she answers with a slow head shake and a barely-audible, "No," before turning to face me. "Riding down into the pit of Hell...it's not exactly what we signed up for, is it?"

"We didn't sign up at all," I remind her with a light laugh I hope she knows is meant to ease her mood and not to mock her. "We're going to be dealing with scenes like this all the time down below. It's the way of the world."

"So what do you say?" War asks. "Are you ready?"

Libra nods, offers up a feeble smile, and slips her helmet back on.

"I can't speak for them, but I'm definitely in!" Ignacio shouts with a clap of his gloved hands and way more cheerfulness than the situation warrants.

"I'll take the lead," War says as he clomps his way back to the Chopsaw. "The rest of you...stay close."

In an orderly, single file queue, we follow War down the steep slope and right up to the cluster of buildings Libra called a "village."

He stops ahead of us, and the rest of us park our Grip-bikes around his Chopsaw at the bottom of a set of steep front steps of the largest, steep-roofed building.

Her breath coming out in big, cloudy puffs, Mattea suggests we go exploring. "You never know," she huffs, hooking her helmet over the handlebars of her bike, "maybe there'll be some supplies or weapons or something we can scrounge for our teachers to use back at the Academy."

War agrees, and Matholook and I are just about to start heading up the steps when I come to a dead stop with my boot hovering in the air.

"What is it?" Mattea asks from behind us, fiddling with her lethal pair of bear claws in her hip holsters.

I point to the steps. What I thought was just piles of ice and splinters of wood from the cracked and broken banisters is actually a collection of more human remains.

War squints at the bones and then up the steps at the lodge. "Maybe this isn't such a good idea after all."

"I'm with you," Libra says, taking a giant step back to stand next to our teacher.

As she steps back, Arlo steps forward and pokes at a sheet of ice with the butt-end of his scythe. The ice cracks and falls apart to reveal a human ribcage.

Arlo sweeps aside more of the ice and debris, and we discover that the entire set of steps is covered in human bones and skulls. Most are in pieces. Others are nearly intact. Whatever is left of their fused flesh has been petrified into hard lumps, barely covering distorted slabs of muscle. All of the exposed bones have been bleached white as snow by the sun.

Sara's got one of her typical unreadable expressions plastered across her face, and I can't tell if it's a grimace of disgust or some kind of weird, perverted thrill at seeing a staircase full of ice-encased corpses. She asks War if we should still go up.

He tells her, "Yes. But don't step on the remains. It's disrespectful."

Next to me, Sara mutters, "I don't know about that. It's hard enough to respect the *living*."

Before I can respond and with Matholook sticking close, Arlo slides past me on my other side.

As carefully as he can, he nudges aside the bones to create a narrow pathway up to the landing at the top of the stairs.

War ushers us along ahead of himself and then follows us up.

Climbing the stairs single file like this, with frozen, long-forgotten bodies in piles on either side of us, I feel like Libra was right: The whole world is a graveyard, and we're all walking through it on our way into Hell.

Matholook asks if this is okay, and I tell him the absolute and totally honest truth: "I have no idea."

I breathe a sigh of relief when we reach the top of the stairs. I'm not sure why. It's not like I'm afraid of the dead or believe in ghosts. It's just that ever since Cardyn and Manthy walked into the *Lyfelyte*, I've been thinking about death as less of an ending and more of...I don't know...a process?

Whatever death is, I don't think it's what I thought it was.

Beaming and with her eyes wide, Sara tells us we should definitely go inside, so I don't have time to follow my train of thought about death. Right now, I've got to concentrate on staying alive.

I really want to hold Matholook's hand right now. Or do I want him to hold mine? Either way, it's nice to know I'm not alone in this.

With War in the lead, we climb the steep, icy, corpse-congested stairs. Getting into the lodge is easy enough. It's got two huge doors—thick and carved with all kinds of swirls and decorations—but one of the doors is leaning off of its shattered bronze hinges. The space between is more than enough for us—even War—to squeeze through.

It's Sara who leads the way.

Once we're all inside, War tells us it's okay for us to go exploring. "Just don't go far. And keep the comm-links from your helmets with you. If anything happens to any of you, Wisp'll kill me."

Normally, a teacher the size of a military jeep wouldn't be terrified of our pint-sized principal.

But then again, these aren't exactly normal times, and we're not exactly a normal school.

"Don't worry," Ignacio promises, giving War an energized double-thumbs up. "We'll be careful."

Sara rolls her eyes at Ignacio and shoos him away with a flick of her hand. "'Careful' is just another word for boring."

"And 'careless' is just another word for 'stupid,'" Libra snaps back at her.

Sara glares at Libra and fondles the darts in her bandolier but otherwise doesn't respond.

Mattea breaks the tension by promising War we'll be as careful and as boring as possible.

"That's all I ask," he grumbles. "You have your weapons?"

We all pat our hips, holsters, and bandoliers to confirm that yes—we're all armed and ready for whatever might come our way.

Nodding his approval, War tells us, "Great. Now go and enjoy your field trip."

Libra tugs at my elbow and asks me where we should go first.

The lobby of the lodge is wide and empty with a set of stairs on either side leading up to an open mezzanine level.

"How about up?"

"I'm going with you," Ignacio announces as he joins me, Matholook, and Libra on our way to the stairs.

The four of us climb the left-hand set of stairs while Mattea and Arlo climb the right-hand set.

At the top, Mattea leans over the bannister and calls down through cupped hands to ask War if we can explore the long corridors leading away from the second floor in opposite directions.

War tells us it's okay and that he's going to stay there in the lobby. "That way, you'll know where to find me if anything should happen. Just make sure you stay with someone from your Cohort and don't go wandering off alone." War plops down onto a thick wooden bench, rubs a hand over his bald head, and belts out a tired sigh I can hear from the top of the second-floor stairs.

Behind us, Sara heads toward a door off to the side of the broken remains of a counter and slips away to go exploring by herself.

War raises a hand and looks like he's about to call out to her to tell her to come back or else stay with one of us, but she looks back over her shoulder at him, and he doesn't say anything.

It's not my place to supervise her, so I return my attention to my own little group of adventurers.

Most of the rooms Libra, Ignacio, Matholook, and I poke our heads into are filled with smashed furniture, huge shards of glass from the tall window frames, and sloping drifts of snow pressed up against the walls.

When we get to a room with a door that won't open, Ignacio rubs his hands together and tells the rest of us to step back.

He rams his shoulder into the door and bounces back ten feet, flailing his arms, tripping over some torn carpeting, and crash-lands on his backside.

Libra and I laugh until we cry. Even Matholook feigns a cough to cover his amused chuckle.

"I don't care how much you go to the gym," Libra giggles to Ignacio. "You're *never* going to be Terk." She makes an exaggerated show of wiping tears from her eyes before telling him, "Here. Let me."

She steps forward and slides her sixteen-pound hickory-handled sledgehammer from the holster strapped to her back.

Even though she's not much bigger than me, she's got some kind of weird Emergent strength she's able to channel into the long-handled hammer.

With her knuckles going chalky white from her death-grip

on the handle, she swings her hammer down in a swooping arc, smashing it against the door's thick silver doorknob. The knob smashes off, clattering with a loud clang to the exposed wooden part of the floor. Libra pushes the door open, and the three of us step into the room.

Like the stairs leading up to the lodge, this room is filled with skeletal remains of human bodies. These are seated with their backs to three of the room's four walls.

Libra surveys the scene. "I think they tried to hide in here."

The entire outer wall is missing, and the wind whips around us in a vortex of stinging ice and debris. The interior walls behind the bodies are charcoal black.

"Those are plasma burns," I tell the others. "From Assault Drones."

Matholook says, "Assault Drones" out loud, but I don't think he realizes it.

"I don't know what's worse," Ignacio says. "Getting killed by drones or wiped out in person."

"That's the thing about being in Hell," Matholook mutters. "It's *all* worse."

Libra tugs the sleeve of my jacket. "Come on, Branwynne. It's creepy in here. Let's keep going."

"Why not?" I agree. "Can't get any worse, right?"

33

CONFIDE

OUT IN THE HALL, Ignacio asks Matholook if he's up for some adventure.

Matholook shrugs and looks at me like I'm supposed to give him permission or something.

I tell him, "When in Rome..."

That makes Matholook laugh, Libra frown, and Ignacio stare at me like I've just started speaking an alien language.

"Go on," I snicker. "Go have fun with your little friend."

Ignacio chortles a buoyant, "Yes!" He grabs Matholook by the shoulder of his jacket and pretty much drags him along as the two boys sprint down the long corridor.

Up ahead and with his shillelaghs in hand, Ignacio leans his head into room after room, calling out, "All clear!" to us, until he's so far down the hall we can barely hear him anymore.

Matholook gives me and Libra a helpless shrug and scampers along to keep up with Ignacio, who is now in full-on rambunctious schoolboy mode.

After offering up matching eyerolls, Libra and I walk along after them, investigating the place as we go.

Most of the doors are either missing or else off their hinges, with drifts of dirty snow sloping out into the hallway.

It's cold enough in here so we can see our breath, and the wind rippling through the place makes a ghostly kind of wail.

Cupping his hands around his mouth, Ignacio—apparently immune to the eeriness of the abandoned lodge—shouts for us to hurry up and starts climbing a set of carpeted stairs leading up to the next level with Matholook still padding along after him.

"They're going to get lost," I tell Libra with a resigned sigh.

She mutters, "Probably" and then tugs the sleeve of my jacket again and tilts her chin forward toward the staircase up ahead. "So...what's up with you and Matholook, anyway?"

"What do you mean?"

"You know what I mean."

"Nothing's up. We're friends."

"Friends don't risk their lives to join each other in the enemy's camp."

"Maybe that's *exactly* what friends do."

Libra stops to take a half-step into one of the rooms Ignacio and Matholook have already inspected and tells me there's nothing in there but overturned furniture. "I hear Trax is jealous," she mumbles as we continue down the corridor.

"Why would he be jealous?"

"Well, you *did* go on a date with him."

"That was months ago. And it wasn't a date. We talked for a while up on the roof. I've hardly spoken to him since then."

"And you think the fact that you *haven't* talked to him helps?"

"I don't think about it at all."

"Maybe you should. I mean, you pretty much ignore Trax—who has a serious crush on you, by the way. And you risked getting kicked out of the Academy to be with someone else. And then you bring that someone else back to school with you."

Libra shakes her head and makes a "tsk, tsk" noise that makes me want to smack her.

Is making up rumors and stirring up trouble an Emergent ability I don't know about? If so, Libra is definitely the Kress of gossip.

"Look," I tell her at last, "I have enough trouble keeping tabs on my own feelings. I don't have time to worry about Trax's."

"So you *do* have feelings for Matholook?"

"No. I have a connection with him."

"Maybe that's exactly what feelings are."

"You're a cheeky little git, aren't you?"

"I'm your friend. And friends are allowed to know each other's business. Fracking hell...it's practically a requirement!"

"You seem to know a lot about relationships. For someone who's spent most of her life in a Spanish Processor."

I want to swallow those words back down even as they're escaping from my mouth. We don't talk much about the fact that so many of the students here spent their lives imprisoned in research labs. In fact, almost every student at the Academy has been captured and tested on by either the Deenays or the En-Gene-eers and eventually freed by Kress and her Conspiracy. Other than being Emergents, it's one of the few things most of the students have in common.

It's kind of a sensitive subject. Fortunately, Libra doesn't seem to be offended.

"War is my mentor," she reminds me. "He lived in Chicago before, during, and after the Atomic Wars."

"And he's been giving you advice on relationships?"

"Sure. Doesn't Kress talk to you about stuff like that?"

"No. Not really. Haida Gwaii sometimes does."

"Wait. So you're getting your dating advice from a bird?"

"No."

"Ha! I think 'Yes.' You've got advice from the birds. Now, you just need the bees."

"Not funny."

"If Kress doesn't talk about relationships, what do you do for your Apprenticeship sessions?"

"Practical stuff. She mostly teaches me how to use my abilities better, how to improve my use of my Serpent Blades, how to be a proper Ravenmaster...things like that."

"How boring. Talking about relationships is so much more interesting, don't you think?"

I lie and tell her, "No." A few days ago, before I spent that time with Matholook, it wouldn't have been a lie. Now...now, I'm not so sure.

And I *hate* being not so sure about anything.

"So what's going to happen with you and Matholook?" she asks, and I swear her eyes sparkle as she gives me a light elbow to the ribs.

"If I knew how to predict the future, I'd be the most powerful Emergent in the Academy. But I don't. So I'm not."

We start up the stairs at the end of the hall, and I'm thinking that'll be the end of Libra's little interrogation. But I'm wrong.

"So....," she asks, "have you kissed him?"

"We've been...talking."

"That's not an answer."

"It's all the answer you're going to get. For now, at least. Besides, Haida Gwaii helped connect me with him, but she hasn't exactly signed off on him as an ally."

"He's really good looking, isn't he? The muscles. Those eyes..."

"I hadn't noticed."

I think Libra's own dark eyes might pop right out of her head when she flicks them toward me and answers with a sarcastic and annoyingly drawn out, "Riiiight."

"He's a Caretaker," I explain. "It's one of their most important

Guilds. They look out for everyone. They're empathetic. He's got a strong protective instinct. I like that."

"The girl you told us about...the one you saved..."

"Gwernna."

"He was taking care of her?"

"Yeah."

"Hey. Can she really bring people back from the dead?"

"I don't know. I spent a grand total of about an hour with her. Anyway, I doubt it."

At the top of the next flight of stairs, we enter another hallway. This one is wider than the one on the floor below. Parts of the roof are missing or buckled in. The walls are coated in an ugly pattern of green and red wallpaper with little white anchors running up and down in vertical columns.

It's not fair. Of all the things that have been destroyed, of all the people who have violently and needlessly died, this wallpaper has managed to survive?

"Where'd Ignacio and Matholook get to?" I ask.

Libra points to the double set of fresh boot prints in the drifts of dirt and snow covering the floor. "They went this way."

She mutters something about Ignacio being too impulsive for his own good, and I snap around to face her when she stops mid-sentence.

Directing my attention to one of the rooms next to us, she points to two bodies—a man and a woman, I think—that are lying in a half-frozen, half-decayed tangle just inside one of the doorways. "At least they died together."

I really want to argue with her right now and tell her dying alone or dying together doesn't matter. It's all the same death. But my brain is on overload from thoughts about what role Matholook, Gwernna, and I could possibly have to play in Epic's contrived war. Plus, this stupid wallpaper isn't helping.

So I push forward, and Libra follows me along as we

continue on and the long, carpeted hallway curves around a corner.

Up ahead, Ignacio, with Matholook right behind him, leaps out of one of the rooms.

Waving frantically, Ignacio shouts back to us. "Get over here!"

Libra and I exchange a look before I call up to him, asking what he's on about.

Stabbing with his thumb back toward the room the two boys just jumped out of, he whisper-shouts, "There's somebody in there!"

34

COUPLE

SHOULDER TO SHOULDER, Libra and I sprint the rest of the way down the hallway. Leaping over piles of rubble and skirting around holes in the floor, we slide to a stop in front of Ignacio and Matholook. The boys' eyes are supper-plate wide as Ignacio clamps his hands onto our shoulders and steers us into the room.

"Look!"

I don't know what they expect us to see, but whoever or whatever is in here, I'm not too happy about Ignacio using me and Libra as his personal human shields.

He points deeper into the room and says, "See?"

The space is big, almost as spacious as our Lounge back at the Academy.

Except for a few wood-framed armchairs with soot-covered cushions, the furniture seems to have been chopped up and stacked into neat piles of pieces of frames and fabric along one wall.

A clunky metal box—maybe an old radio of some kind—sits on a small steel scaffold near what's left of a splintered window frame. The dented box has a glossy sphere on top and a mess of coils and colored wires pouring out of it in all directions like an octopus someone pulled inside out.

The slanted windows above are mostly boarded up, but with gaps in between. A million tiny specks dance in the beams of light streaming down into the room.

On the far side of the room is a chest-high marble countertop with a dozen leather-topped bar stools lined up in front of it. Behind the counter is a wall of empty, broken shelves and a giant, dirt-encrusted mirror with a thick gold frame.

Despite the dust and snow coating most of the room's surfaces, the top of the marble bar is green and polished to a high shine.

I shrug myself out from under Ignacio's grip. "What are we supposed to see, exactly?"

He shouts out toward the counter. "It's okay. You can come out!"

Libra and I exchange a glance.

"There's someone back there," Ignacio hisses at us. "I swear!"

"There really was someone there," Matholook confirms. I smile to myself as he takes a half-step over and tucks himself behind me. As a Caretaker in the Cult of the Devoted, he specializes in things like empathy, planning, conversation, and kindness. Combat is more my thing, and it's nice to know he knows it.

Stepping forward, Libra slides her hammer out of its holster. I take out my twin Serpent Blades, but Ignacio shakes his head and puts up a hand to stop us from doing anything more.

"Wait a second," he whispers. "We're not going to hurt you," he calls out in the direction of the bar.

I'm about to suggest to Libra that maybe our friend is losing his mind when two shaggy-haired heads rise up slowly from behind the long marble-green counter.

With totally inappropriate delight, Ignacio points and says, "See!"

With their hands in the air, a middle-aged man and woman take us in through terrified eyes. Their lips are chapped, and their skin is leathery and raw.

The man's grizzled, stubbled jaw twitches. His facial hair is patchy and different lengths, like he's been trimming his beard himself. With a chainsaw.

Nearly as unkempt, it's the woman who squeaks out a quivering, "Are you from the Patriot Army?"

With vigorous head shakes, the four of us assure her that we're not.

"We're from...a school," I tell them.

The woman gives us a burning squint of doubt, and her hands lower a few inches. "A school?"

"Not too far from here. Who are you? What are you doing here?"

The man's shoulders slump a little, and at least some of the terror drains from his eyes. His faded black peacoat is oversized and crusty with splotches of dirt. "We're surviving. Like you, I suspect."

The woman's pleading eyes lock onto mine, and I nod, giving her the okay to put her hands down and come out from behind the counter.

Cinching up the thick tie on her shabby blue bathrobe, she does, and the man follows close behind her.

Noticing the large kitchen knife tucked into the belt of the man's coat, Ignacio steps forward and tells him to leave it on the counter.

When the man hesitates, I tell him it's okay. "You can keep it on you. If it'll make you more comfortable."

"It would."

Next to me, Libra grabs my wrist and says, "Um...Bran-wynne. Are you sure—?"

"It's okay," I tell her as I beckon the couple forward. "It's bad enough being scared. Feeling helpless on top of that...well, we've all had a taste of that, and I don't think any of us liked it all that much."

The man smiles at this and thanks me. But he still slips the knife out and plants it with a clattering thunk on the counter. "A gesture of good faith," he says.

Returning the favor, I holster my twin Serpent Blades and gesture for Libra and Ignacio to put their weapons away as well.

After a quick grumble, they both comply. Matholook mouths a quiet, curled-lip "are-you-sure?" at me.

"Take it easy," I whisper.

"There are more of us," Libra tells the couple. "Three more of us in this building. And our teacher is downstairs."

"We didn't know anyone was living here," Ignacio tells them. And then adds with a hard swallow, "From what we saw outside, we didn't figure anyone around here was even alive."

"It's not exactly the safe haven we thought it'd be," the man complains. "But safe enough, I guess."

"So you're really from a school?" the woman beams, her hand over her heart.

"Yes."

"I used to be a teacher, myself. My name is Connie. This is Darren."

"And you were both teachers?"

"Not me," Darren says with a grim chuckle. "I was one of the janitors here at the resort. Connie was here on vacation."

"With a bunch of my girlfriends," she elaborates. "It was supposed to be a bachelorette party. I was the only one who—"

"That was a long time ago," Darren interrupts, a gentle hand on Connie's arm. "When the drones attacked, nearly everyone was killed. It's a big building. There were a lot of people. We all thought we could hide here."

Connie puts her hand on Darren's and says, "It wasn't," as Darren nods and explains.

"The Patrol Drones stayed here for months. By the time they finally left, we were too scared to leave, so we stayed here and did the best we could with the supplies we had."

Darren and Connie exchange a look. Connie asks if they can trust us. I assure her they can.

"Because if this is a trick...," she says.

"It's not," I tell her. "We really are students from an Academy."

I don't tell her about the Emergents part. Baby steps, after all.

It's Ignacio who breaks the stiff silence that follows. "We'd better take them to War."

At the exact same time, Darren and Connie shriek, "What!?" and take a giant step back.

"'War' is the name of our teacher," Ignacio explains with a laugh.

I'm suppressing a laugh of my own. I half-expect their eyes to come leaping out of their heads and to go rolling around on the floor like marbles.

"Follow us," Libra instructs. "It'll be okay."

Darren and Connie lean in for a whispered consultation. When they emerge, Connie tells us, "Okay. We'll go with you."

On the way down the stairs, I tap my comm-link and tell War we're on our way back to the lobby. "With company."

War's voice crackles in my ear. "Company?" Even over short distances, communication devices like these are subject to all kind of distortions, and I have to strain to hear.

"Two people," I explain.

"Alive?"

"They sure seem to be."

"I'll round up the others. Just get down here. And Branwynne..."

"Yeah?"

"Be careful."

"Why start now?"

I can't tell if War's response is a laugh or a growl or if the sound I hear is just a storm of static, so I say, "We're on our way" and sign off.

If there are others here, could this be a trap? Could these two be the bait?

With the man and woman in tow, we take a brisk walk all the way back downstairs to the lobby. I'm expecting to get attacked the entire way, but we make it back to where War—with Mattea, Sara, and Arlo gathered up and hovering around him—looms large in the snow and soot-covered lobby.

"This is War," I tell our mystery couple. "Our teacher."

"It's nice to meet you," Connie says, craning her neck to look up at War and then scoping him out top to bottom and side to side. "Hell, it's nice to meet *anyone*."

"How long have you been here?"

"I'm not sure," she says with a light-hearted scratch of her head. "What year is it?"

"What *year*?"

"It's 2048," Sara offers.

Darren and Connie stare at her and then back at each other.

Darren snorts up a skeptical laugh. "We've been here for seven years?"

"I guess so," War says.

"We lost track of time early on. After a while, we just stopped thinking about it."

"This has been our life. We resigned ourselves to that fact."

"That's probably what's kept us alive."

"And sane."

"What's happening? You know—out in the world."

We explain about the Eastern Order. The couple laughs, but it's a haunting laugh, not a happy one.

"We used to debate about whether this whole thing was a hoax," Connie tells us, wagging her thumb back and forth between her and Darren. "After all, we just saw drones. We never saw an actual enemy."

"That's the terrifying beauty of what Krug accomplished," War explains. "He was a fool. But he knew one thing for sure: If you keep people afraid, fear itself becomes the enemy. And it's an enemy as real as any army."

"We heard another rumor," Connie says, her voice going quiet and unsteady.

"There are a lot of those going around," War tells her.

"Enhanced people," Connie says flatly, her eyes skipping around from one of us to the next. "Government programs to create super soldiers. Some people said they were the reason for all of this."

Darren scowls and smacks a fist into his palm. "Some people said this wasn't a war. It was a genocide. An extermination. An attempt to get rid of people like us in favor of these..."

He glances over at Connie who says, "Techno-genetically Enhanced."

"Right. Enhanced. Kids who can kill with a snap of their fingers."

Impulsive as ever, Ignacio stomps his foot and hisses, "That's a lie. And we're called Emergents."

I can't tell if Connie and Darren are skeptical or scared. Either way, War drags Ignacio back by the collar of his jacket and apologizes to the couple. "They're Emergents," he tells them. "And most of them do have certain abilities. But they didn't start the war. In fact, it was their teachers back at the Academy who killed Krug and ended it."

"Wait! Krug's dead?"

"I saw him die with my own eyes," War assures them. "He got knocked off a building and splattered to the pavement in a wonderful puddle of human soup."

Connie and Darren are quiet for a long time. Their eyes are bouncing around the room, and I'm pretty sure I can smell smoke billowing from their churning brains.

"So it's true?" Connie asks. She's addressing War, but her eyes are locked onto Darren's.

"It's true," War says.

"And the thing about the...Emergents?"

War signals to Arlo who slips his scythe from over his shoulder as he steps forward.

Standing in front of the stunned, shabby couple, Arlo pushes up his jacket sleeve and slides the razor end of his scythe across his forearm. Connie's and Darren's mouths hang open in identical, perfectly round circles of shock. Then they're doubly shocked when Arlo grins, and the cut heals almost instantly before their eyes, leaving only a raised, red ridge.

Darren clears his throat. "That's, um...quite the trick."

"No trick," War assures him. "It's just who they are."

Darren starts to say, "We have to tell—" to Connie, but she cuts him off with a hard, clamp-jawed stare.

"It's not just the two of you, is it?" I ask.

Connie takes and holds onto a deep breath. "No," she confesses. "There are more of us living here."

35

LEFTOVERS

"THIRTY-THREE MORE OF US," Darren clarifies, dipping his chin toward the floor. "Downstairs. Basement level."

I don't think Connie and Darren notice, but at the same time, War's hand hovers over his gun, and the rest of us each make a subtle move toward our own weapons.

It's War, though, who comes to his senses first and orders us to stand down. He doesn't bark the order, though. He says it under his breath, but with the strength and soft control of a muffled canon.

As Connie and Darren look on, horrified at what might become of their confession, the rest of us, on War's orders, ease our hands away from our weapons.

"Where?" War grumbles to the quivering duo in front of us. "Where exactly are these other thirty-three survivors of yours?"

Darren offers up a timid, pathetic smile. "We can take you."

Accepting the offer, War says, "I think you'd better."

"Is this really such a good idea?" Matholook whispers to me, his mouth close enough to my ear for me to feel his breath on my cheek.

"War knows what he's doing," I whisper back.

War, I really hope you know what you're doing!

Visibly trembling, Connie and Darren lead us out of the room. Mattea and Ignacio seem to want to dart after them, but War steps in front of them. "Stay behind me," he cautions over his shoulder.

In a snaking queue now, we follow Connie and Darren down two flights of stairs, and into a long, bleak hallway. The air is sooty and damp. A musty funk of body odor and decay hang down in a thick fog, and I have to choke back a cough. What's left of what was once a carpet is worn down to nearly nothing. Parts of the exposed concrete sub-floor are wet with cultures of grey-green mold. With no windows down here, the corridor has the warmth and charm of a crypt.

It's times like this when I'm perfectly happy to have War running point in front of us, his hulking body serving as a protective barrier between us and whatever we're about to stumble into.

Or get *led* into.

Matholook's shoulder brushes against mine, and I smile because I know it's not an accident.

What is it about people being terrified that makes us want to hold onto someone?

Following Connie and Darren, we navigate the long hallway of cracked floors, crumbling walls, and stale air.

Waiting for us at the end of the corridor is an oversized wooden door, reinforced with hammered-on strips of flat, rusted steel. Darren takes a finger-sized black key out of his hip pocket. His hands trembling, he apologizes over his shoulder to War before finally settling himself down enough to turn the key and unlock the door. The tumbler falls with a heavy clank, and the door inches open.

Pushing the door open the rest of the way, Darren mumbles a second apology, this time for the smell.

"We didn't survive well," Connie confesses through a little sob and with her eyes glossy with tears. "But we survived."

War plants a monstrous hand on Ignacio's chest. "Stay behind me."

Following Darren, War steps into the large dark room with the rest of us inching along tentatively behind him.

Libra latches onto my arm. She doesn't say anything. She doesn't have to. If this is a trap…

Telling us she's going to turn on the lights, Connie slips off to the side. "We've gotten used to hiding," she explains, her voice ringing through the dark in a hollow, ghostly echo. "When we heard noises in the distance, Darren and I went upstairs. Our surveillance station is in the bar. That's where we were when you found us."

There's just enough light for me to see her as she scans her hand over an input panel of cracked black glass in the wall. A bank of white-hot holo-lights flickers, fails, flickers again, and finally blasts on, illuminating the room and killing every shadow in sight.

I squint against the sudden burst of light. Libra squeezes my arm hard, and I feel Mattea and Ignacio on either side of me take a giant step back. Even Sara lets out a little gasp.

Instead of the trap or the platoon of armed enemies I'm expecting, we find ourselves face to face with a room full of tired and haggard people of all ages. There are young girls and boys dressed in the tattered, puffy remains of what must have been snow suits at one point. There are teenagers, slump-shouldered and crusty-eyed, staring at us from behind a wall of older men and women, all shaggy-haired and dressed in an assortment of faded, dingy clothes that are about two days away from dissolving into wisps of grimy threads.

Back at the Academy, we've all seen clips from movies about a so-called "Zombie Apocalypse." Thanks to the Auditor—the techno-consciousness attached to Terk and the only real means we have to access the scraps of the country's fragmented digital network—we've been able to watch at least bits and pieces of some of those old films. We always laughed about the idea of the dead rising from the grave with nothing better to do than kill people who are just going to come back from the dead, themselves. War and Mayla assured us that those movies were genuinely scary "back in the day." Personally, we never saw why. "Who needs zombies, anyway?" Mattea once quipped. "Isn't the apocalypse bad enough all by itself?"

But here, standing face to face with thirty-three malnourished survivors in the basement of a long-dead ski lodge, I feel like maybe we were a little too quick and cavalier in our mocking dismissal of the concept of zombies. I've never met a zombie before, but *this*...this mud-crusted, vacant-eyed horde is pretty bloody close.

I take a quick look around, half-expecting to see a wall of weapons or a secret door with a few dozen assassins behind it.

But there's none of that.

There's not even much furniture in the room, just a couple of ratty couches and a few nonfunctioning mag-chairs sitting on top of jury-rigged and rusted bases.

The younger kids who are cowering on the floor snap to their feet at the sight of us and shuffle up behind the older kids and the adults.

"This is what's left of us," Connie explains.

A dark-skinned old man with small eyeglasses and a bristly gray beard steps forward and extends a hand to War. Like the rest of us, War is stunned into open-mouthed silence, and I don't think he even realizes he's shaking the man's hand.

Putting his other hand on top of War's, the old man continues double-pumping War's hand while smiling up at him through tiny rheumy eyes that are barely visible behind his cracked, dirty glasses and the creases and pouches of loose skin covering his face.

His face may be a mess of leathery wrinkles, but the rest of his skin—from his exposed arms under his blood and mud-caked tank top to his spindly legs sticking out from under a pair of ancient cut-off khakis—is dark and glossy as a jar of ink.

"Well...?" Connie asks.

At first, I don't know who she's talking to, but the old man finally ends his handshake, drops his arms to his sides, and looks over at her. His jaw moves a bunch of times like he's not used to speaking. "Authentic." The word comes out in three sharp little pieces, as if his mouth was full of chips of cement. The old man surveys us once and then a second time, his beady eyes lingering for an extra second on mine. This time, his voice comes a little quicker and a little smoother. "They're all authentic."

"Authentic?" Mattea asks from behind War's bulky shoulder.

Connie laughs loud enough to startle us all into a communal jump. "You're not the only Emergents around."

"Emergents?" I ask. "What do you mean?"

"We weren't being entirely honest with you upstairs. We know about Emergents."

"We just needed to know what...*who* we were dealing with," Darren explains, his eyes soft with apology.

"This is Malik Enam," Connie says. "We call him 'Papa Ghana.' He has a very unique ability."

"And a very handy one," Darren adds.

"Ability?" War asks.

Connie and Darren nod in unison, but it's Connie who answers. "He can tell if someone is friend or foe. And he's never wrong. Even if it sometimes takes a while for the person to prove themselves, one way or another."

Taking a step forward and finally letting go of my arm, Libra says, "He's really an Emergent?"

"Or he's just highly intuitive," Connie concedes. "Either way, Papa Ghana has helped keep us alive and together for a long time now."

"Those bodies you saw outside..." Darren explains. "Not all of them started out as enemies. Thanks to Papa Ghana, though, we were able to determine which ones wanted us alive..."

"And which ones didn't," Connie finishes.

They decided the fate of those people based on the vague ability of a suspected Emergent? What kind of training did this man have? How does he know the extent of his abilities? How could he possibly know who to kill and who to spare? And what if he was wrong?

"So, you see," Connie beams, "we're actually no strangers to people like you."

The crowd behind her starts to inch forward. The younger kids seem especially interested in War. And who can blame them? To an eight-year-old, he's a bald, walking, talking grizzly bear.

Sara nudges her way past me, and I'm about to get annoyed, but she slips in front of War and asks Papa Ghana out loud exactly what I was just wondering in my head.

"How do you do it?" she asks. "How do you *know*?"

At seventeen-years-old, Sara exudes a glow and a level of health, confidence, and strength that seem somehow out of place, almost disrespectful in the middle of the cavernous room full of suffering and sorrow.

Papa Ghana, though, takes her inquiry in stride. Pressing his palms together, he lets his eyes wander up toward the ceiling. "I apologize for my mistakes," he mumbles through an oddly solemn smile. "The lives that were theirs should never be lost on account of the mistakes that are mine."

"Picking who lives and who dies isn't a 'mistake,'" Sara says, her hands clenched into tight fists on her hips. "It's a *choice*."

War has his hand on the collar of Sara's jacket and is hauling her backwards almost before the last of the words are out of her mouth. "Please forgive my student," War apologizes to the old man. "She's seen and been through too much for someone so young."

"That's the nice thing about youth," Papa Ghana says through that weird grin of his. "You grow out of it."

That gets a cackling laugh out of the teenagers clustered behind him, and a "You can say that again" guffaw from War.

"You should come with us!" Libra beams. "All of you!" But then she turns a funny shade of red and turns to War. "It's okay, right?"

"He's like us," Mattea agrees, her eyes locked onto Papa Ghana's. "Maybe some of the others are, too."

"We get trained in combat, weapons, everything," Ignacio boasts to the younger members of this clan of survivors. He's answered with a buzz of "Really?" and "Can we go with them?" as the smaller kids tug on the shirtsleeves of whichever adult is closest.

Before War can answer, from somewhere outside and up above, an explosion rocks the room and everyone in it.

36

DRONES

A BLAST of dust rains down on us, covering us with what feels like six inches of ashes and soot.

War's thick bellow of, "Follow me!" rumbles hard enough for me to feel the vibrations of his voice in my bones.

He thunders out of the room and storms up the stairs, taking them three at a time. I bolt after him, with Matholook and the rest of my Asylum dashing up after me.

Halfway up the next flight, another concussive blast rattles the building, sending all of us staggering and slamming into the walls. Arlo and I both stumble and nearly slip down the stairs, but Matholook snags each of us by the wrist and keeps us from falling and cracking our skulls open.

Coughing through a dark swirl of dust, War checks to make sure we're all okay and yells for Matholook to stay downstairs before gathering himself and continuing his thumping run up the stairs. Matholook seems conflicted, but he says, "I'm coming with you," and I don't have time to debate or argue.

With the rest of us hot on his heels, War charges through the lobby where we first entered the building and bursts out onto the wide front porch and into the crisp, cold air.

Outside, we're greeted by a hovering fleet of military Assault Drones, and a small squad of soldiers in pollen-colored body armor. Unlike the weapons I saw back in the compound of the Devoted, these ten men and two women are armed with state-of-the-art stun-sticks and lethal projectile plasma blasters.

Connie and Darren have followed us outside, and War screams at them to get the hell back into the lodge. "You, too!" he bellows to Matholook, who answers with a stubborn head shake. The three of them stand there in the doorway, frozen for a full second, but War breaks them out of their trance by swiping at them with his hand hard enough to knock them out of the doorway and back into the building.

Whipping back around to scan the double phalanx of human and mechanical attackers, I'm horrified, and I can feel every member of my Asylum take a mutual gulp and a full step back as the drones arrange themselves in a hovering arc twenty feet in the air. Not much bigger than a bottle of wine, the drones tilt and bank in the air as their gyrostabilizers emit water-like ripples and an otherworldly hum in the air around them.

The twelve soldiers slip into an arc of their own in the shadows cast by the drones in the mud and snow.

One of the soldiers steps forward, his plasma rifle pointed up the stairs and straight at War's broad chest.

"You're not going to take these people," War thunders down, squaring himself up to form a barrier between the lodge door and the slowly advancing double crescent of soldiers and drones.

"That's not the plan," the soldier grins from behind his glassy, semi-transparent face shield.

"Good," War smiles down at him. "Then you can be on your way, and we can be on ours, and you can leave these people in peace."

The man makes a stabbing motion with his rifle in my direction. "We're not here for them. We're not here for you. We're here for *her*."

War slides over to stand directly in front of me. If I thought he was big before...well...projecting an eclipse of a shadow over me now, he seems absolutely *planet sized*. He drops one hand down, his palm toward me. "Stay back, Branwynne."

I know he's trying to take care of me. It's his job. He's my teacher and a battle-tested member of Kress's extended Conspiracy. I haven't heard all the stories about his past, but I know enough. I know he's a relentless warrior, stronger than any six random powerlifters, and fiercely—bordering on *insanely*—overprotective when it comes to using his off-the-charts strength in defense of the ones he's been charged to look after.

The only problem is this: I don't need a defender.

Because I am one.

Sliding under his arm, I surge forward, catapulting myself off the top steps, my Serpent Blades clamped in each hand. I'm through the air and landing with my knee on the lead soldier's chest before anyone—even the floating, poised, and combat-primed drones—have time to react.

I bury one of my blades six inches deep in the man's neck. His blood is already spattering over the Emergents crest on my armored riding kit before the drones fire their first volley.

Not that I'm worried. It doesn't take a genius (and it's a good thing because I'm not one) to figure out what's going on: These are Epic's soldiers. The Sentinels from Sanctum. I recognize their uniforms, weapons, and even the color of their gear from my short time being held captive in their underground lab. How Epic got his hands on a fleet of Assault Drones...well, I don't know the answer to that, and I definitely don't care. What matters more than anything is this: They want me alive.

Big mistake.

I've already slung my second Serpent Blade in a spiraling arc toward the next soldier in the squad, and it's just passing under his visor and though his carotid artery by the time the rest of my Asylum springs down the corpse-covered stairs into very efficient, very deadly action.

In a marvie flash of silvery steel, Libra's sledgehammer strikes one of the women in her armored chest-plate. With a splintering crunch I can hear from here, the Kevlar buckles and her ribcage cracks and collapses under the weight of the hammer's head, and the woman slams back into one of her fellow soldiers.

In the same instant, six of Sara's deadly darts whip past my ear in rapid fire succession like an attacking swarm of angry wasps. Three of the flashing barbs glance off the body armor of one of the shorter soldiers in front of me. But one of the darts lodges into the back of his hand. One sticks into the tough fabric covering his upper arm. The other burrows shaft-deep into the small area of his exposed throat between his visor and his chest-plate. With a gurgled shriek, he drops to his knees, clawing and fumbling in an anguished effort to tug the needle end of the dart out of the soft hollow of his neck.

The drones overhead have started firing, and I risk a quick glance back up the stairs to see that Matholook—an unarmed Typic—is trying to shove past War and enter the fray.

War clamps his fingers onto the collar of Matholook's jacket, lifts him clean off his feet, and slings him down behind the thick balustrade lining the lodge's front porch.

"Stay down!" War orders.

With Matholook safe, War leaps behind a thick wooden column at the top of the stairs and lays down return fire of his own in the general direction of the drones.

For all his knowledge and size, one thing he's *not* is a sharpshooter. His bullets spray out in a nearly random barrage, but I guess it works perfectly fine as cover fire. At the very least, he's distracting the drones and the soldiers and pulling some of their attention away from us.

Taking full advantage of the sudden onslaught of chaos and the instant disorientation of the surprised soldiers, Mattea unsheathes her bear claws and dives fist-first into the battle.

Deadly as a mountain predator, she unleashes a salvo of deep slashes onto the nearest soldiers. With her fists clamped to the hard black handles of her two sets of razor-sharp hooks, she whirls in a spectacular dance through the enemy ranks, the curved fangs of her steel claws gouging deep, bloody wounds through the gaps in the soldiers' armor.

Not as fast but just as deadly, Ignacio wades into the battle. He swings his twin shillelaghs in a pair of whirling helicopter-blade blurs. The impact of the steel-core of the wooden shafts pings and clangs off the soldiers' armor. He's not doing Mattea-level damage, but he's definitely getting the job done.

Unprepared, unequipped, and clearly untrained in close-quarters combat, several of the soldiers drop to their knees or else crumble to the ground outright, succumbing with agonizing screams to Ignacio's bone-breaking strikes. In a single motion, he strikes the other woman in the back of the neck. The snap of his combat sticks against the bones at the base of her skull is loud enough to be heard over the pumping blasts from War's rifle. With that motion melding into the next, Ignacio slides his second shillelagh under the chin of one of the male soldiers. With his fist on one end of the shaft and the crook of his elbow hooked under the other end, he pulls hard. The man's eyes roll back, and he coughs up a thick spray of bubbly white foam before Ignacio drops him to the ground and moves on to the next opponent.

Oh, frack. He's been practicing!

From a defeated crouch, the first female soldier manages to draw a stun-stick from its holster. She thrusts it at me, and the crackling blue tip of the weapon sends a lightning strike of pain through every muscle in my leg.

Squealing and feeling myself go numb from the hip down, I stagger back, but I don't fall. Instead, I drop into Arlo's waiting arms.

"You okay?" he calls out, his voice dark and deadly from deep under his hood.

I pant out a "Yeah. I'll be okay" lie even as my tongue feels like it's been slathered in battery acid.

Overhead, the drones must have been given an extermination signal because they rain down a flurry of so-called "lava pellets" that sizzle and scorch the ground all around us. They're not trying to capture us. They're trying to kill us.

Ensuring that I'm still alive and steady enough to stand, Arlo dodges a volley from the drones and swings his long-handled scythe, the curved blade slicing in a beautiful silver arc—not just through the air, but also through the thick tendons in the neck of one of the kneeling soldiers.

Holy frack! He just saved my life! Got to remember to thank him for that...

Up on the porch at the top of the stairs, War continues to blast out rounds of cover fire. It's not much, but it's enough to disorient the rest of the soldiers and distract the drones.

The remaining soldiers are trying to regroup, and I'm starting to worry. We're not as outnumbered anymore, but we're still radically outgunned, *and* we're being attacked from the ground and the air at the same time.

You can do this, Branwynne.

I'm trying to shake off the numbness tingling through my leg and hip and am just about to charge back into battle when Arlo and Ignacio step in front of me.

Calling out for the rest of us to get behind him, Arlo swings his scythe in a single, overhead arc. Before our eyes, the air seems to swirl and solidify into a kind of thick, humid cloud.

Dropping to a knee next to him, Ignacio plants one palm to the ground and raises his other hand up, fingers spread wide, in the direction of the overhead drones.

His golden-amber eyes turn crackling blue, and a white web of electric sparks sizzles in the air, leaping its way through each of the drones.

From within the bubble of warm air cast by Arlo, we look out to see the soldiers fighting to move while the drones plink down out of the sky or go spiraling off into the nearby woods. One of the spasming, out of control drones dive-bombs its way right at War, who flips his rifle backwards and swings it baseball bat style at the sputtering machine, whacking it a hundred feet through the air. It skids to a dead stop right near my feet.

With the drones out of commission, the rest of the soldiers have apparently decided that this mission isn't for them, and they bolt away from us, tearing off toward the woods like terrified bunnies.

37

RETURN

THE FIELD outside the lodge is swirling in a smoky vortex of puffy particles of snow and ash.

In a flash, the remaining soldiers start sprint-limping their way over to the tree line where they clamber up onto their armored snowmobiles and go grinding off into the distance.

"We should go after them!" Mattea cries, but War holds her back.

"No. They're headed back to Sanctum. And no telling how many reinforcements they might already have up here or that might be on their way. But don't worry. I'm pretty sure we'll run into them again." War grins down at Mattea, his meaty hand resting heavily on her shoulder. "Soon." Swinging around to the rest of us, he promises we'll get more fighting than we can possibly hope for.

I don't know. I smile to myself. *I have pretty high hopes.*

"That was quite the display," War rumbles through a complimentary laugh. "Looks like some Emergents have been paying attention in their combat skills classes." With a slow pivot, War lets his eyes land on Arlo and Ignacio. "What did the two of you do, exactly?"

Ignacio jabs a playful elbow into Arlo's side. "Just a little something we've been working on in our spare time."

Where the frack did those two find spare time?

"Well," War beams, "if what you just dished out here today is a taste of what's to come, I don't envy Epic or anyone else who risks taking you on."

Exhausted but happy to be alive and with the glory of the moment slowly settling down on us, we share a hearty round of laughter and a whole spate of high-fives, handshakes, and pats on the back.

Matholook bounds down the stairs and joins us, cheering us on and gushing about how he can't believe what he just saw. "How...how...," he stammers to Ignacio and Arlo who tell him, through a pair of cheeky unrestrained grins, that it's no big deal.

"Arlo here is learning how to affect the density of the air," Ignacio brags, throwing his arm around Arlo's shoulders.

"And Ignacio here is learning how to short-circuit electrical systems," Arlo brags back as he drapes his own arm over Ignacio's shoulders.

"And both of them are experts at finding new levels of big-headed hot-dogging," Sara sneers.

"We're a work in progress," Ignacio pretend-whispers to Matholook. And then, turning to the rest of us, pounding his chest, and with his mouth dripping with bluster, he adds, "Brohn's my mentor. He says I'm on pace to be the most powerful Emergent ever and I'll be running this whole school before long."

"Not if I'm running it first," Arlo interjects.

From his towering stance behind Ignacio, War rolls his eyes and gives Matholook full permission to "completely ignore these two braying jackasses."

Relieved and with surges of post-fight adrenaline still pumping through our veins, we all share in another round of happy laughter and mutual praise and admiration for our most recent victory.

Only Sara stays apart, standing with her arms folded and a strange look on her face that's somewhere between bored and smug. I don't care. It's not my place to keep her happy. If she wants to stand alone sulking after our amazing triumph, that's her business.

Our celebration gets a big bucket of ice-water dumped on it, though, when Connie and Darren reemerge in the lodge's doorway with what looks like their entire crew of adults, teenagers, and younger kids huddled up around them in a cluster of wide white eyes and dirt-crusted clothes.

"You shouldn't have done that," Connie complains.

"Done what? Save your lives?" War growls up the stairs at her.

"They weren't here for us," Darren explains through a nervous stammer. "You heard that man. They were here for *her*."

I'm tempted to whip out one of my Serpent Blades and slice that accusing finger clean off his crusty little hand.

"You don't have to stay here," War promises. "Not anymore. Those kids don't have to stay here." War makes a broad sweep with his hand toward me and my Asylum. "These kids weren't lying. They attend a special Academy. I'm sure all of you would be welcome."

From behind War, Mattea half-raises her hand and says, "Um..."

I know what she's going to say. It's called the *Emergents* Academy, not the "Let's Just Invite Any Straggling Group of Leftovers Into Our School Academy."

Of course, I wouldn't say that out loud to War, and apparently, Mattea won't either.

After a menacing glance from our teacher, Mattea's half-raised hand drops like a wilted balloon. Turning back to Connie and Darren, War tells them again that it's okay. "No matter what else, you can't stay here. You'll come with us. Wisp, that's the dean of the school, she'll figure it all out. I can take a few of you in the Chopsaw over there. We have rigs back at the Academy we can use to transport the rest of you."

Connie shakes her head hard like she's just been asked to leap from a cliff onto rotating helicopter blades.

War's voice drops another register, which I didn't think was possible, when he extends a beckoning hand and, one more time, urges Connie and her crew of survivors to join us.

Connie slips her hand into Darren's but otherwise doesn't move.

A tall girl behind them points to the six dead soldiers, bleeding out in the snow. "Are they...are they from the Patriot Army?"

War stares up at her, and I know he's got to be conflicted. These poor people have been living in fear of a lie. But it's a deadly lie, and telling them everything right now, all at once, could make things worse.

"They were sent by a man named Epic," War explains. "He wants these kids, Branwynne specifically, because he thinks they're the key to the future."

"A future he wants to control," I add, feeling slightly ashamed about feeling so stupidly important and giving myself an internally-directed mental eyeroll about the obnoxious pride in my voice.

"They're going to be back, you know," War warns. "Whether Branwynne is here or not. You may not be Epic's primary target. But you're on his radar. And that means all of you are in danger."

Connie begins to make her way down the stairs, picking her way gingerly over the pitted surface of crusty snow, chipped ice, and dead bodies. Darren follows close behind her, also walking with deliberate care, although I'm not sure if he's worried about slipping and falling or else accidentally stumbling over someone he knew and may have even killed.

The tall girl follows them both. Bug-eyed, rail-thin, and wearing gray sweatpants six inches too short for her long legs, she cinches a dirty robe around herself with a frayed cloth belt I figure could wrap around her skeletal waist four or five more times.

Just as she gets to the bottom and with the three "Leftovers" standing in front of us, the shadowy figure of Papa Ghana appears in the lodge's doorway. Stepping forward through the crowd of milling kids and adults, he's stone-faced at first, but then War calls up to him that it's okay to join us.

Papa Ghana takes a hesitant step toward the top of the stairs but then freezes in place, his foot hovering in the air.

Is he afraid to come down the stairs?

Offering up a crooked, consoling smile, Darren waves him on. "It's okay. The soldiers are gone. The drones are gone. These...Emergents...they beat them. They are what you said they'd be."

Papa Ghana's foot drops back down, and he shakes his head. Wagging his finger and dropping his entire face into a creased scowl, he backs away, retreating past the rest of their people and into the darkness of the lodge. As he does and just before he fully disappears, his mouth shudders out a word I can barely hear: "Unauthentic."

"What's with him?" Ignacio asks, poking his thumb toward the spot Papa Ghana just vacated.

"He's probably scared," Libra guesses. "I'm sure you all are," she adds, casting a sympathetic look over at Connie and Darren. "You don't have to be. We're the good guys. War's right. You'll be safe with us."

"I don't see how," Darren sighs. "It sounds like you might be in just as much danger as us. If not more."

Connie nods her agreement before locking her eyes onto mine. "If this Epic person is after you...well, I'm sorry, but I don't think we want to be anywhere nearby when he finds you."

"The Academy's hidden," Libra insists.

"But you're not," Connie points out, a slow burn behind her eyes. "Unless you want to live the rest of your lives like us."

From deep under his dark hood, Arlo's voice is thick with disbelief. "Wait. You're really not coming with us? You really want to stay...*here*?"

"Are you sure we can't persuade you?" War interrupts. "We can protect you."

"We believe you," Connie says, her eyes cooling down a bit, her voice softening as she turns her attention back to me. "But protect her first."

Standing half-hidden behind his bulging arm, Libra looks up at War. "So what do we do?"

"We can't force them or anyone else to do what they don't want to do." War gestures over to our parked Grip-bikes and his Chopsaw before turning back to Connie and Darren. "Last chance..."

Looking torn, like they really want to come with us just as much as they don't, they return War's final offer with a pair of slow head shakes and a full step back.

Trembling and clearly on the verge of sobbing, the tall girl behind them wraps her long arms around herself. She doesn't seem to be sure what to do or where to let her eyes land as she flits her gaze from us to Connie and Darren and then up to the rest of her people still huddled together at the top of the stairs before finally deciding to stare at a spot on the ground between her tattered, shabby boots.

With Connie on one side of her and Darren on the other, the three of them turn together and start to make their way back up the stairs.

What the frack is going on with these people? I've seen people win fights and lose them. This is the first time I've met anyone who's just... given up. How can you convince someone to do what's best for them? And why should you have to?

Honoring their last wish, we leave these "Leftovers" behind to live out whatever is left of their lives.

38

DECOMPRESS

BACK AT THE ACADEMY, we glide our Grip-bikes into their mag-stalls and join War in the middle of the hangar where he's just clambering down from the short ladder on the outside of the Chopsaw.

"Stow your helmets and weapons," he instructs us with a head-tilt toward the long silver lockers lined up against the wall. "I've got to report back to Wisp. I've got to tell her about those people out there. Tell her about the soldiers and the drones." He stops and casts a proud, papa-bear look over us. "And I'll definitely tell her about your prowess in battle. First time I've seen you in action. I think even Kress would've been impressed."

At that, something inside me lights up and sends a warm tingle from my ears all the way down to my toes.

"Those drones," Libra asks. "Those soldiers. You really think they were sent by Epic?"

"I do."

"And you really think they were targeting Branwynne, specifically?"

"There's more going on here than you know," War promises. "Yes. They were specifically targeting Branwynne."

I slip my arm into the crook of Libra's. I'm not usually the clingy, touchy-feely type. But she seems worried, and since I'm kind of the cause, I figure reaching out might be the friendly thing to do.

She gives me a weak smile of thanks and pats my arm.

Meanwhile, War snaps his rifle into one of the weapons racks next to the storage lockers and heads toward the hangar's pedestrian door. "Listen," he calls back to us, stopping and swinging around to give us a soft look of pure pride. "You really did handle yourselves well back there. Maybe not at the level of Kress and her Conspiracy," he adds with a bass chuckle from deep inside his chest. "But I'll be sure to tell them you're definitely closing in on them."

We offer up our thanks, and I can sense our own chests swell with pride as we all stand up a little straighter.

"Oh," War adds, "Branwynne, I need you to be responsible for Matholook while I meet with Wisp and the others. Can you handle that?"

"My mum always said I'd have made a brillie babysitter," I laugh. "I'll take good care of him."

War gives me a thumbs up, takes one more fatherly look at the seven of us, and strides off into the hallway.

"I don't know about the rest of you," Libra sighs, taking a long, exaggerated sniff under her arm. "But I smell like the bottom layer of Death's outhouse."

"I wasn't going to say anything," Ignacio laughs, pinching his nose between his forefinger and thumb.

"You're not exactly smelling like a meadow of spring flowers, yourself," Sara teases, thumping Ignacio's arm with a happy little punch.

"Come on," Mattea urges to all of us. "Afternoon classes will be over any minute. Let's go upstairs, grab a shower, and see if any of those little brats from the Exaltation want to take us on in darts."

"Sounds good to me," Sara gushes. Which she always does when it comes to darts. She's nowhere near as good as Kella on the shooting range. But with a dart of any kind in her hands, she's got pinpoint accuracy. (Which also explains why the kids crawl all over each other to try to get her on their team when we compete in our mixed-Cohorts version of the games.) Despite her expertise, she shrugs off any praise, but I don't think it's out of modesty. I just think *she* thinks she's above any praise a gushing fan is able to offer. I really don't want to think bad about her, but sometimes I feel like she just doesn't give me, or anyone else for that matter, much of a choice.

"What do you say?" Arlo asks Matholook. "Up for a little friendly Emergent-level competition?"

Matholook gives me an "Is he kidding?" stare.

"I'm sure you can handle anything we throw at you," I tell him with a reassuring hand to his forearm. "What do you say?"

"I say it sounds great. But I'm actually kind of wiped out," he confesses.

"Really?" Sara slides her arm into his with all the subtlety of a horny octopus. "I figured we're all on such a rush...let's make the most of it!"

"He's not one of us," I snap at Sara, and then I feel instantly bad about saying that. I didn't mean it to sound like he's unwelcome or something. In a lot of ways, after what we've been through together in a short time, he's already very much one of us. What I meant is that he's not an *Emergent*. Which is to say that he's not a techno-genetically enhanced lab rat who's been designed to be a super soldier adrenaline junkie. He's a Typic. And, at the moment, instead of fear or disdain, he's a Typic I kind of envy. After all, not having superhuman abilities means there's no superhuman evil madman sending soldiers and drones after you.

Why can't this be easier? Why can't all the pieces just fall neatly into place? Why do Matholook and I have to come from such different and warring worlds? And why do I have the irresistible compulsion to be such a bloody jerk about it?

With watery eyes and a lip quiver I can't control, I tell Matholook I'm sorry. "Typic or not, you really are one of us."

He shrugs off my apology, though, and says he thinks he'll just head upstairs to his room in East Tower. "I don't know how much longer I'll be allowed to stay, anyway. Probably best to keep my head down and stay out of the way."

"That's too bad," Sara sighs. "We'll miss you."

"I'll go with you," I volunteer, swinging around to stand face to face with Matholook. "Someone's got to show you how to get back up to the top of East Tower, right?"

It's a pointless offer. I know that. Sure, the Academy is big, with lots of passageways and tucked-away staircases leading back and forth between the main complex and the two towers on either side. But that "pull" is back, and it's telling me to stick with Matholook.

In my mind, I reach out to Haida Gwaii.

Is this the right thing to do?

She doesn't answer, so I try again.

Is Matholook someone I'm being pulled toward, or am I just following some senseless instinct that's as lost as I am?

She still doesn't answer. I can feel our connection in my head, so I know she can hear me. But Haida and I aren't at the level of Kress and Render when it comes to being instantly, constantly, and intimately connected, so I figure maybe I'm just glitchy after the experiences of meeting the Leftovers and fighting for their lives that they didn't want saved.

"Come on," Matholook urges. "Lead the way."

Reassuring my Asylum that I'll catch up with them soon, I take Matholook's hand and lead him out of the hangar, down the access corridor, and toward the back set of stairs that will ultimately—after some twists and turns—lead us up to the top of East Tower.

In his room, Matholook collapses onto his springy cot and throws an arm over his clearly very tired eyes.

"I'm conflicted," he admits.

I ask him what he means, and he tells me he's conflicted about being here.

"If it makes you feel any better," I assure him, "I'm conflicted about having you here."

Sitting up, he pats the bed next to him, and I come over and sit down, happy to have a moment to recover and decompress.

He puts his arm around my shoulder. He doesn't do anything else. He doesn't talk, pull me toward him, or lean in to kiss me.

I love combat and adventure. I've always hated quiet, tender moments. Until now.

What's wrong with me?

Finally, Haida's voice slips into my head, and I start to wonder if she's always there, if she connects with me in times when I need her to, or if she just pops randomly in and out, and it's just a coincidence that she shows up in my consciousness when I need her most.

~ What's wrong with you is the best thing that can be wrong with anyone. You're disconnecting from the Self you thought you were.

It takes me a second, but I think I know what she means. Caught between duty and desire, between Kress and Matholook, between friends and enemies...I'm losing little parts of myself and holding out hope that what I gain will more than make up for what I've lost.

How can a thought like that be so reassuring and so terrifying at the same time?

39

GOODBYE

I STAYED with Matholook and his Cult of the Devoted for a day.

He's been with me and my fellow Emergents for about a day and a half.

I feel like I lived two whole lives during our time together. So why does it feel like it's still not enough?

"What about Bendegatefran?" I ask Matholook as he and I sit together on the edge of his bed and I do my pointless best to stop time from moving forward. "Aren't you worried?"

"We don't worry."

"Maybe that's your Emergent power," I laugh.

"When's your next class?"

I glance at the small chrono-projector by the door. "An hour. Mayla's running a forensics seminar."

"Should I come with you or stay here?"

"I'd rather have you with me."

"I'd rather *be* with you."

"Then we're in agreement," I say with a pat to his knee.

"And what about *your* family?" he asks.

"What about them?"

At first, I think he's talking about Kress and the rest of the teachers and students at the Academy, but when I ask if that's what he means, he gives me a curious, tilt-headed, narrow-eyed stare before clarifying. "No. I meant your family back in London."

"Oh," I say with dismissive wave of my hand. "That's a whole different story. Different world. Different time."

"History tends to repeat," Matholook reminds me. "And the definition of 'family' changes in times of crisis. I'll bet the feelings you have for your birth family are as powerful as the feelings you have for your Emergent family."

"Llyr and Penarddunne aren't actually my birth parents."

"Really? Then you're adopted?"

"Kind of."

"What's 'kind of' adopted?"

"I was...um, discovered."

"I'm sensing a story there."

"Your senses are accurate."

"Tell me."

"London was hit by all the same drone strikes as everywhere else. Krug and the handful of world leaders in his back pocket made sure to wipe out as much and as many as they could. They basically invented enemies, created terrorists, played on people's prejudices and fears, turned people against each other whenever they could. I didn't find this out until later, mind you."

"I understand."

"Anyway, the more health and wealth everyone else loses, the more health and wealth the Wealthies could hoard for themselves."

"The game plan of pretty much every deranged, narcissistic dictator who ever was."

"For sure. And like a lot of kids, I wound up on the streets, dodging drones and the military muscle our leaders sent in to fight what turned out to be a non-existent enemy."

"The Patriot Army."

"We didn't call them that. That was your term for them over here. But yeah, same idea."

"So you hid?"

"Hell no. I *fought*. As best as I could anyway. I got pretty good at finding old weapons or making my own, stealth attacks, surveillance, tracking down food and water. There weren't a lot of places left standing. There was Buckingham Palace, but the Royal Fort Knights took that over. And Kensington Palace and the Garden, but the Banters held onto that."

"And they wouldn't take you in?"

"I didn't *want* to be 'taken in.' They were all just going to turn into the same bunch of violent, shambolic arse-munchers, anyway. So I made my way to the Tower of London."

"And it hadn't been destroyed."

"Not only that, it was locked up tight and secure as a bank vault."

"But you got inside, didn't you?"

"I didn't know how at the time. It was only later I realized something must have gotten triggered inside of me that made me invisible to the heat sensors, motion detectors, and magnetic-wave interference spotters. After that, getting past the rest of the security protocols—perimeter pylons, laser-wire, residency cameras, guest-trackers, drone-deterrents, and some pretty basic lock-bolts on the gates, doors, and windows—was easy. I found my way onto the grounds and that's when Llyr and Penarddunne found me."

"And they took you in?"

"Yes. But only after I'd already been there for what must've been a few months."

"You were living in the Tower undetected for *months*?"

"On the grounds mostly. And undetected yes. But I wasn't by myself."

"Oh. There were other kids with you?"

"Other ravens."

"Ravens?"

"The six ravens who lived on the grounds. Who always have to live on the grounds."

"I know the myth."

"You say 'myth,' I say *reality*. Either way, I lived with the ravens. I ate what they ate. I played when they played. And I hid whenever one of them told me Llyr or Penarddunne was close by."

"When they told you?"

"Well, not all of them. It turns out Haida Gwaii was the one who was talking to me."

Matholook's eyes are open hysterically wide, and I don't think he realizes how much he's leaning forward. When I laugh, he seems to get self-conscious and pulls back. "I'm sorry," I tell him. "You were just looking *really* interested there for a second."

"That's because I *was* really interested there. And for more than a second. So...?"

"So eventually, something in my head told me it was time to stop running. Time to stop hiding. Time to stop fighting."

"And that voice, it was Haida Gwaii's, right?"

"Bonus points to Matholook! Yes. It turned out the voice I'd heard, the voice I'd been hearing on and off for weeks by that time, was Haida's. So one day, when Penarddunne was coming out to check on the ravens, I just stepped out onto the lawn. She saw me. Called Llyr over. And then, just like that," I say with a snap of my fingers for extra flourish, "they were my parents. They adopted me, took me in, taught me how to talk—"

"Wait. You didn't know how to talk?"

"After I lost my parents—my biological parents—and after I wound up alone in the the city, there wasn't really any need to talk. So I didn't. Not until my time in the Tower. I'd been eating and living with the ravens, so I guess I just talked to the birds through Haida."

"So you don't know who your real parents were?"

"Llyr and Penarddunne *are* my real parents."

"You know what I mean. Your biological parents."

"I don't remember them. Not really. Just vague images. I left the Tower a few times to look for clues, clues about who they were, where I lived, if I had any other biological relatives out there..."

"And what happened? Did you find anyone?"

"No. I didn't find anyone. But I was found."

"Found?"

"By En-Gene-eers."

"The techno-geneticists?"

"They got their hooks into me for a short time. They wanted to experiment on me. Test me. Stuff like that. I have to admit, I was curious. I went willingly. At first, anyway. They said they could tell me all the things about myself I didn't know. In the end, I figured out I was just a subject, someone they were interested in for their own purposes, not for mine. So I left."

"You left?"

"Sure. I walked right through the wall of the lab, found my way back to the Tower of London, and never looked back."

"Walked through..."

"It's a little trick I'm still trying to perfect. It's the trick I did to get Gwernna out."

"You..."

"Can walk through walls. Yep. Sometimes. It hurts, so I don't do it for fun. Kress is trying to teach me how to do it right."

"So *that's* how you got her out of there. I'd been wondering."

"Wonder no more. I *traversed* the two of us right through the back wall of that RV-prison the Unsettled had her in."

"Traversed?"

"That's what Kress calls it."

"And she can do it, too?"

"I'm not sure there's much Kress *can't* do if she puts her mind to it."

As if on cue, a knock on the door makes me and Matholook jump a little.

We say, "Come in" at the same time, and the door eases open to reveal Kress standing in the hall. She's got Render on her shoulder, and he barks out a curt *kraa*! of greeting.

In pocket-covered military combat pants and a black, half-sleeved compression-top that shows off her toned muscles and her intricate set of forearm tattoos, Kress looks like she might have just come up from one of her famous marathon workout sessions down in the Fitness Center. Which she probably has. (I don't think she sleeps.)

"I'm sorry," she says, and she sounds like she really means it. "But we've got to send Matholook back."

"Why?" I pout and then feel like a daft cow for my pathetic display of worry.

"He doesn't belong here."

"We didn't belong here, either," I remind her. "Until we got here and made it our home."

Kress slips a small holo-projector out of her pocket and consults the shimmering image hovering above it. "You and your Asylum have a class on Emergency Surgery in a few minutes. Matholook can stay for that. After the class, though..."

Matholook offers up a slow, sad not of understanding.

"It's not personal," Kress assures him. "The truth is, we like you. And Branwynne likes you. From what we've heard, your people were kind to her. Efnisien notwithstanding. But none of that changes the reality of what's about to happen out there."

"What's about to happen, exactly?" I ask. Now that I'm learning about all the activity my teachers have going on behind the scenes, pretty much everything Kress says and every bit of intel she gets back from Render makes me nervous, edgy, and suspicious.

And why is it so bloody easy to go from knowing you know everything to realizing you know nothing?

Kress pins her gaze to Matholook. "Epic is going to go through you to get to us." She puts a hand on my shoulder. "And he's going to go through us to get to *her*. You're either going to die here or die with the Devoted. This isn't a happily-ever-after fairy tale. The world we've been training Branwynne and the other students to save is going to get a whole lot worse before we try to help it get a whole lot better. It's going to be bloody, and you should be with your family when the bodies start falling. Which they will."

"Forgive her," I joke. "She's a great mentor and possibly the most powerful and important Emergent in the world. She's just not especially good at pep talks."

Kress swats my shoulder with the back of her hand, and Matholook lets out a slightly nervous but mostly relieved chuckle.

"Thanks," he tells her. "Thanks for letting me tag along for a bit and for, you know, not killing me."

When she replies, "There was some debate on that final point," her voice is even and matter-of-fact, and I'm expecting her to say she's just kidding, but she doesn't.

"Maybe there's a way we could talk to the Devoted," I plead. "You know, work something out so he could stay a little longer?"

Kress cuts me off with an abruptly raised hand, and Render ruffles his hackles and shakes his head hard enough to send a spray of tiny, black, feathery specks into the air.

"Things are happening the way they need to happen," Kress assures us. "Now, I'll leave you two alone to say your private goodbyes. You won't have much of a chance later."

40

DISSECTION

ONLY AN HOUR LATER, Matholook is with me and my Asylum in one of the fourth floor Med-Labs. We're supposed to be studying forensics and post-mortem medical examination with Mayla.

"If you don't know how a body works," she tells us, "you won't be very good at taking care of your own."

I don't even bother trying to concentrate. As soon as class lets out, I'll go my way and Matholook will go his. And the probability of us meeting again, especially as friends, is bloody low. The two most likely scenarios are either that we never see each other again, or, if we do, it'll be as enemies on opposite sides of a battlefield.

At the lab table across from me and Matholook, Ignacio and Arlo are goofing around, daring each other to stick a finger deep enough into the partial cadaver on their table to twang the hyoglossus muscle connected to the hyoid bone in its throat cavity.

At the next table over—its steel top coated in blood, white goo, and entrails—Libra and Mattea are fiddling around with the sloshy innards of a long-dead racoon and huddling over a Liquid Scintillation Counter as they test for radiation levels.

At the table behind them, Sara is hunched over the headless and limbless body of a dead deer and is elbow deep in its chest cavity as she consults the floating holo-text of notes, instructions, and detailed schematics in front of her.

Our blue scrubs and white aprons are spattered in blood. I should be paying attention to the lessons Mayla's giving us, but all I really want to do is go sit somewhere with Matholook and talk. Or even sit in silence. Or just...I don't know...*exist together.*

As he reaches over to pass me a scalpel, Matholook's hand brushes against mine. It's a little gesture. A tiny touch. Probably accidental. Maybe coincidental. But for some reason, I feel like I might start crying.

You know, Branwynne, for a fearless warrior, you can be a right squidgy and completely mental melter sometimes.

I don't look up. I'm afraid if our eyes meet, I *will* start crying. And that would be the end of any reputation I've been cultivating as the Academy's resident bad-ass.

Fortunately, I'm saved from having to react by a ping from the stationary comm-link over on the wall by the instrument storage cabinets.

Mayla stops mid-lesson, scalpel in one hand and a length of animal tendon in the other and edges her way around us to the panel of black glass with the green indicator light blinking in a rapid-fire pulse. Like Kress's button-sized holo-projector, it flashes a scrolling line of text I can't read from here.

Mayla nods and scans the projector off before turning back to our class. "Kress has just called a special meeting with the Asylum. Matholook, too."

His jaw hanging open, Matholook asks, "Me?" and presses his finger so hard to his chest I think he might pierce his own heart.

Mayla's nod is vigorous and absolute. "Whatever she's got going on apparently involves you. I don't suggest letting her down. Anyway, she wants you all in the Assembly Hall right away. It seems there's been a change of plan."

"Change of plan?" I ask, my pulse surging.

"She said everything else is being put on hold. I think she has a major assignment for you."

And just like that, everyone in our Cohort is a nervous wreck.

We all know Kress sent Render on a scouting mission a few days ago. We know our teachers are trying to locate a new Processor out west, somewhere not too far from here. (We heard it's in Nevada.) And we know they're looking for something that's somehow related to the big war Epic is getting ready to wage.

What we *don't* know is what they're looking for, what Render could have found, why Kress summoned just the six of us and Matholook, or what could be important enough to call us into the Assembly Hall in the middle of Afternoon Module.

(It's just as well. With its VR *and* real-life lessons in bone-setting, arterial repair, and open chest-cavity operating procedures, Mayla's class on Emergency Surgery is turning out to be kind of gross.)

After Kress popped into his room, Matholook and I agreed to say our goodbyes, but now, with this emergency meeting being called, maybe—just maybe—those goodbyes will be one of the things that gets put on hold.

That would be positively brillie!

Who knows? Maybe my pointless wish to keep time from moving forward might actually have been granted.

Next to me, Libra plants her hand onto mine and mutters, "Oh, God. What do you think this is all about?"

"I don't know," I answer back through a smile.

"What if she's sending us out on an actual mission? You know...a dangerous one."

I sure the frack hope so.

And if it involves me and Matholook being together in the same place at the same time—even if it's for just a little while longer—danger be damned...I'm all for it.

41

ASSIGNMENT

IN FRONT OF US, at the slender, silver podium on the stage, Kress clears her throat and scans us twice as if to make sure we're all present. I grin when Matholook, in his seat next to mine, sits up a little straighter and folds his hands neatly on his lap. I don't know why, but it makes me happy to know how afraid he is of her.

Brohn walks in through one of the side doors and sits in front of Kress, his long legs hanging over the bull-nosed trim at the edge of the stage.

Kress clears her throat again and pushes up the sleeves of her jacket, exposing her signature pattern of forearm tattoos. "We called the Asylum here because you're the most experienced of the Academy's five Cohorts. By a lot, actually. Your Emergent abilities are the most developed, again, by a lot. You've now experienced combat and have acquitted yourselves with all the skill and composure we've been hoping for and expecting of you. And, more than the other students, you've seen what's become of the world." She throws in a proud little smile, but it's gone almost before I've registered it. "Plus," she adds, "War assures us that after what he saw you do out at that old ski lodge, you've more than proven yourselves ready for a mission."

From his seat on the edge of the stage, Brohn leans forward, his powerful forearms draped over his knees. "As you all know by now, the Devoted are committed to the past. Epic has his sights locked onto the future. And the Unsettled are always on the move, always trying to find perfection in the present. Well, those three trains are on a collision course, and, from what our sources tell us, they're now less than three days away from one very fatal crash." His baritone voice fills the room in a slow, haunting rumble. "They *are* going to crash," he assures us. "It's inevitable. And, on top of it all, the Unsettled are on the move."

I put my hand halfway up. "The Unsettled are *always* on the move."

He looks at me for just long enough to make me uncomfortable, but it's Kress who responds.

"That's true, Branwynne. But this time, the Unsettled are splitting up. And not just a small scouting crew like you encountered the other day during your impromptu rescue mission with Matholook and Bendegatefran. They're dividing up their entire army into two very large and possibly autonomous armies. Which they've never done before. After you helped get Gwernna away from them, they got more desperate."

"Desperate for what?" I ask.

"For victory. They had to change tactics. They're as afraid of us as they are of Epic. We think they're gearing up for something big, preparing for a flanking operation on multiple fronts."

"And you think we could be one of those fronts?" Libra asks.

"No, Libra. Not yet. We're too high up. They won't dedicate that many resources to us."

"Then what—?"

"We think the Unsettled are going to raid the Devoted compound again—only this time, in much bigger numbers. We think their incursion the other day was a test. They're determined to get their hands on Gwernna. If they do, they're going after Epic and his Sanctum Civillains next in a preemptive strike."

"And if they manage that," Brohn adds morbidly, "then, yes, we think we're next. Either way, the war we've been talking about and worrying about...well, that war is about to happen."

Kress scans us once. Then twice. She seems sad and not at all like the off-the-charts powerhouse I know her to be. "The attack on New Harleck, kidnapping Gwernna...that was the first brick pulled out of a very wobbly wall. We need to act fast because the rest of it is on its way down."

A buzz of nervous excitement rips through our Asylum, and Matholook curls his fingers over the back of my hand.

"Our Conspiracy," Kress explains, "can't be in two places at once."

"So we're sending you out on your very first *official* mission," Brohn informs us. "You're going out as a reconnaissance team. War and Mayla will stay behind with Granden and Wisp this time. They'll look after the Academy's other students. The other Cohorts aren't nearly as far along as those of you sitting in this room." I *think* I see Brohn give us a complimentary wink when he says this, but I'm not sure.

"We'll be off on a mission of our own," Kress elaborates, pressing her thumb to her chest. "There's a Processor in a place called the Great Basin National Park. It's in Nevada, not too far from here. We don't like having to divide our resources, but the Unsettled have made it necessary. Epic's plan requires an important database of techno-genetic code."

"The same code we think went into making us," Brohn elaborates with a sweep of his hand.

"Epic's original plan was to get it from Branwynne. From her DNA and from Haida Gwaii's, actually. Since he couldn't, he's planning the next best thing. He's sending a team to pick it up from the Processor. The good news is, they haven't left yet. If we can beat them there and get our hands on the Database first..."

"We'll put a very large hole in Epic's ability to wage this war," Brohn says with a fist-smack to his palm. "Or at least make it a lot harder for him to win it."

"We need all hands on deck. The problem is that there's now more than one deck. Ours is an acquisition mission. We need that Database. Your mission is *surveillance* only. I'm going to say that again: *surveillance only*. Track down the southern wing of the Army of the Unsettled. See what they're up to. We need locations, movements, numbers, weapons. Everything. And then, report back. We'll rendezvous right here in twenty-four hours. That will give you more than enough time to gather your intel and for us to complete our mission, get back to the Academy, and see if we can use the Database and your findings to help us take down Epic."

"Preferably before he launches his war," Brohn clarifies.

I put up a tentative hand. "Um, what about Matholook? Isn't he supposed to be going back today?"

"I'm afraid we have to put his return on hold for the moment," Kress explains. "We don't have time to see him safely home, complete our mission in the Great Basin, *and* deal with this new threat by the Unsettled. And, if we're right, New Harleck might be about the *least* safe place he could be right now."

"In fact," Brohn says, clapping his hands together before planting them on his knees, "this particular recon mission concerns him, too. You helped him get Gwernna back, Branwynne. Now, we're going to ask him to use his knowledge of the Unsettled to help keep her from falling into their hands and keep his own people as safe as possible in the process."

"I'm not exactly trained for combat," Matholook says. He's sitting right next to me, and I can barely hear him.

Kress, on the other hand, hears him just fine. "This won't be combat," she snaps. "You'll go with the Asylum on this purely observational mission. You'll help them gather intel. You'll all report back. And *then*, Matholook, when the dust has settled and we know you'll be safe in New Harleck, we'll help you get home. I promise."

"Information only?" Matholook asks through a stammer.

"Information only," Brohn confirms. "Leave the heavy lifting to us."

"Easy-Peasy," I whisper to Matholook with a light pat to the back of his hand.

Kress says, "Let's get to work" and taps a panel on the silver podium. A huge, intricately detailed 3D holo-display appears in the air in front of her. Quickly, almost too fast for me to follow, she taps out locations on the display. Under her flurry of inputs, the diagram is populated with an over-whelming cluster of information—everything from topo-graphical elevations in the desert and glowing indicator lines of possible troop movements to potential vehicle vulnerabili-ties to weather patterns and a ranked list of the Unsettled's suspected targets—mostly small outposts scattered throughout the desert. For another hour, she goes over weapons capabili-ties—theirs and ours—and spends at least an extra ten minutes after that reinforcing to us just how important this mission is.

"Don't deviate," she warns. "No improvising. Follow the plan. Get in, get out, try not to get seen or killed. And be back here in twenty-four hours. Got it?"

We all answer, "Yes."

After she's done explaining the rest of the "Xs" and "Os" and making sure each of us knows our specific assignment for this mission, Brohn hops down from the stage and starts striding toward the rear doors.

"Come on," he barks to us. "We don't have time to waste."

Kress and Brohn lead me and my Asylum—plus a terrified-looking Matholook—down to the Sub-Basement where the rest of their Conspiracy is already waiting.

Rain has just finished dropping the Terminus down from its mag-pad and is busy loading it with black bags I'm assuming are filled with their weapons and ammo.

Kneeling on the hangar's cold floor and barely acknowledging our presence, Kella is busy strapping double bands of her own ammo around her chest, snapping her sniper rifle into its case, and slipping an assortment of smaller guns and knives into various holsters and pockets on her tactical combat uniform.

At the silver bank of weapons lockers, Terk hauls out Libra's hammer, Sara's shoulder-holster of throwing darts, Mattea's Bear Claws, Arlo's scythe, Ignacio's twin shillelaghs, and my pair of Serpent Blades.

"Remember," Kress says as she helps Terk distribute our weapons and helmets and the riding gear we'll need for the Grip-bikes, "track and report *only*. No heroics."

"No heroics," we all promise in unison.

"You're going east," Kress reminds us. "We're going west. We'll meet back here in twenty-four hours. Not a second longer."

"Not a second longer," I repeat through a completely unrestrained smile.

She hands me a portable chrono-projector, which I slip into my pocket. "I mean it. Don't be late. Once we're all back at the Academy, we'll only have a couple of days to finalize the rest of our battle plan. And that plan won't work without the Database we're going after and the report you'll give us on the Unsettled."

"Easy-peasy, Teach. It's under control."

On the far end of the hangar, War enters through the pedestrian door and makes his way over to us.

"War will help you with the vehicles, weapons, gear, and all the other prep you'll need. We're leaving now. War will give you a final mission brief and send you off in an hour."

We all say we understand, but I'm disappointed I have to wait a whole hour before springing into action.

Kress and her Conspiracy pile into the Terminus. The huge rig wheezes to a stop just before the big hangar doors leading into the mines.

Leaning out of the open side door, Kress lets her eyes wander over me, Matholook, and my Asylum. "We need you to be half-detective, half-ninja," she instructs us through a grin. "Try not to die, okay?"

With that, she slides the door shut, and the Terminus rumbles out of the hangar, down the mine shaft, and out of view.

Exactly an hour later, with our weapons secured and our helmets and body armor on, War wishes us luck. Giving him our thanks and our combined promise not to die, we mount the Grip-bikes and scan them to life. Like before, Matholook shares a bike with me. The others hop onto their own bikes. (Ignacio grabs the red one again.) The hangar doors open, and I wind up in front of our queue, leading my team down the mine tunnel and out the vehicle exit-hatch.

Outside of the mines and skimming along with the air and the trees whipping past, I'm beyond excited about this mission. And why shouldn't I be? After all, I've got Matholook with me for a while longer, my Asylum is together, and we've had months of training.

With our talent and Kress's detailed instructions, I'm a hundred percent sure this will be the easiest and most painless assignment of our young lives.

I get a chill, a lump in my throat, and a spasm in my heart when Haida's voice slips into my head with three little words:

~ *No it won't.*

END OF CULT *of the Devoted,* **Book 2 of** *The Academy of the Apocalypse* **series**

42

COMING UP...

ARMY OF THE UNSETTLED, **Book 3 of** *The Academy of the Apocalypse* **series...**

In the days before Epic is expected to launch his all-out war, Branwynne and the Asylum have been given their first major assignment: track and report back on the moving caravan of the Army of the Unsettled. What could be simpler?

After the Unsettled destroy a cluster of Survivalist outposts and turn their deadly attention to a small town in the desert,

Branwynne decides that tracking and reporting just won't be enough this time. With their training still far from complete, Branwynne and her friends agree that saving the town is their only option.

After all, that's what the Emergents are in school to be taught to do.

In way over their heads, with no backup on the horizon, and facing an entire army, they're about to discover that there's a huge gap between *learning* about the end of the world and *surviving* it.

Army of the Unsettled is available for pre-order until its release on July 25th, 2021.

43

BUT WAIT! THERE'S MORE!

DEAREST READER:

BRANWYNNE and her friends will be back and ready for action in *Army of the Unsettled,* which will be released on July 25, 2021!

IN THE MEANTIME, enjoy the following bonus chapter from Kress, and be sure to keep an eye out for the return of Kress and her Conspiracy in the exciting new series, *The Ravenmaster Chronicles,* starting with the first book, *ARISE,* scheduled for release on October 25, 2021!

44

(BONUS CHAPTER)

"Kress: Re-Emergence"

I GAVE BRANWYNNE, her Asylum, and her friend Matholook twenty-four hours to gather the intel we'll need to stop Epic in his tracks.

Naturally, as partially trained students, they got the easy job, which is as it should be. I know they need to leave the nest at some point. I just didn't expect to feel quite this mother-bird nervous about nudging them out. As Brohn is fond of reminding me, though, we set this Academy up with the express purpose of teaching our little fledglings how to fly.

For our part, my Conspiracy and I took on the far deadlier task of trying to liberate the Database from a silver-domed Processor deep within the forest of bristlecone pines in Nevada's Great Basin National Park.

I'm not sure what kind of luck Branwynne is having.

Brohn, Rain, Kella, Terk, and I?

We're running like hell for our lives.

Swiftly but still with the same gentle care he might use on a baby bird, Brohn hoists the four kids we just rescued—two boys and two girls—into the waiting Terminus.

Maybe twelve or thirteen years old, three of the kids are malnourished, disoriented, bruised, battered, and glassy-eyed: all the signs of captivity and forced experimentation we've sadly come to know so well over the years.

Unfortunately, we *have* to know it. It's our job to stop it.

The fourth kid, older and woozy but still in much better shape than the others, is a boy named Apex. But because he's an Emergent whose very DNA may hold the key for unlocking the confluence of binary and genetic code that made us in the first place, he's referred to as "the Database."

Terk bellows out to us from behind the controls in the cab. "Everyone in?"

Through cupped hands, I shout back, "No!" and hope he can hear me over the hum of the truck and the sharp crack of gunfire raining down all around us.

Barking out that they've got me covered as I scramble into the rig, Rain and Kella lay down a spray of cover fire. Under a volley of smoke and the hail of discharged shell casings plinking to the rocky ground, they pick off the team of armed En-Gene-eers and another dozen armored guards in combat camouflage gear before slinging their Inferno stock twenty-two rifles over their backs and diving headfirst into the truck.

Grabbing Rain and Kella by their arms and shoulders, Brohn and I haul them the rest of the way in. Brohn slams the sliding door shut behind them, and shouts into the cabin for Terk to get us the frack out of there.

The vibrations from the rig's massive, reinforced wheels on the rocky, pitted access road ripple through our bodies, and we clamp our hands onto the grab-bars, onto the backs of the seats, or onto each other as Terk—his human hand and his Modified hand clamped to the steering posts—navigates the Terminus down into an old riverbed and then up the far side where we go crashing through a dense wall of underbrush.

From outside, Render snaps open the telempathic connection he and I share and warns that we've got Assault Drones on our tail.

~ Three of them. With laser targeting systems, plasma grenades, and energy inhibitors. Nasty little flying beasts. I'm insulted they're in my sky.

Before I've even finished relaying the info to my Conspiracy, Kella has already slid into the truck's firing station.

With our consciousness combined into his body—my training, knowledge, and ferocity mixing with his dexterity and razor-sharp talons—Render and I are able to take down one of the drones. His wings pinned tight to his sides and with his curved claws snapped wide open, he swoops down on the goblet-shaped drone from above.

The strike is fast and deadly, and the thrill I get from experiencing it through Render's eyes and mind sends excited shockwaves down my neck and all the way into the network of digital implants in my forearms.

The drone belches up a slurry of smoky, blue-gray liquid before pinwheeling out of the sky and smashing to pieces on the rocks below.

With the pinpoint accuracy she's become famous for, Kella picks off the other two drones, her shots piercing their mag-grav propulsion ports. Sputtering, the drones join their busted buddy in pieces on the ground.

"Got 'em," Kella exclaims with a celebratory fist-pump.

She really doesn't need to announce the kills. Kella doesn't miss.

Standing behind her and confirming the downed drones,

Rain calls down the length of the Terminus and asks me if we're clear.

Disconnecting from Render, I feel my eyes return to normal. I blink the interior of the Terminus back into focus.

"Any word from our two ravens?" Rain asks, flicking her thumb toward the ceiling.

"Render doesn't see any pursuit vehicles behind us. And Arapaho is flying up ahead somewhere." I close my eyes to focus for a second. Connecting with Render has been second nature for a long time now. My connection with Arapaho—one of two white ravens in Render and Haida Gwaii's six-bird brood—is more of a challenge. He's guarded, mysterious, and fiercely independent. Even when he's cooperating, like now, he can still be pretty hard to read. Doing my best to muddle through the static in my head, I relay what he's seeing to Rain. "He's signaling clear sailing at least up to the dry lake. With any luck, we should be back at the Academy and comparing notes with Branwynne and her crew before dark."

Brohn leans back in his seat and tilts his head toward the rear doors of our big rig. "Speaking of luck, we've really got to stop pushing ours like that."

I slip my arm around the shoulder of one of the girls we just rescued. Small and trembling, she stares up at me with grateful, coffee-brown eyes before resting her head against my arm and slipping her hand into mine. I give a head-tilt toward her and the other three scared but now-safe Emergents. "Pushing *our* luck," I remind Brohn, "helps them with theirs."

That may be true, but I still don't think I take another breath until the Terminus is safely parked on its mag-pad in the Academy's vehicle hangar.

* * *

After getting our four new recruits settled in, Brohn and I meet with Wisp and Granden to discuss Apex and our next moves as we prepare for a final showdown with Epic.

"Any word from Branwynne and the others?" I ask.

"Not yet," Wisp informs me.

"Okay. If they're not back by morning, I'll send Render out to find them."

Brohn glances up at the ceiling and offers up an exasperated sigh. "Count on Branwynne to turn a simple recon mission into something complicated and nerve-wracking."

"I'm sure they'll be fine," Wisp assures us, glancing down at the holo-clock in her desk. "They've still got a couple of hours."

"And, remember," Granden reminds us with a comforting smile, "they've been trained by the best."

Brohn and I thank him and Wisp for the encouragement and ask them to notify us right away when Branwynne and the others return.

"Absolutely," Wisp promises. "The second they're in the door."

I'm exhausted as Brohn and I trudge up the stairs toward the room we share in West Tower. I know Brohn is just as wiped out —physically and emotionally—as I am. Which is why I'm surprised when he suggests we stop off at the Third Floor Combat Skills and Training Room of the main building for some quick sparring.

"You're kidding."

"Nope. We've got a little time before Branwynne and the others are supposed to be back."

"We just got back from a mission, ourselves," I complain.

"We need to practice if we're going to keep teaching these kids."

"Ugh. I never thought being a teacher would involve doing so much homework."

Laughing, Brohn stops on the landing. He slips his hand around my waist, pulls me close, and heaves a happy sigh. "Did you ever think it'd be like this?"

"Like what?"

"You know...us being teachers instead of test-subjects."

"And being Recruiters instead of being recruited?"

"Exactly."

"I never *expected* it. But now that it's here, I'm really enjoying it."

"Do you worry at all?" Brohn asks after a moment's pause.

"About what?"

"You know. The teaching we're doing. What we're training these kids to be."

"You're worried we're going to turn them into the world's next batch of super villains, aren't you?"

"No. Maybe. Kind of."

"It's a risk. But it's also a challenge. Sure, they've got abilities we're committed to enhancing. But that's not all there is to them. Empathy can be a superpower, too, you know."

"You really think so?"

"Absolutely," I assure him. "It's possible to be *better* without being superior."

"Hm. Interesting point. So...what do you say? Are you up for some more training or not? After all, it's when we're at our most tired when we need to be at our most powerful."

"I don't know...," I pretend-sigh as we continue up the stairs. "I guess you *do* need a chance to catch up."

"Hey! You may be up in Jeet Kune Do—"

"*Way* up," I remind him.

"But I'm winning eight to seven in Krav Maga," he brags.

"Baloney. I won that last fight."

"With an illegal eye gouge," Brohn whines, pressing his palm to his eye and grimacing like he's just been run over by a train. "Which really hurt, by the way."

"Hey. All's fair in love and beating the crap out of each other, right?"

"So..." Brohn says in his most taunting, provocative drawl, "what do you say, Kress?"

"I say, let's fight."

The door to Room CSTR-3 whooshes open, and the motion-sensor lights go on as we step into the empty training facility.

Easing our way into the sparring ring formed by the glowing pink circle embedded in the floor, Brohn and I perform our ritual palm-over-fist bows before taking a breath and squaring off against each other.

We've been training, sparring, and working out together for years now. Although the goal is to stay in shape and develop improved teaching strategies for the Academy's five Cohorts, I know we both get a secret thrill from the competition. Plus, there's an intimacy about fighting like this. It's a sweaty, physical, close-quarters dance and just about the most fun you can have with your clothes on.

We know this routine well by now. We've trained together nearly every day for over five years. And we're pretty evenly matched.

It always comes down to my quickness and agility against his physical strength and bulletproof skin. I'm not supposed to channel Render, but I usually do, anyway. All's fair, after all.

I draw my hair into a tight ponytail and then I throw a quick, testing jab, which Brohn deflects and redirects with his open hand.

"These kids..." he says as I shuffle my feet to regain my balance and find my center, "...they have it easy. We have to teach. All they have to do is survive."

He counters my attempt at a knee strike with a reverse leg sweep.

"Do you really think they were ready for a mission?" he asks.

I hurdle his leg sweep with ease and skip around in an effort to outflank him.

"It's a simple recon mission," I shrug before attacking his unprotected ribcage with a flurry of jabs that he shrugs off like they were nothing. "*Render* could do it."

Brohn throws a half-hearted elbow, but I don't react. I know it's a bluff.

"Maybe we should've sent *him*, then. He's the best reconnaissance resource we have, after all."

Brohn sends an arcing left-hook toward my jaw. I feel the wind whistle past my ear as I dodge the blow.

"You know we need him with us," I remind him. "Besides, what sense does it make to train these kids and then not give them a chance to do what we trained them *for*?"

Brohn's quick front-kick hits my forearm. It hurts, but not enough to stop me from landing an uppercut to his solar plexus. He winces but shakes it off as I dance back. He offers up an unnecessarily loud chuckle to prove to me that he's unfazed.

"Hey, Kress. Do you think Apex really is what Epic thinks he is?"

"Wisp will run her tests. But yes. All signs point to it."

Brohn wipes sweat from his forehead with the back of his hand. "What about Micah? What are you going to do when we find him?"

I slide in close, hoping to counteract his extreme reach advantage. "He's my brother. I don't know where Epic found him or how he got his hooks into him, but I'm going to save him. Same as he'd do for me."

"And if he chooses not to be saved?"

"I'll save him anyway."

Brohn tries to latch onto my wrist, but I slip away. "And Epic?" he asks.

"He took Micah from me. He's a killer, a mass-kidnapper, a torturer of children, and he's gearing up to commit genocide in the name of peace. So...I'm going to kill him."

"Killing him won't make the world any better."

"Sure it will."

My leg sweep happens way too fast for Brohn to register it. By the time the move's completed, he's on his back, and I'm straddling his chest with his arms pinned under my knees.

He makes a big show of thrashing around, but even he's not strong enough to overpower what I turn into when Render and I are connected like this. (So, yeah. I'm cheating.) For all their hollow bones, ravens are incredibly strong. Render can carry nearly his entire body weight in his beak with another full load in his talons. With his relative strength added to and enhancing my own, pinning down a nearly two-hundred-pound man isn't all that hard.

Giving Brohn the most wicked smile I can muster, I ask, "Give up?"

Squirming, he drops his head back and taps his hand against the side of my thigh, so I release my grip. As soon as my knee is off his arm, his hand shoots up, his fingers curling around the back of my neck in a totally unfair, underhanded sneak attack.

I'm just about to clock him—I'm thinking a forearm to the throat, a side-hand blade strike to the carotid artery, or maybe a sharp elbow to the eye—when he pulls me close and kisses me.

It's nice to know, no matter how messed up the world gets, that kisses still happen. And this is a *really* good one. It's warm, soft, and slow...and a very nice end to a *very* long day.

"Ready for some rest?" Brohn asks at last.

"Definitely," I tell him. "Once Branwynne and her crew get back, our Conspiracy is going to have get back to work."

"Five of us and a raven jumping into a war between three armies. Are we crazy?"

"We've faced worse odds before."

"Um. No, we haven't."

Laughing and hand in hand, we head upstairs to our room for some well-deserved rest.

Over the past six years, Brohn and I have been a lot to each other: Recruits, Rebels, Survivors, Travelers, Teachers, and Lovers.

We could have been killed at nearly every step of the way. But we survived together and lived for each other.

Tonight, I'm stressed, sore, and exhausted.

As one of the founders of this school and with everyone looking to me for guidance, I already felt like I had the weight of the world on my shoulders. Now that we've just added four new students to the Emergents Academy—including one who could conceivably alter the course of human evolution—and with a three-way war about to break out any minute down below, the weight has just gotten a whole lot heavier.

But I've got Brohn, I've got Render, I've got a world to save, and I've never felt better in my entire life.

45

A NEW CONSPIRACY SERIES!

FOR FANS OF KRESS, **Render, and the original Conspiracy: A new series is coming your way!**

In a spectacular crossover event of re-emergence, Kress and her original Conspiracy leave the Emergents Academy on a daring mission to free four Emergent children being held captive in a high-tech Processor in Nevada's Great Basin National Park.

When Epic—the villainous, marble-skinned techno-geneticist—threatens to use her own past against her, Kress will need to fight, not just for her life, but for the fate of every living person on the planet.

PRE-ORDER the first two books on Amazon:

Arise (Coming in October 2021)
Banished (Coming in January 2022)
Crusade (Coming in April 2022)

46

AN EXCITING NEW DYSTOPIAN SERIES:
THE CURE CHRONICLES

BEFORE THE BLIGHT, becoming an adult was something teenagers looked forward to.

But now, turning eighteen means certain death.

Unless you prove yourself worthy of the Cure.

On her seventeenth birthday, Ashen Spencer is blindfolded and escorted to the massive, mysterious building known as the Arc to begin her year of training and testing in hopes that she can earn the Cure—a powerful drug given only to those deemed worthy to survive beyond their eighteenth birthday.

Ashen has a chance to rise up from her former life of squalor and be granted a place in society, if the Panel—the mysterious group of powerful men and women in charge of the Arc— deems her year a success.

She's assigned to work for twelve months as a servant for a wealthy family whose son is the most alluring—and confusing —young man she's ever met.

At first, Ashen is thrilled for the opportunity to earn her place in a society she's always dreamed of inhabiting. But as time passes and she begins to learn the truth about the people she admires so much and the home she left behind, she realizes she has a choice:

Be part of the disease...

Or be part of the Cure.

PRE-ORDER THE BOOKS on Amazon at a special temporary discounted price:

The Cure (Coming in June 2021)
Awaken (Coming in September 2021)
Ascend (Coming in December 2021)

47

ALSO BY K. A. RILEY

IF YOU'RE ENJOYING K. A. Riley's books, please consider leaving a review on Amazon or Goodreads to let your fellow book-lovers know about it.

Dystopian Books:

Resistance Trilogy:

Recruitment
Render
Rebellion

Emergents Trilogy:

Survival
Sacrifice
Synthesis

Transcendent Trilogy:

Travelers
Transfigured
Terminus

Academy of the Apocalypse Series:

Emergents Academy
Cult of the Devoted
Army of the Unsettled (July 2021)

The Ravenmaster Series:

Arise (Coming in October 2021)
Banished (Coming in January 2022)
Crusade (Coming in April 2022)

The Cure Chronicles:

The Cure (Coming in June 2021)
Awaken (Coming in September 2021)
Ascend (Coming in December 2021)

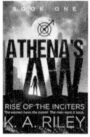  

Athena's Law Trilogy:

Book One: *Rise of the Inciters*
Book Two: *Into an Unholy Land*
Book Three: *No Man's Land*

FANTASY BOOKS

Seeker's Series:

Seeker's World
Seeker's Quest
Seeker's Fate
Seeker's Promise

Seeker's Hunt
Seeker's Prophecy (Coming in 2021)

To be informed of future releases, and for occasional chances to win free swag, books, and other goodies, please sign up here:

https://karileywrites.org/#subscribe